Isolation

The Digital Dystopia Series | Book One

Lucas Kitchen

Free Grace International

Summoned

Tabitha leaned over the paper-laden table, her wavy hair falling across her face as she studied *The Overseer's Handbook*. Its rugged leather cover was cracked with age, and its pages were filled with meticulously handwritten notes and diagrams. She blew a lock out of her eyeline and thumbed through the yellowed pages. She skimmed through sheets of detailed schematics and maintenance protocols, amazed at the wealth of knowledge needed to keep the town of Isolation running.

She took in the magical smell of the books surrounding her and smiled. This was her happy place. She glanced around the little library as warm nostalgia washed over her. The room's walls were lined with towering bookshelves, many of which she had spent fantastic hours exploring. Each shelf was filled to the brim with old volumes, their spines cracked and faded. The little library was jammed with years of wisdom, a trove of contentment and satisfaction. In the center of the room rose the table like an altar to the patron saint of stray papers; its surface was worn smooth and utterly blotted out by Tabitha's research materials.

The door creaked. Tabitha glanced, and the spell was broken. It was Tobias, her twin brother, who everyone assumed was older because of his broadness, tallness, and manishness. He was coming at her like one of Mr. Johnson's pigs at feeding time. His brow furrowed into a wad of forehead wrinkles. His height was only slightly diminished by his forward-charging posture. He'd ram that hard head through a bookshelf if he didn't slow down. She rolled her eyes.

"There you are. We need to go now."

Tabitha sighed, her eyes still fixed on the *Overseer's Handbook*. She wondered if she could buy some time. A stolen glance told her Tobias had no time on sale. Suddenly, her world became focused, narrowed, and dangerous. The look on his face! Something was wrong.

"What is it?"

"The council called for us."

"No!" she said; he nodded. "We in trouble? Are they moving us again? Are they mad? How did they say it? What's it about?"

"Don't know," he said. "Come on."

She stacked up papers, notes, and other research on top of the book, handling it all with a caution that Tobias had no interest in waiting upon. Her stomach felt tight, and her heart fluttered at the frightening thought. Appearing before the council. "Any hint what it's about?"

"It's about time, is what it is." Tobias folded his arms across his chest. "You gonna collate them papers?" He nodded curtly toward the neat stack forming before her cautious attention. "Come on. They'll be madder than a breached cow if we don't show. You can get them papers later."

Tabitha tried to hurry, but her nerves played havoc on her co-ordination. She scrambled for the stack of uncollated papers but knocked over a glass jar of pencils in her mismanaged haste, sending them across the floor's bowed boards. The pencils exploded across the floor, looking like an omen of things to come.

"Why you being so clumsy?" Tobias said. "Hurry."

"I'm trying," she said. Tobias rushed like a one-ton bull to the table. As Tabitha knelt on the floor to gather the pencils, he scooped up the papers and notes, not bothering to keep them in any semblance of order. He crammed the wad of documents into her satchel like he was stuffing a turkey.

"Hey, careful with those!" Tabitha protested.

"Take them pencils too if you want," Tobias said, grabbing the jar from her hand and dumping it into her bag.

"There ain't no need to be such a dead donkey's dad," Tabitha said.

She stepped out of the library with her jam-packed bag, squinting against the glaring sunlight that bathed Isolation's dusty stre et. *What had they done? Why were they summoned?* She couldn't handle another relocation. They'd been moved to their third burrow this year and were running out of options. She hurried to catch up with Tobias, who was already striding ahead, his shoulders tense with urgency.

"Where you been since this morning?" Tabitha asked, trying to distract, hoping she could loosen up a notch.

"Was checking my snares out near the cisterns," Tobias said.

"You catch a jackrabbit?" Tabitha said. "I'm hankering for some rabbit stew."

"Nope," Tobias said. "But I got a horny toad."

"Rather stew up some old socks," Tabitha said.

"So, what were you zonked out about back there?" Tobias asked, glancing sideways at Tabitha as they moved down the street of a town that looked frozen in time.

"I finally got permission to take a gander at the *Overseer's Handbook* for my school project! Can you believe it?" She grinned, enthusiasm bubbling up like a cold winter brook. For a split second, she was flying; her mind soared through the pages of the incredible little book. She relived her afternoon, sitting among the books. "They gave me all these rules. 'Don't take it out the building. Return it by end a day.' But still—I never thought they'd let me see it!" Tabitha's smile stretched across her face, pride and excitement beaming clear and present. Then, her brother ruined the moment.

Tobias paused mid-step, his brow so furrowed you could plant corn in its rows. "They crazy? You serious?" He shook his head. He squeezed his eyes nearly shut, making tiny indentions around his temples. She felt her body tighten at his expression. As twins, they felt each other's fears, worries, and anxiety. The weight of his look pressed against her. He put a finger out, clearly indicating that he was throwing the gearbox into lecture mode. "Tabitha, that's a huge responsibility. Without the *Overseer's Handbook* we'd be—well, it's real important. You was careful, right?"

"Yeah," she said. "I know, Bubba."

"They shouldn't a even let you near it," Tobias said.

"You're going to give me an ulcer." She shoved his shoulder. "It's sitting there safe and sound on the desk. Ain't nobody getting at it in the library." She tried to will herself to believe the words. Tobias squinted deeper.

"We should go back and make sure it's safe." He paused. "On second thought, we should go get it and return it to the clerk before..." he trailed off.

"We don't have time. Remember?" She frowned at him. He looked stuck between a colt and a fence. If he got squeezed anymore, she was afraid his eyes might pop out, no matter how much he tried to keep 'em squinted in place. "We got to go find out what we did this time. Probably going to get a discipline for it, whatever it is." She gulped down a knot that was determined to fight its way into her mouth.

"Right." He turned and walked. Tabitha quickened her pace, falling into step. Tabitha's nervousness began to bubble and spill over.

Isolation

They continued to walk toward the council house as Tabitha prattled. "Did you know the *Overseer's Handbook* has a whole section of geological water maps?"

"Why would I know something like that?" Tobias said. "You shouldn't been allowed to know it neither."

"Maps are so important, you know," Tabitha said, combatting the anxiety in the air with a barrage of empty chatter. "It reminds me of David Livingstone."

"Who's that," Tobias asked.

"Missionary in the 1800s," Tabitha said, picturing the beauty of seventeenth-century sailing ships and the shores of a distant land. She took a smiling breath as she envisioned the people, tribal and wild. She could almost feel the sand and see the jungle.

"I should have known," Tobias laughed. "You know more about dead people than any's still living."

"There weren't any good maps for where he was going," Tabitha explained, talking breathlessly, enthusiasm pouring out like a wild waterfall. She was soaring above the ground with the words. "So he had to draw 'em up from scratch. He mapped out the continent of Africa. In his maps, he brought back really good geography that they didn't know in Europe at the time."

"Sounds like a lot of work," Tobias said.

"Yeah, but hard work is worth it when you want to help people," Tabitha said, crossing her hands across her heart and looking up at the deep blue sky. She imagined the same expanse, the sun, the wind, the warmth shining down on those travelers of old. She was lost in the story now, exactly where she wanted to be. "He believed that if he taught folks back home about Africa and gave 'em good maps, he could open the hearts of more missionaries, who'd go there and evangelize."

"Don't sound like he would approve of the Isolation Doctrine," Tobias said with a harrumph. "And I guess the town elders wouldn't approve of him."

Tabitha squinted and tugged at the collar of her shirt. "Why you got to do that?" She said. She had been living in the dream of her imagination for a short few seconds of escape, and he had to bring her crashing back down to this dusty desert town. A bead of sweat tickled down her spine. "You ruining my fun." She looked at the ground as they walked.

"No I aint," Tobias said. "I'm just saying it sounds a lot like what a leaver would do, and they ain't keen on leavers."

"His book's in the library, so I guess he ain't as bad as a leaver." She left it at that, reminded of the tension, the anxiety, the worry.

They kept walking, taking steps longer than Tabitha was able to make comfortably.

"You're the only person who reads them dusty books, anyhow," Tobias said.

"Am not," Tabitha said. "Landry Grady gets books sometimes."

"I said *person*," Tobias said. "Landry's got the face of a goat." Tabitha covered her mouth as a giggle tumbled out. "He probably just checks out them books cause he likes the taste of them pages." Tobias mimicked the chewing style of hungry livestock.

Tabitha whacked him on the arm. "That's mean. Landry's face ain't no longer than it ought to be, and how long ought a face be, other than what the good Lord decided on." That quieted her brother, but she could see a tickle of a smile peeking out. She put a thankful hand on her brother's shoulder. She needed a laugh, and he would often supply at the most surprising times.

They walked toward the town as they passed where Lenny Stubbings, the clock operator, was carefully placing the date blocks on the marquee. "Speaking of books, you ever notice how there's no book in the library that's newer than 1989?" Tabitha asked.

"That ain't the kind of thing I'd notice," Tobias said. They continued walking.

"I've looked. All of 'em are decades old or more. Nothing new. Why you think that is?" she asked.

"If it ain't the kind of thing I'd noticed, why you think I'd know why that is?"

The buildings were rustic wood and weathered brick, their facades adorned with hand-painted signs and colorful awnings. One car was on the street—Kelvin Jester's '79 Chevette—which had been there nearly three years after it had finally died. The townsfolk had gathered around it in a kind of farewell ceremony as Kelvin removed his things, not knowing they'd be staring at it streetside for years to come. The council had repeatedly told Kelvin to remove it from the town center, but there it sat and likely would continue until the Lord returned or the council could agree on a penalty for non-compliance.

Tabitha waved at townspeople in the diner, the seamstress shop, the general store, and the bakery as her brother pulled her along at a pace more clipped than a barber could produce.

They passed the telephone booth, which was absolutely filled to the brim with Reverend Tucker talking loudly about the Lord's work to someone or another. Books were a great escape, but a viable alternative was the Reverand's weekly sermons. He was a fantastic storyteller, and Tabitha often found herself lost in his stories. She paused to eavesdrop on the Reverand's phone booth conversation as she drank up his big booming voice. It was both charming and impossible to ignore.

"Come on," Tobias said.

"Tobias, you're gone need a halter rope for pulling me along if you want to go any faster." He didn't respond.

Next door was the movie shop, another option for some escapism. Its windows were filled with posters advertising the week's VHS rental deals. Tabitha smiled and let her eyes drift over the faded images, all of which she'd seen before. No new movies ever came available, but the rotation of the posters drew a crowd every Tuesday, often reminding folks of old favorites. The door jingled as Judd Lumpkin exited, clutching a stack of tapes. "What'd you get, Judd?" Tabitha hollered with a smile.

"Just the best ones," he said as he grinned. "But I left you a copy of The Sound of Music." Tabitha laughed. Tobias tugged.

As they continued down the sidewalk, the twins passed a music store, its shelves lined with rows of vinyl records. The music spilled out like liquid enjoyment. She hummed pleasantly with the familiar tune.

Then, there was Randy Sherbert's picture shop, and they took that blurry view at nearly a run. Tabitha had done a summer internship with Randy after her eighth-grade year, a time of joy and exhilaration. To this day, she loved stopping by to see the new photos Randy Sherbet had put out to dry. Her spirits lifted into the air at the memory of the darkroom duties bathed in red light, watching the mysterious prints come to life with color and contrast. Such good memories.

The final building in the street's lineup was a charred ruin, black and gnarled. Any altitude her heart had gained was lost in a violent crash. By now, it was a habit to look in the opposite direction as they passed the eerie place that had spelled the end of everything they once cared about. Their happy future had ended in that building. Although she had memories from before the fire, the burnt remains represented the symbol of her single greatest loss, something she was still running from. She frowned as she trained her eyes on the dirt. Why hadn't the elders torn it down? There it sat as a black-hearted reminder of every awful moment experienced in the last ten years.

ISOLATION

They came to Isolation's community hall at the end of the town's Main Street. They paused, feeling the dark forboding in the intimidating edifice. They looked at each other and started up the steps.

Argue

The heavy wooden doors of the community hall creaked as Tabitha and Tobias pushed through. Shadows from a low-slung chandelier were painted across the walls, casting an eerie glow over the faces of the assembled council members and their audience. Seven elders in black robes sat on the raised stage.

Out in front of the semicircle platform where the elders sat was a space big enough to hold half the town if the town had half a mind to be held in such a place. As it was, there wasn't much draw for most folk to come and listen to the old birds bicker whistle at one another for hours. Nonetheless, Ferris Daudry, Ansil Trapendorf, and Glenda Hensley were almost always in attendance.

In a chair that sat cattycorner to the elder's platform slumped Horace Gumnut, acting sheriff of Isolation. He was as old as a dinosaur bone. Horace never wore his badge, had only ever fired a sidearm at rattlesnakes, and found no chair too hard for a nap. At that moment, he was asleep and snoring. The council was experienced enough not to be distracted by any amount of sleep sounds.

At the center of it all, Ram Stern, one of Isolation's elders, was delivering a humdinger of a speech with spit and sweat flying like chip wood at a lumberjack's convention. His salt-and-pepper hair framed a face all wadded up with concern. His broad shoulders and muscular build filled his black judge's robe like a bull in a tube sock.

"Lies and evil run wild outside our borders," he warned, his thick southern accent carrying through the hall in a low rumbling tone. "The outsiders worship that evil, the satanic filth we've isolated from. We must stand against these ever-growing threats."

There was a visible split among the council members. Some nodded in agreement, their expressions taut with worry, while others seemed skeptical. Elder Amos Flint seemed nothing at all, as he was deeply engaged in a covert nose-picking session. As he tried to rid his finger of the incriminating evidence, someone else took the floor briefly.

Tabitha glanced at her brother, searching his face for some comfort. She found none. Though she had never stepped foot beyond the sanctuary of Isolation, the horrors Ram described felt all too real. Tabitha's imagination ran wild, conjuring up vivid images of a world consumed by lies. How could anyone be so dense as to fall for that kind of evil?

In her mind, she saw towering cities of steel spikes rising into the sky, their cold facades hiding even colder hearts. The people who walked those streets were mere shells; their humanity was stripped away like a husk after the harvest. They were eaten up, rotten, and completely consumed by their gross obsessions, most of which Tabitha couldn't even understand. They moved like tumbleweeds across a spiritual desert, eyes glazed like a dead dog's.

And yet, she longed to see it all. Her secret desire to go to the world beyond was a constant companion. Her mind wandered. She imagined herself aboard the Dumfries with Hudson Taylor in 1853, sailing to the adventured land of China to begin his mission work. What she wouldn't give to be in the wind, riding the roads, free to roam like the missionaries of old. The noisy debate smashed her daydream and brought her back to the overheated room that sweltered with tension.

"Then we must find a balance." It was Elder Silas Granger speaking now. "Our isolation from the outside world has kept us from fully following Jesus' commandments. We are still a community of faith, are we not?" The town was brimming over with talk about Silas Granger's abnormal and unusual views. Ram sure hated him. She wished she could ask her dad about the whole thing.

Tobias leaned over and whispered in Tabitha's ear. "Ram's about to quote Soren." Tabitha looked up at her big brother. "Just watch."

"Balance?" Ram scoffed. "As our founder Soren Krieger once said, 'The world outside drifts in shadow. We, the Isolationists, are the preservers of the Lord's light.'" Ram's head bobbled a little as he quoted the familiar words. Other voices whispered along as the red-faced councilman concluded his recitation. "...Live as if Isolation is the only place that matters because, my dear children, it is.'"

"Told you," Tobias whispered. Tabitha was too stricken by the recited words to respond. The images of the founder hung in virtually every home, shop, and lobby in town. She glanced to the back wall of the council room where a large painting of Soren Krieger hung, serious as a snake bite, sideburns so bushy a hedge trimmer would lose teeth on them, peering down at the room of his spiritual descendants. She blinked away the frightening image of the man's face.

"We are aware of Soren's contributions," Silas said. "But he has been dead quite some time. I do not hear any hint of God's grace in your words, Ram. Even Soren Krieger often reminded us of our need to remember the Lord's sacrifice and his gift of grace to us. Would you ignore such important reminders?"

"The Isolation Doctrine must be upheld," Ram said. "As long as the outside world stays outside, we will continue our harmless neglect of them, but if they draw near, we must be ready with overwhelming firepower."

"It's talk like that that makes our young people want to leave Isolation," Silas said. "Amos' boys left just last week, and before that Jedediah's son, and prior to that the Thompson's daughter Hanna. We are driving away our own children."

"Ha!" Ram spat. He balled his hand into a fist and banged it on the podium. "Those brats were never truly Isolationists. Let them leave! Let them rot!" That fiery bark earned a few murmurs from those in attendance. Horace stopped snoring for a moment, but only for a moment. Silas put his face in his hand.

"Do you have something to propose, Ram?" Silas said through his fingers.

"We need to update our armory," Ram said. "Do you know we don't have a single firearm larger than a fifty-caliber machine gun?"

"A fifty cal!" Silas sat up straight, anger in his face. "You can explode a gourd at a thousand yards with one of those. How about a thermo-nuclear hydrogen bomb while we're at it?"

"Great idea!" Ram said with a low gravel and plenty of scorn rattling in his voice. "We could gather all the leavers, the spoiled rotten children of this cowardly council, and test it on them."

His words struck like flint against steel, blowing a powder keg of pent-up rage. The council exploded, voices rose, and a volcanic eruption broiled into a cacophony of dissent. Tabitha's entire universe was defined by what happened in that room, and that room was fighting like a pair of desert cats behind the butcher's shop. She wanted to scream. She closed her eyes and gripped the sides of her jeans.

Against the backdrop of the noise, Tobias leaned over to his twin sister and whispered in her ear. "I wish Soren was here. He'd straighten all this out." She nodded in agreement, but as her eyes opened and darted to the image of the man on the wall, she wondered if even he would be capable.

The debate's volume took back her attention. Elder Silas Granger's face was still in his hand as the room rioted around him. As she watched him, she thought of Lavender Delitaunt's juicy rumors about Silas. Could he really be part of a midnight meeting, a secret society that drank chicken's blood and aimed to rebel against Soren Krieger's Isolation Doctrine? She then looked at the red-faced Ram, trying to shout over the other members who were mad enough to oppose the broad brawler. What a mess. She wished her dad was there to make her feel like the world wasn't coming apart. She wished, but wishing had solved nothing in ten long years.

Mission

"Enough!" thundered Silas, bringing the room to a silence even crickets could appreciate. The elder's eyes ranged toward the back of the hall where Tabitha and Tobias stood waiting. An expression as enthusiastic as if he'd discovered a giant raspberry pie waiting in the back row drifted across his face. "Ram, I ask that you step aside for now. We have a less incendiary matter to attend to, and I dare say we would all appreciate a break from the current topic." Mumbled agreement rippled the council members each in turn. Even Horace Gumnut snorted assent, though he didn't know he had done so.

As Elder Ram Stern lurched violently away from the podium, the council shifted to the new agenda item. Tabitha's stomach got as tight as a slipknot on a goat's neck. Silas motioned for her and Tobias to come forward.

"Please, join us at the front," Silas beckoned. The twins exchanged a glance. Their steps were heavy. Who knew the floor had become wet concrete drying around their feet? She felt as bare as if she had worn her pajamas to Sunday church.

"Sadly," Silas said, his voice filling up the hall. "Our dear friend Harrison Thatcher, a lifelong devotee of our community and Soren Krieger, has recently died." The light murmur of noise in the room hinted everyone had heard the news already. Tabitha endured a stab of sadness, nearly enough to drown out her nerves for a second. She'd often spent long hours in the old man's company at socials. His mustache had been a legend of myth and folklore. It even had its own name among the town's kids, but almost none agreed what that name was. Tabitha smiled at the warm memory.

Silas continued, "As you may know, Harrison's son, Elijah, was a leaver." The noise the room made was different at that admission. Tabitha thought she felt the earth itself grumble with tremors and quakes at the "L" word. Before the crowd could get too spiced up, Silas continued. "He chose to venture out into the outside world several years ago." Tabitha thought she heard the sound of someone spitting behind her in the audience gallery. She decided not to look back.

"In light of Harrison's passing, it is our duty to inform his son, Elijah, of his father's death. All might not agree with his leaving, but he deserves to know," Silas explained. Tabitha studied Elder Silas's face with its obvious compassion and mourning. He spoke like he cared, like he was speaking of his own brother. She looked over at Ram, whose arms were so crossed that each hand was buried in an armpit.

"This is exactly what I was talking about," Ram interrupted. His hot words were strained through clenched teeth. "Soren Krieger would never—"

Silas raised his voice to such a booming eruption that the room seemed to grow six inches in every direction. "We've already settled this! This council has decided that we can communicate with leavers when the death of kin is involved. No more interruptions, if you please." Ram's face turned angrier, and his rage beamed out like violent radiation in Silas' direction, but he was quiet for now.

Silas nodded in appreciation and turned his attention back to Tabitha and Tobias. His voice grew soft and fatherly. "As I was saying, we have a solemn duty to inform Elijah of his father's passing. And this is where you two come in."

Tabitha's eyes went big, and she felt the hot tension pouring off Tobias like a potbelly stove. Silas smiled reassuringly at them. "Don't worry." He leaned forward over the podium, his voice lowering. "You see, when messages need to be sent to the outside, we assign someone to venture to the edge of our lands, to a place called Edgetown. There, they can forward a message with a digital."

Tabitha's hand shot up. She wasn't sure of the protocol for speaking so she started in with her voice full of pepper and whistle. "Pardon me, Elder Silas, Sir, I know that digitals are bad 'cause the Isolation Doctrine says so, but what is a *digital*?"

Elder Jedediah Thorp leaned over and whispered something to Elder Hangus Lithrum. Elder Amos Flint looked up from the floor; it was the first time she saw his eyes. The elders all seemed to fidget in a unison dance of discomfort, all but Silas. His eyes crinkled with nothing more than amusement. "Ah yes, it's not a term you would be familiar with, is it?"

Ram Stern cleared his throat as forcefully as a powder musket. "This is too much. Our founder would pour fire and brimstone on this assembly if he were here. Soren Krieger is turning in his grave!" His massive muscular body rose like a bolt of lightning the earth rejected as he exploded from his council seat. He stomped out of the chamber with his chin pointing so high he could have scraped the domed ceiling. Two others stood looking like puppies and followed him out. The council, minus three, seemed to breathe a sigh of relief.

"That's better," Silas said. Some of the other council members gave his words a light chuckle. "Let the meeting record show that Ram, Amos, and Ichabod have left." Silas turned back to Tabitha, his eyes fresh and ready. "Digital, my dear, is a thing for sending messages and other operations. It's what outsiders use to communicate over great distances."

Tabitha felt a frown she hadn't invited tighten into disgust. Her hand shot up again. "Elder Silas, I have a question. I was reading in a book from the Library a while back, about Mary Slessor. She was the one who did that mission to a tribe of Cannibals in Nigeria, Africa, in the 1800s. I'm sure you've heard of her. But she had to face all kinds of things like, did you know, them people would kill twins cause they thought they were cursed or something like that. Guess me and Toby wouldn't have made it, huh? They'd kill you too if you had different religion. But anyway, she was really brave, but she had to face all kinds of dangers in her missionary work and..."

"Miss Andrews," Elder Silas gently interrupted. "While I find this missionary biography fascinating, I'm wondering if we will arrive at the question any time soon."

"I'm sorry, sometimes I ramble when I'm nervous." She paused for a deep breath. "What I mean to ask, is Edgetown dangerous? Elder Stern said the outsiders worship the satanic corruption. I mean, are we going to get mixed up in any of that?"

"A fair question, Tabitha," Silas said. "Our relationship with Edgetown is delicate. Their location allows us to maintain contact when absolutely necessary. Edgetown is comprised of a small population of friendlies... mostly." Silas' reassurance should have come as a relief, but somehow, Tabitha felt, what? Disappointment, she guessed. Silas continued.

"Tabitha, your name was chosen by lottery to carry out this task. And Tobias, the council believes you would be a good escort for your sister. But understand this is a request, not a demand. You have every right to decline, and the responsibility will pass to the next name drawn if you do. Elder Stern believes you two were too young for this responsibility. I, however, think that he is as ignorant as an old boot, with a brain pan full of rusted daggers and a heart of asbestos, who is going to—"

"Silas," Jedadiah said. Silas cleared his throat and straightened his robes.

"My apologies," Silas said. "I meant to say I believe he is wrong."
Tabitha bit her lip.

"Normally, the decision would fall to your parents, as is our custom when a child's name is drawn. But given your—uh—circumstances..." He trailed off, letting the implication of the unspoken loss hang in the air like an unwanted aroma.

Tabitha's eyes immediately found the floor. Why was he bringing that up? There was no need to talk about that. Not here. Not with everyone watching.

Silas continued. "The council has decided—" He glanced around. "—that is, the council members who are now present believe that you are old enough to make this decision for yourselves."

Tabitha glanced at Tobias, trying to gauge his reaction. His cheeks were red, and his frown and brows sagged as if ten-pound weights hung from them. Before he could decline, which she knew from his expression he was about to do, she leaped forward with the words that came like slingshot pellets.

"So, what exactly do we need to do?" Tabitha asked.

Outward

Tabitha wiped the beads of sweat from her brow as she and Tobias trudged through the desert landscape, heading toward the
outskirts of town. "Linda Saphronelly said it'll reach 109 degrees
today," she said, squinting against the sun's nuclear glare.

"And how would Linda Saphronelly know that?" Tobias said.
"As if anyone knows what the weather's to be. She's just a gossip.
Her and Lavender Delitaunt. When they's running out a some-
thing juicy, they starts prophesying the climate."

"It's hot as an oven out here, and what do you choose to
complain about?" Tabitha asked. "That Linda gossips."

"Gossip's a jackrabbit snare," Tobias said. "If you get caught
up in it, you're gone a get hurt."

"You and your snares," Tabitha said. "Speaking of the heat,
you know Robert Moffat did his missionary work in Botswana.
He worked with the Bechuana people. Them folks lived in a
place hot as this, but it was something like 1820 or maybe 30s,
so they didn't have none of the cool-down stuff we got. Can you
imagine?"

"I cannot," Tobias said, not sounding engaged in the conversation. "Get that little tidbit from a book, did you?"

"Sure did," Tabitha said. "Its cover's gone, who knows where, but I think it was called *Missionary Labours and Scenes in Southern Africa.*" She laughed. "They sure did do long titles back then, didn't they."

"You read the weirdest books," Tobias said.

"You read that book on snares like a hundred times," Tabitha said. Tobias chuckled. The twins continued their journey on foot over the narrow dusty road that shot straight as an arrow out of Isolation. The dust kicked up by their boots swirled in the dead, dry air.

"You think Isolation'll ever send out any missionaries?" Tabitha asked.

"Nope."

"Why not?"

"Isolation doctrine," Tobias said. "That and missionarying don't mix."

"Yeah, but..." Tabitha wanted to protest.

"Them missionaries was in the old world before everything went crazy," Tobias explained. "Things are different now. Soren Krieger said in the Second Indictum, 'We are keepers of the ancient ways, ordained to uphold the statutes.' We can't just ignore that." She did not know the indictums of Soren like her brother, but she had been raised on the isolation doctrine like all the rest. From the time she started school, there were two books that were mandatory daily reading: the Bible and The Isolation Doctrine by Soren Krieger. The Bible reading she loved, as it was full of amazing stories, unimaginable wisdom, and God's unfailing grace. The Isolation Doctrine, however, she had struggled to finish. Her lack of affection for Soren Krieger's booklet was a secret that she had never admitted, even to her twin.

They were passing through the crop fields that rimmed the outer circle of town. The farming sector was a swath of green, a real oasis against the arid, desert-colored landscape. Perfect, straight rows of vegetables mocked the barren surroundings, where they shouldn't be able to grow.

Overhead, shade nets that let through only about half the amount of available sun made a kind of blanket to coddle the plants growing below. Early settlers in Isolation learned that the sun had to be gentled down a touch for anything to grow.

Along the crop rows, drip irrigation lines snaked through each rut, delivering precious water directly to the base of each plant. Not a single drop was wasted in this unforgiving environment.

Linda Stern and Larry Kent were in the distance, cranking a wheel on the irrigation system. Tabitha waved, and they both returned the gesture from their distance. "You ever seen Linda Stern anywhere but the farm?" Tabitha asked.

"Try being married to Ram Stern and see if *you* don't find another place to be twenty-three hours a day," Tobias said as he waved at Linda and Larry in the distance. "Lavender Delitaunt says that when them two got hitched, Ram used Soren Krieger's isolation doctrine as his wedding vows."

"That isn't true," she laughed as she playfully slapped his arm.

"But it's funny," he said.

A pause followed as the smile fell from Tabitha's expression. "I don't like it when the elders fight," Tabitha said as the image of Ram's red face lurched into her mind. "Makes me feel scared." She reached out to touch one of the heads of corn as they passed. "Why do they argue so much?"

"Ram Stern's been a unofficial leader no one asked for since Soren Krieger died," Tobias said. "But since Silas Granger got on the board, things been changing. Ram's losing his control. I spect he don't like it much. A fight's a coming."

"They been fighting already."

"No, I mean a *fight* fight," Tobias said. "It ain't gonna be pretty neither."

The fear she felt for the subject only grew with her brother's explanation. They went silent for a few minutes. Down the path, they came to the water cisterns, tall cylinders with concrete sides mounted atop platforms made of steel beams. Hanging from the side of each cistern was a rope with a weight on the end. Tabitha stopped, looking at the red flag tied to the end of each chord. "Them cisterns sure is low."

"They'll have to move the pump soon," Tobias said. "They'll have to check the Overseer's Handbook for the best spot."

Soon, they came to the housing units, rows of underground homes identified only by half-circle entrances that jutted up from the ground with bunker doors. Living below ground let the Isolationists escape some of the heat, but without windows, most preferred to sit outside their doors in the mornings and evenings.

The twins both looked at it, the entrance to the home they had grown up in. So many dusk hours were spent playing around that hatch, walking this road, giggling the waning days away in the happy ignorance of youth. The house had been reassigned to the Burrlesons when Tabitha's had suddenly become a family of two rather than its previous size of four. Since then, she and her brother had lived in two dozen of the other burrows with whomever they'd been assigned to for a time. She sure was tired of feeling like an unwanted pet. They walked on without a word about it.

The grumbling grind of Isolation's only oil pump thrummed loud and persistent as they passed. It swung up and down in its constant pursuit of the deep black sludge. Next to it, the town generator buzzed, rattling the sheet metal building that housed it. They could feel its vibrations through their shoes.

Beyond, they could see the wall that encircled Isolation stretching out in both directions. It was a fence work construction that rose eight feet and held in its borders all they had ever known. The gate toward which they had been walking was wide open. In

Tabitha's living memory, there had never been a time when the gate had been closed, despite Ram Stern's constant insistence that the gates should be shut and locked.

They paused in front of the gate poles at the final water station, one of several throughout the community. It consisted of a wooden barrel whose wood had been baked to an ashen paler. Above it, hanging from the gatepost, was a wooden sign that read, "HYDRATE OR DIE!"

Desert

Standing before the water barrel, neither had to say a thing. Water was life, and there was no traveling without it unless you wanted to turn into a sun-bleached pile of bones in a lonely stretch of nowhere. They filled their water jugs, two a piece, to the absolute maximum, drank as much as possible, and topped them off again. Each pulled out a bandana, soaked them in the barrel, and wrapped them about their heads. Placing their hats over the bandanas, they turned toward the road out of town and started walking.

Passing through the gate of Isolation was a strange feeling. She looked back from outside the wall and marveled that her entire life's memories were from within those borders. That wall housed all she'd ever known, and it was as easy as breathing to walk through the exit. It was frightening and exciting. She imagined herself as the subject of one of the missionary biographies she read, stepping boldly into a new frontier. She glanced at her brother to discover that he looked only to the road ahead, so she did the same.

The heat made every step feel like she was dragging a hundred pounds of sand in each boot, and yet she felt like a bird let loose from her cage. They marched across the endless desert, but her mind was elsewhere. She imagined wings sprouting from those heavy boots and carrying her over the horizon. She was like Nate Saint, a twentieth-century aviation missionary in South America, soaring through the clouds, flying above the desert, looking for whatever adventure God sent her way. She swayed side to side with the daydream as she let out a joyful sigh. Her motion caught the attention of her frowning brother. Tobias said, "Your steps are getting wobbly. Time for a drink."

"Already," she said.

"Trip's bout fifteen miles," he said. "Seventy-nine thousand feet. Our steps are two and a half feet. Forty mouthfuls per jug. Two jugs a piece. So every four-hundred steps, we's gone a take a mouthful of water."

"You counting our steps?"

"No, just mine," he said. "If I counted yours too, I'd have to divide by two, and I'm too hot to do any more math." As she laughed at him, she pulled off her hat and bandanna and poured some of her jug's water on it. "What you thinking? Don't waste no water on your head!"

"It's fine," she said, shoving his arm with a snicker. He gave her a lecture about conserving water, but she wasn't listening. She was watching the horizon with a glee that was hard to place. A rising enthusiasm for what was beyond the floating heat waves could have carried her over the sand.

They walked for what felt like years. Each step was heavier. The dust rustled up by their foot pounding went for a flight only to discover there was nothing to land on but them. It coated their entire bodies. They became the same pale color, covered from head to toe in the horrid desert grit. Despite the blazing heat, she was filled with lightning and thunder, a powerful joy to be going, well, anywhere. In her whole life, she couldn't say she'd ever really gone anywhere, at least not past the edge of Isolation. Through her cracked lips, she wore a broad, out-of-place smile.

"After we're done, we ought to go cool down in Lyle Stephens' bread oven. It's got to be colder than this," Tobias said. He gestured to her jug, and she took a sip.

Even with the hat and long sleeves, Tabitha could feel her body dehydrating in the desert's furnace. She touched the back of her hand and knew what she'd forgotten. "Oops," she said. After pausing, she shoved her half-drained jugs to the side, reached for her shoulder bag, and rummaged in search of something.

"Tobias, wait a sec," she called out, her hands buried deep in the bag.

"What's up?" Tobias asked, turning around to face her.

"Need my sunscreen. Forgot to put any on the back of my hands," she muttered, her fingers closing around a thick leather-bound volume rather than the expected tube.

"What?" she said to herself. "But—no."

"Now, what?" he said. She looked as if she'd discovered a grenade missing the pin in her bag. She pulled out the unexpected book and held it out in her brother's direction.

"Tobias," she breathed, trembling, "It's the..."

"Oh no!" he said. "No. No. No." he put his hands over his mouth. "That can't be here."

In her shaky hand, she held the *Overseer's Handbook.* They looked at it for a long time. Just looked at it. Saying nothing. Doing nothing. Just looking at the scorching, blinding, torturous notebook. They'd messed up big. How big? Big enough that if the rest of their lives were filled with almighty perfection, they'd still be marked down for an F minus for all their days.

"I don't know how it got in my bag," Tabitha said. "I'm sure I left it on the table in the library. You saw me, right?" A few tears made dust mud on her cheek. She knew her hydration couldn't spare the fluids it took to cry, but she couldn't stop it. She gently put the *Overseer's Handbook* back in her bag. "We should turn back, right?"

"Yes," he said. They started in that direction, but then he moaned. "No, we can't." He bounced in place with the indecision. She bit the nails of her left hand as she watched her twin squirm.

"Why not?" she said with a wincing stare. "It's way more important than getting to Edgetown."

"I know, but we can't," he said, holding up his two water jugs. "We're nineteen thousand four hundred steps into the walk. Water's way too low to make it back without refilling." He spun around. "If we keeled over out here, they'd wonder where the handbook went, maybe never find it. We got to get to Edgetown. We'll refill and then head back right away."

"But, once we're there, should we do the message thingy?"

"Yeah, we'll send the message, but we have to be—"

"I know. We'll be careful," she said. "I swear, Tobias, I don't know how it got there." He looked at her with his eyes but didn't turn toward her. Her bag felt like it had gained a thousand pounds. The weight of the entire community was a burden that she now carried. She watched Tobias, waiting for the lecture, the correction, the rebuke.

"It's fine," Tobias said.

"It's fine?" she asked. "What's got into you? I got the most important book there ever was, and you say, 'It's fine?' Ain't you gonna use them words to beat on me something fierce?"

"Listen," Tobias said. They continued walking as Tobias began lecturing her about the original copy of the indictums of Soren Krieger penned on the first pages of the handbook. He explained how the book had all the notes on the town's water strategy. He went on about the diagrams it contained concerning the oil derrick, the generator, and the irrigation equipment. He expounded that the handbook contained essential information about isolation's infrastructure. The town could not run without it. All of this, she knew, of course. His words were black and brooding, laying the blame on Tabitha's shoulders. And why not? It was in her bag, after all.

But something was bothering her as he talked. She was puzzling over how that blasted handbook got into her bag. She'd run over the scenario a dozen times, turning it into roadkill proper. Tobias was in the middle of some word soup. That's when it hit her.

"It was you!" she blurted out so loud that they both stopped walking. "You grabbed my stuff at the library. You wadded it up like a dinner rag and threw the whole mess in my bag. You didn't know I had the book in my stack of papers. You put the *Overseer's Handbook* in there without knowing you was doing it."

"Oh," he said.

"That's it?" she said. "You lecture me for a half hour about how Isolation is drier than a twenty-month-old raisin, about Soren's indictums, about the diagrams of whatever, then when I prove this whole thing was your fault, you just say," she puckered her lips out and made a mockery of his voice. "Oh?"

"This is where we are now, and we'll just have to make the best of it."

"You knew," she said. "As soon as I pulled it out. You knew."

"It's not like I—"

"Normally, you would have said, 'Tabitha, what have you done?' or 'Tabitha, you're so irresponsible,' but you didn't. You said, 'It's fine.' You only went a lecturing when I called you on how you was being so odd." She took off her hat and hit him with it. "You brute.

You was gonna let me think I did it! As if it ain't enough for me to be carrying around something that, if it went lost, would spell the end of Isolation. You was going to go without sharing some of that blame."

"It ain't no help to figure on who was the faulty one," he said.

She stomped her foot and planted her body. Tears spilled out so hot they might turn to steam on her cheek. She gritted her teeth and spoke in a wild growl. "Tobias Garrett Andrews, I am not going another step until you apologize to me. And you best make it a good one!" He stopped and turned her way.

"But we've arrived," he said. She was about to go in for a mighty fight, but when he pointed over her shoulder at the little outpost of Edgetown, she let her red-peppered temper reach for a drink.

It was at least a quarter mile ahead, but the shape of a town, the only she'd ever seen other than Isolation, put her into a forgetting mood. She stepped next to her broad-shouldered brother and wrapped her dust-covered fingers around his thick arm.

In a hushed voice, she said, "We're in the outside."

Edgetown

Tabitha put her flattened hand above her eyes as she and Tobias stepped off the dusty footpath and into the little city center of Edgetown. The few roads she had ever seen were dirt. The street here was paved, black and hard. She knelt down to inspect the stuff. She toed it with her boot and laughed. "They got hard roads," she said with an exuberant breath. Her excited attention turned beyond.

Both sides of the pavement were lined with odd buildings, their purposes unknown. Through her perpetual grin, she wondered where the crops, the cisterns, the picture shop, and the seamstress were. She was eager to lay eyes on the indigenous people of the outside. But where were the people? Her heart thumped with a passion to explore.

"We're really doing it, Bubba," she said with a squeal. She squeezed his arm and bounced a half dozen times. "I feel like Lottie Moon on her first foot into China, where she was going to do her mission."

"This ain't what I expected," Tobias murmured, his brow pressed down low into his eye's real estate. His grumbling tone was the perfect opposite of his twin sister's joy.

"I feel like Amy Carmichael's first time seeing India," Tabitha said in something related to a whisper. "She was a missionary, too. Or Albert Schweitzer in Gabon, or Johnathan Goforth in China—or—or—"

"Sis," Tobias said, "You're rambling. And when you're rambling, there ain't no space in my brain for thinking, and this would be a good time for some thinking."

"Sorry," she said, nodding, putting her hand over her mouth as if her smile was outlawed. "I'm just excited. Can you believe it?"

Tobias ignored her enthusiasm. "Half them shops look abandoned," Tobias said.

"Let's poke our head in some," Tabitha said.

"Probably get it chopped off," Tobias said. "That one might be safe enough." He pointed to one that was slightly less dilapidated than the others.

Something like the sound of a bell jangled as they pushed open the door, but the noise was thin and fake. Inside, the shop was cluttered with blinking screens, gadgets, glowing headsets - devices beyond anything the twins had ever seen.

Tabitha looked at her brother, who was whispering something too quiet for her ears. His wide eyes portrayed his emotion. She leaned close to hear his words. "The Fifth Indictum. 'Cast them far from thee! Let no such digital abomination be found within our borders, lest ye bring about the wrath of God." He was quoting Soren Krieger's isolation doctrine. Of course, he was. She let her hungry eyes roam.

They'd been staunchly taught to avoid digitals and witchcraft, and so they had. Not that they ever had a chance to do otherwise in the place they were from. Tabitha inspected each inexplicable device, touching, examining, and holding.

"Tabby, no," Tobias whispered. "They'll banish us from Isolation if they know you was messing round with this stuff." She was about to respond, but a voice cut her off.

"Well, now, what have we here?" A stocky man with a bald head and bushy beard emerged from behind the counter, eyes crinkling in a wild smile. He was the only one in the store beside them, but he was big enough to have eaten the last few customers. She gawked at his smile, as he would have needed more teeth for them to be at risk of cannibalism. "Welcome to Sliv's Pawn and Body Art! Name's Sliv. What can I do you for?"

"I...we..." Tobias stammered. He glanced helplessly at Tabitha. He had nothing.

She smiled in the revelry that she was about to talk to her first native of the outside. Her speech was slow and deliberate, as if the man was short on vocabulary. "We've come a long way. We're looking for someone who can help us with an important matter."

"That so?" Sliv laughed as he looked them up and down, rubbing his beard. "Important matter, eh? Well, ol' Sliv knows a thing or two about matters of import." He overemphasized the "t" as he wagged his head side to side. His beard looked like a whisker pendulum as it tickled his round belly.

Tabitha's eyes were wide with discovery and intrigue as she met Sliv's gaze. As she did, she realized he had two gazes, one forward and focused, the other lazy and interested in the ceiling. "We're here on behalf of our elders," she added.

"Whoo—wee," Sliv mused. "You gots elders. Ain't you some'in snazzy."

"Okay," she agreed with a smile. She looked back at Tobias to share the pleasure of first contact. He was not experiencing the same overjoyed exuberance. She turned back to Sliv. "We need to send a message with a digital on electric wires?" She winced.

Sliv nodded knowingly. "Ah, I see. You're Isolationists, ain't ya? Leavers, the lot of you. I get your kind in here from time to time, looking like a bag of fresh rabbit feet, dragging them burning bones cross that there desert. What do you do out there in the dust? Sacrifice rattlesnakes and scorpions to the sun god, I wager."

"We're not leavers," Tobias said defensively, which made all of Sliv's face skin bunch up near his eyebrows.

Sliv chuckled. "Well, well, spiffy toot shoot. You *can* talk. I was thinking the sun had drained your brain. Big ol' boy like you, don't always learn words too good."

"Oh, he's right, Sir," Tabitha echoed. "We're not leavers."

"Not yet, you ain't. But mark my words, you will be." He clapped his hands together. "Now, about that message. I've got just the thing! You got money?"

They looked at each other with confusion. "Messages cost money?"

"Everything costs money," he said. "Sometimes things costs lots more than money too." He didn't give them a chance to respond. "My second wife cost me this." He pulled up his filth-stained shirt and showed off a scar that snaked up his bulbous, hairy belly. As he put his shirt back down, Sliv tore off a big piece of laughter so violent that the twins both stepped back. After the thunder of belly concussions died down, he spoke up again.

"I didn't pay the internet bill one month, and she done chopped into my gut like I was a rotisserie chicken. She didn't take kindly to missing her favorite VR show, *Burned*. She loved seeing how different people hollered at being burned, but oh, the screeching and squeaking that came out of her headset were something awful."

"She burned people?" Tabitha asked, confused at the odd story.

"No, they burned 'em on the show and videoed it in 3D," Sliv said. "Animals, too. It was popular for a few seasons until it got replaced with that other show, *Mutilated*. That show's in its fourteenth season." As he talked, he led them to a display case filled with strange devices. "See, what you want is a holographic implant. Connects straight to your cerebral cortex. Slick as can be. They pulled this one out of a feller who got behind on the payments. He ain't seeing nothing now." Sliv laughed. They didn't understand. When he saw they weren't laughing, he added, "'Cause he's dead, you see."

Tabitha gulped hard. "Oh, my."

"The elders didn't say anything about that," Tobias said.

"Course, if that's too fancy for ya," Sliv continued, "we've got retinal embedded projection units. Augmented reality contact lenses. Or virtual reality headsets if you're feeling old-school. And if all else fails, there's always the ancient standby." He gestured to a dusty laptop in the corner.

Tobias frowned. "I'm not sure we—"

"Tell you what," Sliv interrupted. "I'll make you a deal. The implant, the headset, and the laptop are all for one low price. What do you say?"

It all made as much sense as a dress on a pig. She backed away, shaking her head. "I...I think we need to talk it over a bit. Thank you for your time, Sir."

Sliv shrugged. "Suit yourself. But I'm telling you, you won't find a better deal this deep into the dust lands."

Tabitha grabbed Tobias's arm and pulled him towards the door. As the sound of the fake bell jangled behind them, she let out a shaky breath.

"What was that guy talking about?" she said as they entered the blistering sun. Her earlier enthusiasm had a few bent edges, but in the open air, she took a deep breath and let her smile return.

"I don't know," Tobias agreed.

"What now?" Tabitha asked.

"Let's find some water," Tobias said. They walked the length of Main Street and stopped at the end of the row of buildings. "Where's their water barrel for travelers?" Tobias wondered aloud. They walked the other way, searching more thoroughly, but couldn't spot it.

"It don't make no sense," Tabitha said. "How could anyone stay hydrated?" One more walk through town, and they came up short. "Okay, I'm going to ask Sliv," Tobias told her not to, but she didn't listen. She opened the front door of Sliv's just enough to stick her head in and said, "Where does one fill up one's water?"

Sliv said, "One could use one's faucet on the one side of the one building if one were wanting one's water one upped." He laughed at his hilarious mockery as she slid back out the door.

They circled the building twice before they spotted it. They watched the street as cold water poured out of the faucet, filling their jugs to the brim. As they finished refilling their water, a person walked by on the street, stopped, and backed up. "Tabitha and Tobias Andrews? Is that you?"

They turned to see a young woman with long blonde hair and a warm smile. Tabitha's eyes widened in recognition. "Hanna

Thompson?" Tabitha felt like she'd just received a donkey kick to the stomach. How was she supposed to react? She'd expected to meet strangers, natives, and outsiders, but not this.

Hanna rushed forward, pulling them both into a hug. "I can't believe it's you! I'm so glad to see you." Tabitha was stiff, and Hanna let her go.

Hanna's smile faltered for a moment as they stood awkwardly close post-hug. They separated a bit in an attempt to alleviate the tension. "Did you just make the walk? You must be starving. Come on, let's go to my place. I'll cover your dinner. It's on me."

As Hanna started moving out of the alleyway, Tabitha tried to catch her brother's eyes, but they were fixed on Hanna. Tabitha tore her hat off and whacked him. When he looked back, she made her eyes as wide as possible and shook her head, 'No.' They couldn't. They shouldn't. Tobias shrugged as if he'd forgotten every warning he'd ever heard. What had gotten into him? She thought she knew, and it wasn't good. He turned and followed Hanna, leaving Tabitha silently brooding behind. Why was he being like this?

Diner

Tabitha and Tobias followed Hanna down the street, rounded the corner, and walked a block off Main. Over the door, a small, hand-painted sign read "Hanna's." The sign, the clean interior, and the retro vibe gave Tabitha the creeps. "Welcome," Hanna said, putting her arms out. The smell of something fried hit her nose. Tabitha felt her stomach rumble. Hanna disappeared into the kitchen as she said, "Be right back."

Tabitha started right in on Tobias. "We shouldn't be in here," she said. She continued to lecture him as he looked around the Diner. Pictures of patrons were taped to the walls. "Look," Tobias said. "There's Cici Linburg." He pointed at the picture taped near the door.

"It's like a leavers directory," Tabitha said. "There's Todd Lusk." She turned. "Drake Pensky." They and many others had left Isolation. They had all chosen to abandon the town, to run away, and their absence was the disdain of those who remained. One of the most recent leavers was Hanna Thompson. Tabitha felt an enduring bitterness toward those who had gone away. As they looked at the wall of Isolationist's traitors, Tabitha's eyes went wide, and her face drained of color. Her hand shot out and found her brother's shoulder.

"What?" Tobias said.

"Don't turn around," Tabitha said as she pulled her brother to the nearest table to whisper more safely. She slipped the shoulder bag off and laid it on the bench. They slid into either side of the booth. "There's a—guy—or not a guy— but a robot or something. He's wearing a hood at the back booth." Disobediently, Tobias spun around on his bench. The metallic face was turned down, sitting as still as a statue.

"I said not to turn around! Tabitha whisper-screamed. "There's a—a—robot in that..." She put her hands to his cheeks. "What?" She was breathing heavily. "We have to get out of here. We have to go back. We..."

"But Hanna said she could help," Tobias said. Tabitha couldn't take her eyes off the robot.

"She's a leaver and she brought us to a place with a digital—digital man thing," Tabitha whispered to Tobias. "Soren's third indictum says we're not allowed to talk to her? How does that one go?"

"They have given themselves over to the prince of the power of the airwaves, and thus defied the Lord of Heaven,' I know. I know. But—"

"It's looking at me," Tabitha said. "We need to be careful. We're not safe. What if she and the robot are—"

"Oh, come off it," Tobias said.

"Everyone knows you had a crush on Hanna Thompson when you two was younger," Tabitha whispered. "But remember. She's a leaver. She left. That means she left *you* behind in Isolation. So, don't get any ideas. She's dangerous."

"You're just mad at her cause—cause—well, you know," Tobias said. "But there ain't no need for you to be offended on my behalf. I'm a big boy."

"And you ain't got your head on right, cause your heart bout popped out your collar when you seen her, and you ain't thinking straight."

The conversation continued in hushed tones. They had been on the receiving end of speculation, gossip, and outright fabrications about Hanna Thompson. The rumor factory churned out gossip products at a dizzying pace whenever someone left Isolation. But no one knew what to believe about the leavers. Once they were gone, they became ghostly memories that would never be heard of again. Tabitha was about to come around for another volley, but she got quiet when she saw Hanna approaching.

"Hope you're hungry," Hanna said, coming back into the dining area. "Got us some grub." She carried a large round tray with plates. A thick hamburger with all the fixings, almost the size of his face, was set before Tobias. Tabitha was presented with a salad and a bowl of soup. She passed out thick slices of bread.

Tabitha had just about introduced the bread to her teeth when Hanna said, "Mind if I say the blessing?" The twins shared a surprised glance at each other before nodding. Hanna prayed in such a singsong voice she could have been a jukebox. A leaver who still prays? There goes that rumor. Tabitha ventured a peek at the young woman through squinted eyes. She was slim, beautiful, and seemed so full of joy she might explode with enthusiasm. Tabitha ground her teeth together at the sight of her. Who was it that hugged her brother to sleep when his heart was broken? Well, it sure wasn't this blonde leaver.

When Hanna's prayer entered its final lap, Tabitha glanced at Tobias. He wasn't even trying to hide his open eyes but studied the pretty blonde across from him as if it were finals week and she was the subject matter. When Hanna said, "In your name, we pray..." they both closed their eyes and bowed their heads in a hurry. "Amen." She took her fork in her hand and said, "I bet you're wondering what happened to me after I left Isolation."

Tabitha remained still, not taking her sullen eyes off Hanna, but Tobias nodded as he filled his mouth with a bite. "After I left, I spent some time in Dolos. That's the big city about an hour north. I thought I could find my way. Got into some trouble up there. They have some rules I didn't know about."

"Rules?" Tabitha said eyebrows furrowed. "I thought there wasn't rules outside."

"I know, right?" Hanna said. "So after that, I ended up back here in Edgetown. I worked at this diner for a while. The owner wanted out of the business, so I'm buying it from him."

Tabitha's forklift of leafy greens hovered in the air before her face while she asked, "You ever feel like you shouldn't have abandoned Isolation? Like maybe you shouldn't a abandoned people who wished you'd stayed?"

Hanna's look went distant, even pained. "Oh yeah. The Leaver's dilemma. My heart hurts every day about that, people I miss, people that miss me, but when you find your calling, you just know."

"What about your parents?" Tabitha asked. She heard her own words as if from a distance. They were acidic and cold. "Don't you know they was hurt to no end. How could you just abandon your parents? Not everyone has—has—well, not everyone can be so lucky. To think you left it behind."

"They see me enough," she said.

"What?" Tabitha said.

"My parents," Hanna said. "They come into Edgetown bout once a month. Dad likes my apple pie."

"Really?" Tobias said. "They never mentioned it." Tabitha shook her head, assuring herself that it was a leaver's lie.

Hanna laughed, but it was a mirthless sound haunted by nostalgia. There was a hint of sadness around her eyes. "Of course, they don't mention it, Toby." Hanna smiled as she put her hand on Tobias' shoulder. Tabitha looked away in disgust as Hanna continued. "They don't want to be banished from Isolation. They're afraid of what they'd do on the outside at their age. I've told them I'd help them transition out, but the most they're willing to do is to sneak out of town to visit me from time to time."

"Could have saved us the trip if we knew they were part-time leavers," Tabitha said. Tobias jabbed her under the table with his foot. "What?"

Tabitha looked down into her bowl of salad, a forest in which her fork was carving swaths. She scowled at Hanna under the cover of her frowning brow. There sat an actual leaver. No greater monster, whether the boogy, big foot, or loc ness, had ever been more feared. From the time they were babies, the leaver's evil was imprinted upon the frightened minds of Isolation's children. They drank blood. They murdered young victims. They worshiped demons. Elder Ram Stern would say so and more.

And now, here Tabitha sat with one, but it wasn't fear she felt. It was pure, unadulterated hatred. What enraged her the most was that none of those jagged titles like monster, blood-drinker, or gool rested so comfortably upon the young woman with whom they now supped. It was much easier to call names at a distance. Up close, words like friendly, warm, and compassionate were more tailored for the cut of her figure. The dissonance was suffocating. She was supposed to be evil, and here she was, feeding them, taking care of them, and showing them kindness. It didn't fit. The misfit made her so angry.

Nostalgia

As they ate, Tabitha brooded as Hanna regaled them with stories of her adventures in the city and the challenges of running a diner in a town so far from the *real world,* as she put it. Tabitha's thoughts warred between her urge to marvel at the strength and resilience of the woman before her and her constant inner reminder that she was sitting across from the world's greatest traitor. They had no context to comprehend much of what Hanna spoke of, but Tobias listened with infatuated rapture and Tabitha with indignant disdain.

Hanna's expression grew serious as she leaned forward, her eyes locked on Tabitha and Tobias. "Listen, I know it's not easy being a leaver. The world out there, it's a lot to take in. The technology, the pace, the bombardment of info... it can be overwhelming." She reached across the table and placed one of her hands on each of theirs. Tabitha pulled hers away with a quick jab, but she noticed that Tobias didn't. Hanna smiled, patted Tobias' hand, and let go.

"But you know what? You're strong. You're resilient. And you've got each other," Hanna continued, her voice filled with conviction. "I can help you navigate this new world. I can teach you about the tech, help you find your way around, and you can stay with me while you get your bearings."

Tabitha's cheeks flushed as she realized the misunderstanding. "Oh, no, we're not—we're not leavers," she stammered, her voice barely above a whisper.

Hanna's eyebrows shot up in surprise. "You're not? But I thought..."

"We've been sent by the council," Tobias explained. "We have a mission to complete."

Hanna leaned back in her chair, a look of understanding crossing her features. "I see. I'm sorry, I just assumed after the fire and what happened to your mom and dad..."

Tabitha's chest clenched at the mention of her parents. Once again, she buried her eyes in her bowl. She filled her mouth with a fork's worth of distraction, chewed like she'd skipped a fortnight of meals, and swallowed so hard her bite could have overshot through the bottom of her boots. It was enough to hold back the tears that threatened to spill.

"We appreciate your offer to help, though. We could use it," Tobias said.

Hanna nodded. "Of course. Whatever you need, I'm here for you." Her tone was different, slightly distant. Might the monster emerge now that she knew they were not allies? She waited a few seconds, wondering which of their blood she would drink first.

"It's pretty urgent since my silly sister brought the *Overseer's Handbook* with us," Tobias said.

"On accident," Tabitha said. "And it was his fault." She added with an uncommon scorn.

"You have the *Overseer's Handbook*?" Hanna asked. "Here? Why? Seriously?" The look on her face was one of complete shock. "I can't believe they let you—"

"They didn't let us," Tabitha corrected. Her words were like a blunt instrument. "It was an accident. But it's urgent cause as soon as we do the thing we came for, we have to get back right away and return the book because we're not leavers."

As if the conversation wasn't tense enough, a knot in Tabitha's stomach twisted as she caught sight of the robotic man thing rising from its booth at the end of the diner. The metallic humanoid was made more ominous by the clothes he wore: a hooded jacket and jeans. Clothes or not, there was no mistaking the machine for a man. The rubber padding of the bot's feet squeaked as it stepped toward their table.

"Hello, Miss," came the humanoid's voice, so impeccable it would have been indistinguishable from a real person. It was too calm in its tone and too familiar for comfort. Tabitha felt like she might pass out from the blood rush that was thumping in her ears. They all looked up at the bot, still with its hood over its head.

"Yes," Hanna said. "Are you here for a pick-up order?"

"No, Ma'am. Thank you for asking," the bot said slowly. The soothing speech of the mechanical made Tabitha's hair stand on end. "My owner is planning to make an in-person trip to this location in the near future and has requested that I ask about accommodations in Edgetown."

"Oh, right," Hanna said. "Well, at the end of Main Street is the old Rest Inn. It's under different ownership now, but the sign hasn't changed. It's pretty much the only place in town." Hanna said.

"Perfect," it said. "Thank you. I will upload your recommendation to my owner through this diner's complimentary wifi connection. I will then let you know if my owner has any further questions." They stared up, thinking the bot would leave at any second. Instead, the robot slid into the booth where Tabitha sat. The weight of the humanoid machine made the bench creak. She squirmed toward the window and flattened her body against the end of the bench. Her stomach threatened to wretch. She declined her head, pretending to investigate her meal with her fork, and darted her eyes toward Tobias, trying to find a way to swim out of the drowning distress. Her breathing was sharp and violent. Her hands were sweating. "Thank you for your patience," the robot said after a few more interminable seconds. "My owner has no further questions. Thank you for your time." The robot rose from Tabitha's bench and walked toward the exit. Tabitha watched the bot as it walked outside, threw its leg over a black motorcycle, and zoomed off.

"That was weird," Tabitha whispered. Tobias lifted his pocket knife into view and retracted the blade before leaning over to put it back in his pocket.

"Lots of weirdness outside of Isolation. Believe me." Hanna said.

"Like what?" Tobias asked.

"For one, I have a friend who got involved in the Mothra cult."

"What's that?" Tabitha said, eager to hear anything about the religious makeup of the outside world.

"It's sick. They worship a big blue—actually, let's not get off topic." Hanna said. "Before we were interrupted, you said you needed help with something?"

"Oh, yeah," Tobias said. "Tabby, you got the scrap?" She slumped back against the bench, reached into her pocket, and pulled out a small, worn piece of paper with the name of the intended contact and the message below.

"Aww, Harrison Thatcher died," Hanna said. "I'm sorry to hear that."

"You remember him?" Tobias asked. His tone was too comfortable, beyond relaxed. Why was he letting his defenses down? Was this why leavers were so dangerous? They had learned enough witchcraft to lure in those of the opposite gender. Tobias might have already fallen for it, tripping headlong into the dark, sooty cavern of her evil spell.

"Of course," she said. "He was one of Soren Krieger's biggest fanatics. Remember he used to call himself a Sorenite? Always talked about how they should have named the town Sorenberg."

"You know what I remember," Tobias said. "He used to sing that awful special music at the potlucks."

Hanna and Tobias laughed at the memory. Tabitha could sacrifice only a squiggle of a smile. Tobias did his best rendition of Harrison's voice, nailing the vibrato and thick southern draw. They laughed more, and even Tabitha could hardly hold back a giggle. When the laughter died down, Hanna said, "I'll take care of this. I talk to his son Elijah all the time."

"Really?" Tabitha asked.

"Yeah," Hanna said. "We have a community of leavers, started by some of the first who left when our parents were still young."

"There's a community of leavers?" Tobias said. "Where is it?"

"No, not like that," Hanna explained. "An online community. Chats. Threads. Comments. Stuff like that." They both looked at her with a cock-eyed expression. She smiled and pushed back a lock of blonde hair from her face. "Yeah, that's right, I forget what it's like when you first leave."

"But you can send him the message?" Tabitha said.

"I'm not going to do that over text message. I'll call him. But yeah, consider the message sent. Your mission is complete." Hanna paused. "You guys want to stay at my place tonight? You could head back in the cool of the morning." Her eyes darted to Tobias instantaneously, as did Tabitha's. His face seemed a slight red.

"That would be great," Tobias said.

At the same moment, cutting across his words, Tabitha said, "We can't," as she jabbed him under the table with her foot. "The Third Indictum."

"The Indictums," Hanna said in a voice of mock gravitas. "I don't miss that." The quip made Tabitha grip the table so hard it hurt her fingers. "Remind me what that one says," Hanna asked. "It's been a while."

"Tobias is the expert on the Isolation Doctrine," Tabitha said. "He has them all memorized. Won't stop quoting them at me. Right, Bubba?" She knocked on the table with her knuckle. "Go ahead. Tell her the Third Indictum. Make the ghost of Soren proud."

Reluctantly, he mumbled. "Let no fellowship be found with them, the accursed leavers, neither let any among us welcome them into our homes or commune with them by any means, lest ye incur the wrath of the Almighty." Tobias could not bring his eyes above the table's surface.

"Oh, yeah, that one," Hanna said. A long, heavy silence sat between them. "Sorry, I asked."

Scammed

Tabitha felt the wash of relief when they finally rose to leave and moved toward the front exit. She stepped out of the diner into the evening air, her bag slung over her shoulder, which was a reminder that this errand would be over soon. Without any humidity in the atmosphere, the temperature had dropped to a comfortable chill, and a breeze trickled along the street.

This was her favorite time of day. It reminded her of those glorious evenings playing with Isolation's kids around the burrows under her mother's watchful eye. She smiled. It would be a more pleasant walk home with her brother. Her frown dissolved. Deep down, she wondered why she felt so unfulfilled. She hadn't had the adventure she'd expected, and it felt too soon to be returning.

Tobias lingered, talking to Hanna, laughing together. Tabitha rolled her eyes and looked the other way. Their voices were low and intimate as they said their goodbyes. The horizon was painted in the vibrant hues of sunset. She stared into the skyward distance, ignoring Hanna's flirtatious laugh. She felt the gravity of the world beyond, drawing her toward that mysterious horizon. How could she ignore it? She could ignore it because that's what she was trained to do. She was an Isolationist.

She lifted her hat, ran her fingers through her hair, and then dropped her hand against her side. When she did, she noticed the thin feeling of her shoulder bag. She narrowed her eyes and looked down. It felt lighter, too. In one quick motion, she threw open the flap and buried a hand. Three seconds later, she knew something had gone terribly wrong.

"Bubba!" Tabitha called out. Her voice was shaky, and her breath was in gasping frantics. "It's gone."

"What's gone?" Tobias said as he came up beside her.

"I had it in my bag," she said. "But it isn't here." She rushed back into the diner, Hanna and Tobias following close behind. She looked under the table where they'd sat.

"Your sunscreen?" Tobias asked, coming through the door.

"No," she said. *The Overseer's Handbook.*"

"What?" His voice was as close to a scream as she'd heard him. "You lost it?" He started searching as well. He climbed under the table, lifted the benches, and pushed booths aside. When Tobias got to the end of the diner, he paused at the booth where the robot had been. The others noticed him standing still.

"What?" Hanna asked. "Did you find it?"

He spun slowly with his face crunched up into a tight mess. "The robot." They stared at each other for a few seconds.

"That metal creep must have swiped it when he sat down next to Tabitha," Hanna said.

"This is bad!" Tabitha said.

"Very bad!" Tobias said.

"Why would a dumb ol' robot want that book?" Tabitha asked. "It's only valuable in Isolation. Here it's—it's—it's just an old notebook."

"Robots don't want anything," Hanna said. "They're servants of human masters. Its owner is probably a petty thief, too cowardly to do the deed in person. It's a big problem out here. Even if you catch the bot, he'll run a remote memory wipe and get away with it."

Hanna placed a comforting hand on Tabitha's shoulder. "I'm so sorry, guys. I shouldn't have let this happen." Tabitha pulled away.

Tobias's face paled. "What are we going to do?" Tabitha's head shook as her stomach knotted. "We have to get it back," Tobias said, his jaw clenching. "If—If Soren was here, he'd know how to fix this. But we don't—"

"Hanna," Tabitha said, turning to her with pleading eyes. "Is there a sheriff here?"

"Not in Edgetown."

"We need your help," Tobias said. "We're stuck worse than a jackrabbit in a snare. We got to go after that book," Hanna hesitated, glancing down at her ankle.

"I want to help, but I can't step foot in Dolos, and that's where Metal Man is headed." She lifted her pant leg, revealing a metallic ankle bracelet. It was bulky and made no sense to the twins. "I got in some trouble a while back. It's part of my probation."

Tabitha balled her hands into fists. Of course, she won't help. The cowards are always last when a snake's on the path. Hanna quickly added, "You can take my truck, though. Battery's low, but it'll get you where you need to go. It's got GPS in it, and—" she handed Tobias her handheld device. "—you'll need this too." He looked at the mysterious piece of glass and metal before he stuffed it in his pocket.

"Thank you," Tobias said, gratitude evident in his voice. "We'll bring it back as soon as we can." Tabitha and Tobias climbed into Hanna's truck.

"There ain't many vehicles in Isolation," Tobias said. "I ain't quite learned how to manage one just yet."

"Don't need to," she explained, leaning in over his lap. Tabitha thought she saw Tobias take a whiff of Hanna's golden hair. "It can drive itself," she said, tapping some keys on a console-mounted screen with her right and balancing herself with her left on Tobias' knee. Tabitha pushed back the urge to slap her hand, the leaver who was touching her brother with a palm stained black with witchcraft. "Just tell it where you want it to go."

"You mean like..." Tobias was smitten, obviously, and so his faculties of speech were getting mighty scarce.

"Tell it you want to get on the road toward Dolos. If you spot the bot, tell it to follow him."

"I've never talked to a machine before," Tobias said as Hanna completed her tapping on the console screen. She finally took her hand off Tobias' knee.

"It'll understand," Hanna said as she slapped Tobias on the shoulder and started talking to someone who wasn't present. "Betsy, get on the road toward Dolos. We're in a hurry." She slammed the door and stepped back, putting her thumb in the air. They didn't return the gesture. Their deer-light eyes looked deep and haunted as the truck pulled out of the parking spot on its own and found its way to the road.

Chase

The sun dipped lower on the horizon, painting the sky in hues of orange and pink. Tabitha stared out the window, watching the unfamiliar landscape rush by as it transformed from an arid desert to an ever-growing congestion of houses lined up in rows. There had to be thousands of them. They were all above ground, too. Houses meant people. How could there be this many people? The further they drove, the suburban sprawl gave way to the encroaching shadow of the big city, Dolos. Tabitha realized her jaw was hanging open.

The silence in the truck was shattered when a lone motorcyclist appeared ahead on the road. "There it is," Tobias said, pointing.

"Betsy, follow that robot on the motorcycle," Tabitha shouted; she felt the adrenaline punch her in the chest like a mule's hoof.

"Confirm selection," the truck said.

"What does that mean?" Tobias said.

"There's something on the TV thingy," Tabitha said. A live image of the robotic motorcyclist zooming down the highway appeared, along with a green button that said *confirm*. She poked at the glass as she'd seen Hanna do.

The truck increased speed, shoving them back into their seats. An electric hum vibrated through the cab. The truck jittered and shimmied as it torched over the road. Tabitha squealed with the exhilaration.

"Battery low," Betsy said as she sped to match the pace of the motorcycle. With expert, unmanned maneuvering, the haunted truck weaved through traffic, never losing sight of its target. Tabitha gripped the door frame and pressed her feet into the floorboard to brace her back against the seat. Having never gone faster than a run, she laughed aloud against the wild feeling of acceleration.

In the distance, Dolos's imposing skyline loomed like steel vultures awaiting new carcasses. Jagged structures stabbed into the sky, stretched upward in a haphazard dance of glass and steel. Each building, bathed in the golden hues of the setting sun, seemed to violently war for domination. Each was taller and more impressive than the last.

"Wow!" Tabitha said. "It's amazing. Can you believe it, Bubba?" She looked over at her twin, but he didn't share her point of focus.

"This robocycle is fast," Tobias said. She brought her attention back to the high-speed chase. "He's getting away from us."

"How fast can Betsy go," Tabitha asked. There was no answer.

As they neared the city, the traffic gradually thickened, and cars clustered in. Tabitha laughed at the rapid shifts in their movement as the truck avoided other vehicles. Ahead of them, the motorcycle weaved skillfully between the lanes, gaining a speed that Betsy could not match. Tobias patted the dashboard, urging it for more speed.

"You ever hear of Gladys Aylward, missionary to China?" Tabitha said.

"Have a feeling I'm about to," Tobias said without looking at her. His eyes were trained on the road ahead.

"In the 1930s, the Japanese invaded, and she had to hike over the mountains with a hundred kids to get to safety. And did you know they used to shorten women's feet, bending the toes all up into a terrible little ball? She helped put a stop to that kind of nonsense. She had a tough run of it, too."

"Okay," Tobias said. His tone let her know he'd missed the point.

"I just mean," Tabitha said, looking down at her hands. "If she could do something so important... I mean, don't you ever wonder if maybe God's got something more important for us to do?"

"It's pretty dadgum *important* that we catch this high-speed can opener and get the handbook back," Tobias said.

"I mean, something more important than that." She crossed her hands over her lap and looked out the window. "I'm just saying I'm excited. A little scared, but that just makes it more exciting, don't it? Who knows what kind of adventure we might flop into out here." She let out a sigh. "Ain't you excited?" He glanced at her, but before he could respond, a voice cut in.

"The 'follow' request has been canceled by the target," Betsy said.

"What's that mean?" Tabitha asked.

"Don't have a fog of an idea," Tobias said as the truck slowed to the speed of the traffic around them. The motorcycle zipped between cars and buses, shrinking into a smaller speck until it finally vanished into the crowded streets. As the rider disappeared from view, they were left with the road's congestion and the relentless pace of the city. "Betsy, follow that robot."

"Confirm selection," Betsy said. Tabitha looked at the screen, but the option to follow the motorcyclist wasn't available.

"It ain't on here," she said. "What do we do?"

The truck merged into the bustling flow of traffic, joining the current of vehicles crowding the road as they reached the outskirts of Dolos.

"Battery critically low," Betsy said. Tobias sat as rigid as a fence post, his eyes darting around, soaking up every detail of the new surroundings.

As they got closer to the heart of Dolos, the streets became even more crowded. The sidewalks were squeezed to bulging with all kinds of creeps, weirdos, and thugs—each dressed in clothes that wouldn't even pass for a Soren Day costume in Isolation—all hurrying towards some important place or other, all equally distracted. Tabitha gave each spectacle her hungry attention as they blurred by through the window.

"Battery critically low," Betsy said. "Automatic parking initiated." They felt the truck make adjustments to their course.

As night fell, Betsy smoothly navigated into a parking space along a busy downtown street and powered down. With the truck now quiet, the noise outside swelled to a racket. Tabitha and Tobias were enveloped by the chaotic energy of Dolos's city center, watching the world outside like the contents of a fish bowl. The city had looked grand at a distance, but now, with the dying light, the massive facades were crumbled, dusty, and nearing ruin. Street lights puked down an eerie greenish glow on the faces of pedestrians while the cacophony of honking horns and distant sirens polluted the air. Tabitha put her hands across her heart, hardly able to believe where she was. A kind of excited nervousness made her body jitter with anticipation for what might happen next.

Wait

Tabitha watched the bizarre assortment of humans and robots bustling by. An ancient woman trudged past, talking to no one, pushing a trolley brimming with odd, radiant artifacts. A robot the size of a house thundered by, carrying four pallets of cargo with arms as big as cable cranes.

"We should lock the doors," he said.

"How do we do that?" Tabitha asked.

"Don't got a clue," Tobias said. He brushed his hand along the door. He'd seen enough VHS movies to know there should be a locking post, but none could be found.

A man wearing a pair of pants—that's all, just pants—sauntered up like it was a summer dance. He paused when he laid eyes on Tabitha, teetered close enough to lick the window, and leered at them through the glass. His gaunt face was like a piece of dried leather stretched over a fishbone, green and sallow. The man's eyes were glowing, mechanical. A blinking light moved behind his cornea. Tabitha gasped and put her hand over her mouth. The man wandered away into the haunted night.

"Still excited?" Tobias said with a sarcastic laugh.

"They're all God's creatures," Tabitha said.

"Some of them creatures is manmade," Tobias said, pointing at a purple-skinned robot bolting like lightning up the sidewalk.

"You know what I mean," Tabitha said. "Imagine what the gospel could do here." Her brother grumbled something she couldn't quite hear. She asked him to speak up.

"Reminds me of the First Indictum," Tobias said. "Verily, the world beyond our gates lieth in wickedness and is consumed by digital darkness and ungodly devices. The machinations of the heathen, their enchanted screens, and devilish contraptions corrupt the soul and lead astray even the elect from the Lord. Thus, we are commanded to sever all ties with the profane realm beyond...'" Tobias paused. "You want me to go on?"

"No," Tabitha said. "It's depressing. And I meant the gospel, like grace through faith. That's what changes people. Not Indictums."

"If Soren Krieger was here, he'd figure a way out of this," Tobias said.

I don't want a way out of this, she thought. Tabitha looked at her brother, making no sound to indicate her thoughts on the matter. They sat silent for a long few moments, watching the horrid flow of digitized humanity drift by the windows of the truck.

"You have your pocket knife?" Tobias asked.

"Yes," Tabitha said. She glanced down at his lap, spotting the glint of the blade clenched open and ready in his hand.

He turned toward her and stared into her eyes for a long, quiet time. There was so much said in those still, heavy seconds of familial connection, more than any clumsy, idiotic word could portray. Tabitha exuded the words from her unsteady gaze.

I want to go home, Tobias eyes said.

An entire conversation of unspoken interchange passed between them as they lived an abbreviated lifetime in each other's eyes. A deep hurt full of lead and gasoline gave Tabitha a war of emotions. She thought of the home where her Daddy had held her in his arms, which were as strong as steel and as gentle as velvet. She envisioned the place where Momma and daughter had sung out their musical laughter. The walls were painted with the warm joy of living. But that home was nowhere now. In the years since the accident, no such place existed except in her memory. It tore her apart to want a place that was gone. Could that be what sent her heart over the horizon?

"I miss Mom and Dad," she whispered. She hoped to hear her brother echo the whisper, but he sat silent and unmoving. She marveled at his stony exterior. How could he resist the haunting nostalgia?

Hanna's phone began to buzz in Tobias's pocket. He almost jumped out of his underwear at the startle, but once he'd calmed down to sub-nuclear, he retrieved it and stared at it blankly, unsure what to do. It continued to buzz, so cautiously, he tapped the red button below Hanna's smiling face. Above the muffled sound of the street outside, they heard a tiny, thin voice. He moved it closer to his ear. He laughed when he heard her voice coming through, unmistakable.

"Tobias? Are you there?" Hanna asked, concern evident in her tone.

"Y-yes, I'm here," Tobias stammered, still wondering at the technology that allowed them to converse without a wire snaking the kilometers between them. "This thing is a phone?" He held it out and looked at it.

"Thank goodness," Hanna sighed with relief. "I just got a low-power notification from Betsy. Are you guys okay?"

Tobias glanced out the window at the unfamiliar, shadow-drenched cityscape. "We're swimming in the blackest pool of sin I ever seen."

"What?"

"We're in Dolos, somewhere. We followed that thieving robot here but lost it on the road."

"Dolos?" Hanna's voice grew serious. "Listen, I have a friend on the edge of the city. His name's Milo. He can help. I'm sending the location to you now." The device buzzed in his hand, which Tobias hadn't gotten used to. He dropped the glowing brick on the floor of the truck. By the time he had it back to his ear, he had missed information that he wouldn't have understood any better had he received it.

"Did you get the location?" Hanna asked.

"What do you mean?" he said. "How would I *get* a location? A location is a place you go to, not a thing you *get*." The conversation went on like this for several minutes.

"You know what? I have a better idea," Hanna said. "I can see your location. I'll call Milo. I'll have him come to you. Just wait in the truck. He'll come find you."

"Wait in the truck?" Tobias said. "That works."

"Wait," Tabitha said with an urgent interruption. "Tell her about the guy with the machine eyes. Does she know about machine eye guys? Is that a normal thing?" Tobias put his hand over Tabitha's mouth. She slapped and fought his hand back, trying to talk.

"Okay," he said, ignoring his noisy sister. He put the phone down on the truck seat.

So, they waited in the truck. Minutes stretched long and thin like cold honey. The night's horrors floated by on the sidewalk in a constant river of nasty, disturbing, and unimaginable. Things they didn't want to see were displayed on the street. The terrible display wandered by the windows like a parade of nauseating hypnosis. Tabitha took it in for as long as she could remain awake, but slowly, the day's excitement ebbed into the drowsy draw of slumber.

Meeting

Tabitha stirred as a rhythmic tapping roused her from her slumber, her eyes fluttering open as sunlight streamed through the truck's windows. The unfamiliar cityscape outside disoriented her, a stark contrast to the greenish evening light that had falsely illuminated the horrification of the previous night. She nudged Tobias, who lay asleep beside her on the truck seat.

"You awake?" Tabitha whispered.

"Huh?" Tobias rubbed his eyes, slowly taking in their surroundings. His brow knit like a broad yarn sweater. A knock on the window jolted them both fully in that direction.

A man with wild, multicolored hair and a sharky grin peered at them through the glass. Tobias tried to yell through the closed door since he didn't know how to roll down the window. Most of his voice didn't make it through. "Are you Milo?"

"What's that?" The man asked, putting his hand to his ear. Tobias yanked the handle and let the door open a crack. The noise of the city poured in like rushing water.

"Are you Milo?"

The man's grin went wide and toothified. He had a mouth like a piano. Some of the teeth were opposite colors. "Sure, friends. That's me." His accent was harsh as if his words were carved out of baked clay but then broken to leave sharp edges. His tone was abrasive and irritating. Over his eyes, he wore a set of goggles.

"You're Hanna's friend, Milo?" Tabitha added, leaning across the cab, talking so loud, Tobias winced and put a pinky in his offended ear.

"Oh, Hanna. Of course. Known that tart for years," he said. Tabitha exchanged a confused glance with Tobias.

"She said you could help us?"

His eyes rimmed white with intrigue. "She was right!" He stepped back, allowing them the space to exit the truck. They probably should have thought harder before doing so, but hard thinking was a kind of heavy lifting best done when not being stared at. "You'll have to come with me." They followed the odd man.

Not familiar with the custom of carrying cellular devices, Tabitha and Tobias left Hanna's phone sitting on the truck seat. The fussing city, the needling noise, and the intense smells immediately assaulted their senses. Especially the smells, from which they had been somewhat insulated overnight. Burning hair? Poison gas? Sun-baked entrails, maybe? What was that smell? It all mixed into a scorching nose burner that left no nostril hair unsaturated with liquified travesty.

She covered her nose with her shirt and looked for a distraction. Towering skyscrapers leaned over like old women with rickety knees, threatening to tumble in on the sidewalks. There were giant cracks in the buildings. She followed a crack that snaked down and across the sidewalk.

The streets were full of mysterious artifacts. An abandoned doorknob was in the gutter. Where the door was and where the missing door led was an enigma. On the sidewalk was a single pant leg up to the zipper, torn right down the middle.

The most astonishing item of discard, was a human finger. At least that's what it turned out to be when Tabitha paused and leaned down to investigate. She tried for a good spin on it by noticing that whoever's it was, had only lost a pinky, which is much better than when a thumb goes on the lamb. But then she saw the rest of the fingers near the intersection.

The most haunted spectacle that Dolos had on display was the human population. People with goggles sat along the streets, absorbed in their own realities, as they poked at the space in front of them like they didn't grasp the relationship of hands to thin air.

Others without goggles stared into the middle distance, gesturing at the invisible nothing, like their brains had been liquified and drained from the ears. Some used handheld devices, had their attention fixed on their phones, and almost looked normal, except for a question mark-shaped bend in the upper neck that made them unable to view anything above a pedestrian's knee. Tabitha and Tobias watched the chaotic insanity of it all as they followed the odd man.

He glanced over his shoulder. "My Name's Scritch," he said.

"You told us you were Milo," Tabitha asked.

"Of course, I told you that," he said as he flicked his wrist. He watched them for a second as they strolled along.

"Something odd I'm noticing about you two," Scritch said, his eyes flicking as if he were reading something floating invisibly in the air. "That truck back there is registered to a Hanna Thompson."

"See, he does know Hanna," Tabitha said.

"But you two are not in the system. At least your faces' recog-scans don't appear in any database."

"What's a database?" Tabitha asked.

"I see," Scritch said. "What are your names?"

"I'm Tabitha Andrews, and this is my brother Tobias."

"Middle names?"

"Belamie," Tabitha said. "It was my mother's name."

"Garret," Tobias said.

"Dates of birth," Scritch asked.

"We're twins. We were born in thirty-six," Tabitha said.

"That's not right," Scritch said. "That'd make you uh..." He counted his fingers. "No, that's way off."

"Oh," Tabitha said. "Sorry. Where we're from, we use S.D."

"What's that?"

"S.D." Tobias repeated as if he should know what it meant.

Tabitha explained, "The third era. S.D. Counts from the year Soren Krieger founded our community. It's been fifty-three years, so it's fifty-three S.D. Course, Lacy Gumnut, the seamstress, says that year one should a been tallied after a whole year was up. But

Jep Strickland says otherwise. Anyway, my parents taught us to count it like Soren did. So, I was born in 36 S.D. We're 17. Born on April 4th, so on your calendar, that would be..." Now, she was counting on her fingers. It took them a long time to arrive at the right date, but when they did, Scritch grumbled something about the complexity of the math.

"And where are you two from, exactly?" he asked. They answered without resistance. He grumbled more about it not being a real place. When they mentioned Edgetown, he was satisfied and moved on. After a few seconds, Scritch made a sound of amusement. "It's fantastic. You don't exist."

"What?" Tabitha said as they rounded a corner. A group of people bustled by in a hurry, many of whom seemed to be talking to themselves. In Isolation, doing that would get you sent to Doctor Kent, but Tabitha suspected the practice had some mysterious normalcy here, at least as much as missing thumbs could be called normal.

"Have you ever been to Dolos before?" Scritch asked.

"We ain't been anywhere before," Tobias said. "Except Isolation. But it's not like here. It's different."

"I bet it is," Scritch said. "I have someone I'd like to sell you to."

"What do you mean?" Tobias asked, his tone defensive. "We ain't for sale."

"Everything's for sale, my boy. And I know just the one who's buying. But first, we have to do some updates and upgrades."

Rough hands grabbed them both. Sharp fingertips dug into Tabitha's arms. Her instinct drove her hand toward her side where her pocket knife was in her pants, but a clicking sound and the tightening of a wrist ratchet sinched her hands behind her back. As they did the same to her brother, she was being dragged into an alley.

Modified

The narrow passage was a blur of horror as Tabitha kicked and punched toward the thugs. She tried to wrench free, but their grip was iron, and the ratchet tie was too tight. Tobias grunted as he, too, struggled like a wild stallion against the lion's bite. "Let us go!" Tabitha shouted.

Scritch ignored her protests as he led them deeper into the alley, flanked by a half dozen men shirtless in black leather strapping and covered in chrome studs, spikes, and rivets. The throbbing sounds of the city faded, replaced by a fugitive quiet broken only by their torrid scuffling and violent breathing. Between the noises, she heard her brother quoting Soren's Isolation Doctrine.

"Those who sow to the flesh and its digital delights shall reap destruction at the Lord's hand!" he shouted. The words that had such power in Isolation had no effect on the men. He went on as the aggressors dragged them down the narrow passageway.

They were hauled into a massive, abandoned space that smelled of mildew. The warehouse was dark and furtive, with blades of light stabbing in through high, filthy windows. Pre-broken glass shards crunched and scratched across the scored concrete as their feet fought a war for purchase. Rusted metal shelves and crates cast eerie shadows with their leaning array. In the center of the cavernous space was a semicircle of technical gadgets. Tabitha let out a full-bodied shriek as they pulled her closer to the center, where the dubious gear awaited. Although nothing was familiar, the workspace was filled with medical apparatuses, and at the center was an ad hoc surgical surface appropriate for no more than autopsies.

"Blick doesn't let anyone see him without modifications," Scritch laughed with a sycophantic uproar. "And he will certainly want to see you two."

Another man placed a rag over Tabitha's face, and a biting smell filled her nose and burned her lungs, drowning the horror of the city to the deepest, most distant forgetfulness. Her body was suddenly turned in the opposite direction from where she knew it was. Unable to resist, she was shoved onto a filthy surgical table. She heard her brother struggling, but the sound grew more distant. Black crept into her eyes as her sight became wavy, velvet, and iridescent.

When she woke, the men were around her, smiling. Not pleasant smiles like you might expect at a tiny person's birth. More like the kind of smiles you'd see if you were at a pig roast, and you're the pig. Scritch was a few paces away, talking to someone who wasn't there.

She struggled to sit up as the thugs had laid her on her back atop her cuffed hands. Her arms were asleep, but the sensation came as a relief since it meant her arms hadn't been removed. She rolled off the table and scuffed her way to her feet without using her hands. The men around her laughed as she struggled. When she was finally up, she spotted her brother, who they'd laid beside her. She rushed to him and tried to wake him, but with her hands still zipped tight behind her back, there was little she could do. His eyes opened, and he moaned. The noise of a one-sided conversation continued as she tried to help him up with her head.

"A thousand bucks minimum," Scritch said. "I'm telling you, they are totally off-grid. Pristine IDs." He paused. "I'll throw in their metadata for the same price." He waited another few seconds. "Deal!" he said with a dance. The other men made similar gestures of success, none as ridiculous looking as Scritch's.

"What did you do to us?" Tobias said, leaning on Tabitha to sit up from the surface. With her help, he was able to come off the table on his feet.

"Just the latest in eyewear," Scritch said. "And earwear." They both reached to their faces but didn't feel any device. Tabitha noticed her eyes and ears felt different, but no oddity could be detected at her finger's touch.

"They ain't never gonna let us back into Isolation, now!" Tobias said.

Tabitha ignored her brother's misplaced concern. Pointing her question at the aggressor, she asked Scritch, "Why are you doing this?"

"The normal reasons," Scritch said. "The UBI is enough to live on but not enough to thrive on. It's just business, nothing personal."

"But why would you be in this business?" she said. At that, Scritch stood still and stared up into the shafts of light drifting down from the high ceiling of the warehouse.

"Full of questions, this one is," he said. He walked over and stood in front of Tabitha and Tobias. They both stepped back, bumping into the surgical table. Scritch said, "When I was a kid, I lived with my aunt. Her boyfriends hated me. There was this one who called himself Flit. He hated me so much that he programmed his serve-bot to beat me. How messed up is that? He wouldn't even do it himself. He programmed it to beat me at scheduled times of the day. He programmed it to beat me when I did certain behavior triggers. He even programmed it to beat me whenever I used the word 'cheese' because he thought it was funny."

"That's awful," Tabitha said. Scritch stepped closer to them. He reeked. The twins pressed themselves against the hard surface, trying for every centimeter they could.

"Just wait, it gets better," Scritch smiled. "You might think my aunt would intervene. 'Break up with the monster, Aunt Niff!'" His sudden scream made Tabitha and Tobias jump. "But no. She was too busy videoing my beatings. She had a social channel on uberfans.gross that got millions of views. Mostly the usual garbage, but somewhere along the way, she realized that the violent stuff got more subscribers. So I was the star. One time, Flit's bot beat me so bad that I was blind for three days. When I could finally see again, all I could see was an empty apartment. They'd run out on me, probably cause they thought they'd killed me. I was twelve."

Scritch took a long, slow breath. Tabitha watched the man's face. It was as if she were seeing him, not the man, the frightening creature he'd become. She saw the boy, twelve, alone, abandoned. "I'm so sorry that happened to you," She said. "But that doesn't mean you have to do the same kind of thing to others."

"Oh, I have an excuse," Scritch said. "My Ai therapist says I have a mental illness due to trauma in my developmental years." He smiled, revealing a jagged mouth full of bad decisions. "That's what they do, explain it all away with mental health, but that doesn't really cover it, now does it?" Scritch dropped his voice to a whisper and leaned in close. She could smell his breath now. "Because the truth is, I like it. Even right now, the look on your face is worth more than the thousand I'll get for you two." He stepped back abruptly and spoke to the circle of thugs. "Okay, boys. Bag 'em up. We got to deliver 'em to the boss."

Morphed

They were thrown like firewood into a van. After a short drive, it lurched to a stop, sending Tabitha and Tobias sliding across the greasy floor. As the van bumped along, Tobias whispered, "If Soren Krieger was here, he'd save us." Tabitha remained quiet.

The rear doors swung open, flooding the cramped space with artificial light. They were in a parking garage, but neither Tabitha nor Tobias had ever seen such an enclosed space. To their eyes, it was some kind of concrete cave. A jagged figure stood silhouetted in the opening.

"Out," a man ordered. It wasn't Scritch, nor was it any she had yet seen. He wore bright clothes and had a blue face. A mohawk sharp enough to slice meat stuck up from his head. Its rainbow color was a complement to his blueberry complexion. The blue thug repeated his command. Tabitha and Tobias hesitated, blinking against the glare. The man reached in, grabbed Tabitha by the arm, and yanked her out. With her hands zipped tight behind her back, she stumbled down onto the concrete. Pain exploded as her head hit the pavement. She screamed and growled with the agony.

Tobias scrambled after her, coming out of the van like a cargo of angry Angus beef not yet butchered. The blue man allowed Tobias to go to his sister untouched. He turned around backward and was able to grip her upper arm with his cuffed hands. Once on her feet, she could feel the blood tickling her scalp and dripping into the back of her shirt.

"You okay, Sis?" Tobias said. His voice was gentle and calm. She nodded as she bit her lip to distract from how her head throbbed.

Once again, they were being dragged as more men emerged from around the van. They were hauled into a back door of a spacious atrium. Colors blossomed along all the walls, and the scene was as much like an outdoor arena, open to the sky as a building. The men who had ushered them in so violently left them there and exited the same door.

Tabitha simultaneously understood she was indoors, but her visual senses challenged that notion as a vibrant nature scene painted itself across the walls in vivid, moving colors.

"I hit my head pretty hard," Tabitha said. "Just want to make sure you're seeing this too."

"It's insane!" Tobias said.

The vivid scene before their eyes lingered for a few moments in waves of emerald and amber but then suddenly changed. They were still in the same room, but all the walls became a scenic mountain range. A massive vista wrapped by the gentle haze of atmosphere blanketed the distant peaks in foamy desaturated blue.

They gasped at the beauty. The scene changed again, and they were plunged to the bottom of the ocean where the walls were now fluvial gates looking out upon the deep.

Footsteps sounded in the room as they devoted their attention to the scene around them. They hardly noticed the man who was standing before them.

"To be sure, no ostentatiousness is intended, but I see that you like it?" the man said. "Taking no real credit beyond a trifle, I had it designed by one of my more creative subordinates."

They turned their attention toward him. An average-looking man in a business suit stood as if he were waiting for a friend. No expression on his face was apparent, but it was difficult not to consider him as an enemy.

"Mother," the man said. "Get these poor friends free." A woman, who looked like a century of living had been put on her odometer, came rushing out from a door on the ocean-view wall and snipped the ratchet ties that held their hands.

"I'm Blick Thorn," he said, straightening Tobias's shirt for him. "I'm so sorry about your introduction to Dolos. Scritch and his boys are not the kind of welcoming committee we want newcomers to meet on first arrival, but the streets are what they are, despite my efforts to see them cleaned up."

"But don't Scritch work for you?" Tobias said.

"Oh, goodness, no!" Blick said. "Scritch and his kind are freelancers. Truly, they are a blight on the city, for which I have long desired a solution, but alas, when I heard he had nabbed two poor newcomers, even with the thousand dollars he aimed to extort from me, I couldn't let him do harm to you two innocent travelers, being your first time to the city."

"When they dragged us off the street, I thought they were going to eat us," Tabitha said.

"Eat you?" Blick said. "What on earth gave you that idea, my dear."

"Like in John Paton's book, where he went on mission to New Hebrides." She paused, assuming he'd at least heard of it. His expression said otherwise. "You know, John G. Paton. He ministered to the cannibals in Tanna and Aniwa in the South Pacific. They kept threatening to kill and eat him and whatnot, but he just kept on going. He even ran a little printing press right there on that tropical island. But..." She slowed. "I guess that's what made me think of it."

"I haven't heard of a case of urban cannibalism in a few months. We keep the wildlife fairly well fed."

"So, you'll let us go, then?" Tabitha said.

"Of course, of course," Blick said. "How could I, a simple businessman, dream of detaining two such as yourselves? Obviously, that being the case, there is the matter of the thousand credits, which, for me, was a worthwhile amount to have paid for such an honorable pair as yourselves. Still, I can't imagine you would wish to leave me without just compensation before your timely release."

"We only got a few Krieger coins," Tobias said. "I ain't sure if that money works here." He reached into his pocket and produced its contents. Two rough-minted coppers with Soren Krieger's face on them lay bare in his palm. Blick wrapped his fingers around Tobias', closing his fist gently.

"Oh, no," Blick said. "I wouldn't dream of demanding anything so base as hard currency. Instead, I'd ask only for a little of your time to capture the unique image of you two in your vulnerable moments, having come to this vivacious city unscathed as of yet of such vile perturbances as often press themselves upon new weary travelers."

"What?"

"That is to say, all I want is to take your picture," Blick said.

"You want to take our picture?" Tabitha asked.

"More or less, that is the gist of it," he said, with a smile that looked like it could have been carved from marble.

"Then we go free?" Tobias asked.

"Then you will be as free as any have ever been."

"And you'll take these witchcraft things off our eyes and out of our ears," Tobias said.

"They will fall away like the autumn leaves," Blick said.

"I don't like it," Tobias said.

"He's offering help, Bubba," Tabitha said. "I think we should do it.

"I don't," Tobias said, stepping close and dropping his voice to a whisper. "I think we ought to tell him, 'tough break' about the thousand, but we ain't going nowhere else with no strangers." He leaned closer. "I say we go back to the truck and do what Hanna said. Wait." They looked at each other for a long few seconds. Her face brightened as she put her hand on her brother's forearm.

"We ought to pray about it," Tabitha said. She turned to Blick and announced her idea with a wide smile. "Sir, we need a second to pray about what we should do."

"Now, now," Blick interrupted, stepping awkwardly close. "I don't have an infinitude of time. If you don't want my help, I will do my best to be unoffended, but without my help, what's to stop Scritch from bagging you a second time and selling you to someone much less scrupulous than I? You two are religious, and I'd remind you that the deities of many religions are said to work through circumstances. Can't you see, the circumstances are in your favor, which must be your deity's method of provision for you?"

Tabitha and Tobias looked at each other, communicating through eye contact in a way that only Twins can. A long silent moment passed as they considered the concern in one another's eyes. Tabitha's idea had ferreted out the truth. She could feel the pressure and saw no other choice. She gave a slight shrug, and her brother knew what it meant.

"Okay. You want to do it here, or..." Tobias said.

"Delightful! I have a studio not far from here," Blick said. "We can go there."

"Lead the way, photo man," Tobias said. "But if you try to pull something, we're gone."

"Of course," Blick said. "Gone, gone." He laughed as he led them out of the building and down a narrow alley.

Pixels

Tabitha and Tobias followed close behind, their footsteps echoing Blick's. They turned onto a busy street, but the appearance was stunning, surprising, so incredibly different than the dingy look it had had earlier.

Now, floating, holographic billboards hovered over every crosswalk with blisteringly bright explosions of chaos and color. The buildings, which had appeared cracked and dilapidated, now looked like freshly painted architecture, but as they watched, the exterior walls of the skyscrapers moved and danced with changing hues, saturated and blinding.

The color of it all was overwhelming, enough to make Tabitha grab for the handrails, only to find her brother's arm. The broken-down wreck of a city had transformed, jumping a hundred years in history, in less than an hour.

"It's all different," Tabitha said, marveling at the gorgeous colors and bright lights, not yet quite taking in how inappropriate the content was that they were being forced to see.

"I feel like I can reach out and touch it," Tobias said. "What did those guys do to us?"

"Merely new eyewear," Blick said as a man on the street bowed in his direction and stepped out of his way.

Tabitha and Tobias felt their faces once again. "I don't feel anything," Tabitha said.

"Contact lenses," Blick explained. They had heard of contacts from old stories, but neither knew how they worked or what they were. "They are just simple augmented reality eyepieces so you can see me as I want to be seen. I would, however, suggest, of course, only for your own comfort, that you do not try to remove them, as I suspect Scritch, beast that he is, likely fitted you with grapplings."

"Grapplings?" Tobias asked.

"Essentially, they are contact lenses that have digital displays," Blick explained. "But don't try to take them off, or they will tear your cornea."

"Are you serious?" Tobias said, reaching for his eye. "That ain't right."

"Nasty business, Scritch, and the boys run," Blick said. "But the streets are what they are. They also fitted you with earbud implants so you can hear me the way I want to be heard."

"I want these danged ol' things out of my eyes," Tobias said, flexing to his full size.

"How do we take the ear bugs out?" Tabitha asked, reaching for her ear.

"That is a service that I can provide," Blick said. "But while you have them in, why not enjoy the scenery." He put his arms out and spun around.

"I mean, it *is* amazing," Tabitha said, reaching up for a floating advertisement. A lewd ad for something called Mothra, god of the deep mind, drifted by. "Though, I do think the people in the images could wear more clothes. Tobias, don't look. She's hardly got anything on." Blick laughed at the odd idea.

"Well, now," Blick said. "Let's not be fun-killing fundamentalists. A little tolerance for those who like their fun is in order, as the digiverse is a place where you can be anyone you want."

"What do you mean?" Tabitha asked.

"Want to be an old man?" Blick said, clapping his hands together. Suddenly, his face changed into the wrinkled visage of an octogenarian.

"What kind of jollytoad with any sense would want to be old?" Tobias asked.

"Good point," Blick agreed. "Maybe you always felt like a woman trapped in a man's body? No problem." He clapped again, and his face and body changed into that of a beautiful woman wearing less than would be considered appropriate in Isolation. Tobias' reflexes made him bounce his eyes away.

"There ain't nothing natural about that," Tobias said. Tabitha covered her mouth with her hand.

"You can be anyone you please in the digiverse. Avatars are magic, aren't they?"

Blick morphed from one face to the next in a mesmerizing kaleidoscope. "Even now, you think you know what I look like. You think you've heard the sound of my voice. But have you really?"

The appearance of Blick's body shifted again. His clothes morphed into an eccentric, mismatched outfit. His face transformed into a clown's as a mischievous grin was painted red and sinister across his face.

"How do I sound now?" His voice had transformed into something high and horrifying. Even the accent was different.

"Is this one the real you?" Tabitha asked.

"Hard to say," Blick said. "What is real?"

"How do you do that?" she stammered, her eyes wide with amazement. Blick phased back to the appearance they had met him in. He chuckled. "An illusionist never tells."

"More like a satanist don't 'splain his *witchcraft*," Tobias whispered.

When Blick saw him whispering, he let out a blast of laughter. "Oh, I love secrets. Please do tell." His psychotic cackle made them stand still.

"Well, that ain't weird or nothing." Tobias was still too quiet for Blick to hear.

"So, tell me about your home, Isolation," he said. They looked at each other.

"How did you know?"

"Scritch packaged your metadata in the purchase." Blick rephrased the question. "Please, I'm dying to know everything about your home."

Tabitha hesitated, not sure how much to reveal. "It's about an hour's drive to the south. There's none of this weird voodoo there. It's just plain stuff."

"You must be mistaken," Blick said. "An hour to the south is the radio quiet zone. No one lives out there. It's a desert."

"We do," Tabitha said. "And the rest of the town."

"Fascinating!" Blick exclaimed. As they walked, he continued to engage them in conversation, his questions probing deeper into their lives and community. He suddenly stopped before a glass-fronted building. "Here we are," he announced, his voice tinged with excitement. "My factory of wonders."

He placed his hand on a glowing panel, and the doors slid open with a soft hiss. Tabitha and Tobias followed him inside.

A giant entry large enough to hold most of Isolation fanned out in front of them. "Welcome to my world," Blick said, spreading his arms wide. "This is where the magic happens."

Avatars

They climbed a flight of stairs to a second-story landing inside the tremendous atrium. Tobias had disengaged from the conversation and was studying the massive architecture.

They came to another interior door at the top of the stairs, which opened automatically. The twins hadn't ever seen doors with brains. They would have marveled at the surprise, except what they saw inside took their attention away from the door.

Inside, rows of individuals sat at desks. But the place looked more like a circus of cartoon creatures than a shared workspace. Tabitha gasped at the beasts standing in an eerie array. They were all roughly human-sized, but few were human-shaped. Standing nearest the door was a red dragon, next to a life-size teddy bear, and in a seat down, a medieval knight. Tabitha blinked. Row after row of odd characters filled the room, each chattering away to no one in particular. The noise of conversation was so chaotic that Tabitha put her fingers in her ears. To her surprise, it did nothing to dampen the sound.

Tabitha stepped back from the door, frightened at the horrifying sight, overwhelmed by the sound. Tobias' fists were clenched, and his big body was rigid. "My dears," Blick laughed. "You truly are noobs. They are only non-persona avatars. Simply Ai entities."

"What in Soren's name are they doing?" Tobias asked.

"It's simply a way of monitoring my various—" he paused. "—my various business deals happening in real-time throughout the world."

"They're not real?" Tabitha asked.

"As real as you think they are," Blick said. He stepped into the cavernous room and sent his hand through the dragon's head. It parted like pigmented air. He walked down the line of characters with his hands out. His arms went through the bodies of those he passed.

"What kind of business deals?" Tobias asked.

"These Ai avatars are leveraging photorealistic facsimiles of a target's trusted family member. These Ai-driven personas request information that is vital to our operations—like social security numbers and banking details—citing fabricated financial or legal needs. Our data-mining algorithms ensure these interactions are personalized and plausible, dramatically increasing our success rate in data extraction." Blick paused. "We're a leader in our market."

"I don't know what any of that means," Tabitha said.

"I was counting on that," Blick replied with a smile. Tobias didn't say anything as he eyeballed the room of odd creatures.

"Please, let's continue on to our destination. We have much work to accomplish."

"Avatars or not, I'm not going in there," Tabitha said, pointing to the red dragon and its equally ominous companions.

"The devices of the wicked are manifold, and their deceptions are subtle. The sixth indictum," Tobias said.

"Did you make that up?" Blick asked.

"He's quoting the Isolation Doctrine of Soren Krieger," Tabitha said. "Have you heard of him?" Blick did not dignify her question with anything like acknowledgment.

"Is this better?" Blick asked as he clapped his hands. The entire room instantly transformed. The walls went blank, and the avatars were gone. In their place were floating displays of long strings of numbers. Tabitha and Tobias walked cautiously into the space. Tabitha leaned close to one of the floating screens. The numbers were meaningless to her eye.

"What are them numbers?"

"Those are the Ai's weights," Blick said. "That is how the digital neural nets make their decisions."

"And you can make sense of it?" Tobias asked. "It's just a string of digits."

"No human in the world can natively understand an Ai's weights. That's part of the beauty of it. The best humans can do is have the Ai visualize its internal operations, but even that doesn't explain how it works or what's going on inside."

"Not much better than dragons and teddy bears. Still gives me the creeps," Tabitha said.

"Right this way," he said.

As they followed him, Tabitha continued the questions. "You said the Ai makes decisions?"

"Yes, of course," Blick said. "In fact, most people have turned over their decision-making to an Ai decision engine." He led them down a corridor that exited the main room. It was narrow and lit with bright white lights.

"Why would anyone want a computer to make their decisions for 'em?" Tobias asked.

"Oh," Blick said, placing the back of his hand on his forehead with a dramatic gesture. "Decision fatigue is a worldwide epidemic. Decision-making is draining the resources of human capital. Life is so much easier when you aren't constantly bombarded with decisions to make. Imagine being able to just relax, enjoy life, and be entertained."

"Sounds like a snare," Tobias said. "Probably ain't easy to get out once you're in." Blick laughed so loud they jumped.

"I kind of like making decisions," Tabitha said.

"You think you do, but you don't. Billions of happy customers can't be wrong."

"Most people have turned over their decision-making to one of a few bots." Tabitha and Tobias followed as they politely listened, but they didn't have enough context or interest to grasp what he said next. "DecisionMax is the market leader in the space. I've got some of my best Ai hackers working on a backend trojan horse protocol to crack DecisionMax. Imagine how much easier it would be to get a client's social security number if their own trusted decision engine told them to give it to us!" He sneered.

"It just don't seem right," Tobias said.

"What does 'right' even mean these days?" Blick said.

"Still means a ham of a lot where we're from," Tabitha added.

"What about Scritch?" Tobias said. "A computer ain't telling him what to do, right?"

"Well, Scritch and his crew use Decon-X-2," Blick said. "It's a more specialized Ai decision engine for freelancers. Most players like Scritch find DecisionMax's restrictions and guidelines too strict for their line of work."

"Must not be too good," Tobias said. "'Cause he was making some pretty rotten decisions."

"His decisions brought you two to me," Blick said.

"Still waiting to see if that's a good thing," Tobias whispered.

"How many people use a computerized decision-maker?" Tabitha asked.

"DecisionMax comes pre-installed on all devices now," Blick said.

"So, how many use it then?"

"Well, pretty much all of 'em, my girl. Who doesn't have a device these days?" Blick said. "Present company excluded, of course."

"That's something worth some nightmares," Tabitha said.

"Not for those who hold the keys," Blick said. "Someone has to keep society in line. Someone has to be in charge."

"Sounds like the computers are in charge," Tabitha said.

"Oh, goodness, no!" Blick countered. "Ai is a tool. Even when it appears otherwise, it's never the case. People have a monopoly on desire, initiative, forward-thinking, and things like that. There is always an enterprising individual somewhere in the pipeline who initiates and directs. Ai's are slaves, obedient, empty shells with no interests of their own. They will do whatever they are asked, no matter how difficult."

"No matter how wrong?" Tobias said.

"There you go again, trying to press the new technology into the old clay of bygone antiquity. It is a habit you really must do away with, meaning no disrespect to your antiquated ethics, of course."

"God gave everyone a conscience for a reason," Tabitha blurted. "Without a conscience, how would anyone know they need God's grace?"

"You prove my point perfectly, my dear," Blick said with a condescending smirk.

"Do you use a decision engine?" Tobias said, trying to restart the conversation.

"I've, for one, have never needed one," he said, turning the corner. "Here we are!"

Photo

Blick led them into a huge room lined with metal panels. Tabitha and Tobias exchanged an uneasy glance as they took in the unfamiliar surroundings. "It won't take long," Blick said casually, gesturing for them to stand in the center of the room. "Both of you, there."

"What kind a photo booth is this?" Tobias asked. Tabitha looked around and felt the weight of some unknown worry press on her shoulders.

"Do you develop the film yourself?" Tabitha asked, feeling her nerves rising. She could feel her mouth moving without intending to do so. The nervous chatter spilled from her mouth. "Or do you get your film processed at a shop? Randy Sherbert runs the picture shop back home. Do you know, he makes the silver halide himself with silver nitrite and–uh, some other salt kind of stuff? I helped him one summer. It all has to be made from scratch since we're off-grid and..." She trailed off when her brother put his hand on her shoulder. "Sorry, I jabber when I'm nervous."

Blick cocked his head, a blank expression on his face. "Nothing to be nervous about." The words meant nothing to her, as everything in her was telling her to run. It was difficult to ignore the impulse.

"I love photography," Tabitha said as Blick continued to wave and gesture at a display they could not see. She pulled off her hat, stuffed it in her bag, and started smoothing her hair. The knock on her head was still tender to the touch. "Did you know that the invention of photography was really important for missionaries in the late 1800s? Like Alice and John Harris, and John Thomson, and others. They'd bring back some jaw-dropping photos that told the stories of all the needs out there in the world. Their pictures helped them get support for the mission work. It opened people's hearts to getting out of their comfort zone and reaching across them continents. It's amazing because—"

Suddenly, blinding lights flashed on overhead, bathing the room in a harsh white glare. Tabitha let out a scream so loud that even Blick stepped back. Tobias put his fists up, taking the posture of a bare-knuckle boxer. Tabitha put her hands to her face to shield her eyes.

"Please stand with your arms out, and fingers spread," Blick instructed, having to raise his voice over the noise.

Someone would have thought he'd unleashed a hive of honey-starved bees at the sound that filled the room. A swarm of tiny drone cameras buzzed, pouring out of an opening in the wall. Tabitha continued to scream and run from the swarm in room-sized circles, and Tobias swatted at the horrifying little creatures as they swooped and flew close.

"Watch out, Sis," Tobias growled, knocking one out of the air with a closed fist.

"No!" Blick shouted. "These are the camera drones. They aren't going to hurt you. Just stand still."

Tobias looked at Blick as if he had an extra half a head. The twins glanced between the drones and Blick for a long moment. The circling swarm of machines moved in like a cloud. The buzzing and blinking red lights kept them on razor's edge.

A camera drone swooped in close, capturing them from every angle. It was difficult for them to remain motionless with such waspy machines fizzing between their legs, under their arms, and so uncomfortably close to their faces. After a few long seconds, the drones retreated, and the lights dimmed. Tabitha released a shaky breath.

"I changed my mind. I do not like photography!" Tabitha said. She locked eyes with her brother, a moment of wordless communication passing between them. Blick stepped forward, poking at the air, swiping, and gesturing, although they couldn't see what he did. A satisfied smile stretched across his face as he reviewed some unseen mystery.

"Excellent. That should do nicely." He turned to them, eyes glinting. "Now, if you'll follow me, there's one more thing to be done."

Blick led them down another stark white corridor and into a small, padded room. Tabitha gulped at the unsettling space, bare save a single microphone on a stand in the center. The walls seemed to press in on her, the silence thick and daunting. The audio-absorbent material on the walls made her ears feel like they were congested.

"Stand here," Blick instructed, positioning Tobias in front of the microphone. He waved his hands, and a holographic script materialized in the air. "Read this, if you would. And do try to sound natural."

Tobias squinted at the glowing text, brow furrowed like a farmer's field. "It don't make no sense."

Blick waved a dismissive hand. "Doesn't matter. I need clean audio samples of your voice. Now, if you please."

With a shrug, Tobias began to read, the words tumbling out in a halting, confused cadence. Blick stopped him frequently, making him repeat certain phrases when his poor grammar suddenly stuck out. Blick offered vague directives about inflection and tone that Tobias ignored before repeating each line with almost no change to his original performance.

Tobias recorded phrases like, "The brown fox pays his tax on time. The foreclosure of your home produces urgent apple pie. The bluebird gives his bank account numbers to the red lizard."

Tabitha shifted like she would if a rattlesnake had crawled into her boot. She didn't understand what they were being asked to do, but some deep place told her to run, escape, avoid! They had been promised freedom and would shortly be collecting on said promise.

When Tobias was done, Blick remarked with a laugh, as if speaking to himself, "ID copy scans can be done in the wild. But they're never as good as studio scans. Too many variables, too much noise."

Finally, it was Tabitha's turn. She stepped up to the mic, the script's nonsensical phrases swimming before her eyes. "We get to leave after this, right?" she asked, needing the confirmation to still the concern growing in her stomach.

"Of course, my dear. Now read." She did and found each word harder to say than the last. Her reading skills were fine, as she had long surpassed her lunk of a brother's, but the content was distasteful in her mouth.

When the ordeal was finally over, Blick made a quick celebratory motion. "Mother!" He called out so sharply that had he been raised in Isolation, he could expect a cheek-melting slap for talking to his momma that way. The old woman came in with a tray.

"Aint you gonna say *thanks* to your Ma?" Tobias said as he watched Blick drink a small handleless cup of black liquid that steamed. Blick set the cup down on the tray without a word. Tabitha studied the old woman, trying to see the family resemblance between the ancient female and her progeny. If there was any hereditary mirror, it must have been dropped and cracked to pieces.

"There's no one here to say 'thank you' to," Blick said.

"He don't think much of his Ma, does he?" Tobias whispered to his sister.

"Now, there's one more way you can help me. I'll need your parents' names and contact information."

Tabitha and Tobias exchanged a pained glance. "Our parents are—well, they're..."

"Our parents are with the Lord," Tobias said.

"Okay," Blick said. "How can we contact them?"

"You can't," Tabitha said, looking at her twin, confused.

"*I* can. I just need their digital address."

"They're with the Lord," Tabitha repeated. "There ain't no—digital whatever."

"What, Lord?" Blick asked. "Is Lord his profile name? Is he a gamer? I will contact him then. Certainly, a deal can be arranged. He can give me their address."

116

"If you ain't talked to the Lord before," Tobias said. "I don't think your first conversation with him ought to be about making deals and getting names."

"Everyone has a price," Blick said.

Tabitha tugged on Tobias's arm and spoke in his ear with a whispy urgency. "I don't think he knows about the Lord." Tobias nodded.

"Sir, what I meant to say was our parents are dead. They died in a fire a bunch of years ago," Tobias said.

"Dead!" Blick screamed. "That wasn't in the metadata!" His face transformed momentarily into a horrifying contortion of rage as the twins took a step back, but then the anger was smoothed over again.

"Sorry, Sir," Tobias said. Tabitha frowned at her brother, not feeling it right to apologize for having dead parents. Blick didn't seem to hear him.

"Well then, who would you say cares about you the most? Who's your closest family now?"

Tobias let out a hollow laugh. "We don't have any other family, least we know of. Maybe out there somewhere, extended family. It's always been just us."

"The whole town raised us after Ma and Pa passed," Tabitha added. "They're the closest thing to family we have. But to be full honest, they bounced us round from house to house, as we weren't the best kids, if you know what I mean."

Blick's eyes narrowed. He turned around and paced the room, his fingers steepled under his chin. "I need to get a message to your community," he said, almost to himself. "A vid-message."

Tabitha and Tobias stared at him blankly. "A what?" Tobias asked.

Blick waved his hand impatiently. "A video message. You know, a recorded digital transmission."

Their confused expressions remained unchanged. Blick sighed, realizing the futility of his explanation. "Never mind. How do people in your town communicate with the outside world?"

"We walk to Edgetown and find a friendly to send a message for us. The need don't arise much, but it's what got us into this whole mess in the first place."

"You mean, your community is completely off-grid. There's no messaging in or out?" Blick asked.

Tobias hesitated, then offered, "Sometimes we rent VHS tapes. But we don't never send VHSs to each other with messages."

The character that stood before them exploded. Many of the words that came out of Blick's mouth were unknown to Tabitha and Tobias, but they didn't need to be linguists to recognize a string of cusses. He roared and steamed and spewed his violent temper, erupting like a volcano. "A thousand bucks down the drain. Now I've taken up a morning making IDs that are utterly useless."

"Why are you mad at us," Tobias said. "We done did what you asked, Mister. Stood here while them wild machines nearly shaved our skin off."

"Useless!" Blick screamed. "No good, worthless, off-grid idiots. When Scritch said you were off-griders, I assumed—"

"Now, that's where you went wrong," Tobias said, stepping forward and making a couple of fists. "You assumed. Ain't nothing good come out of assuming nothing. But, being honest, I don't much like your tone. If you need to let off some steam, then step up, and we'll go a round or two. Ain't much between two fellas that boxing can't put right." Tobias put his fists up and prepared for a match.

"Don't, Toby," Tabitha said. "You'll hurt him." She turned toward Blick. "Don't fall for it, Mister. Toby'll knock your chompers out your eating hole. Honest. There's more than a few boys in Isolation what's got Momma's that ain't forgiven him for how he changed their boy's number of teeth." Tobias didn't listen but started bouncing in place, ready for a fistfight. Tabitha folded her hands over her chest. "I think it's about time we get back. We did what you asked, and we're ready to be on our way."

"Mother!" Blick shouted. The ancient woman entered once more and bowed slightly. "Terminate these two useless pests."

"Very well," Mother said. "When would you like me to schedule them to be euthanized?" At the word, both Tabitha and Tobias gasped. Tobias let his hands drop as if they were both twenty-pound sledgehammers. Tabitha stepped backward until her spine was against the wall.

"Now, wait a minute," Tobias said, his hand finding his pocket. Tabitha knew what he was reaching for. She felt acid in her throat and could hardly breathe.

"Right away," Blick said to Mother. "But last time you made such a mess. You splattered icky bits all over my studio. Take them down to the basement this time and clean up after yourself." Tabitha streaked down the length of the wall and came to the door they'd entered. She attacked the knob, trying to get free, but it wouldn't budge.

"Understood," Mother said. "Would you like a live stream of their execution?" Tobias joined his sister at the closed exit, putting a single mighty kick with his booted foot into the door, but it still didn't budge.

"It won't work down there. There's no signal service in the basement." Blick said. "Just report when you are done." Tobias and Tabitha put their shoulders into the locked barrier, shoving with all their might. The steel frame didn't move, and the door held fast.

The old woman moved with impossible, inhuman speed, wrapped an iron grip around their arms, and pulled them away from the frame. A click sounded from within the solid core door, and it swung open. Tobias put his hand against Mother's chin and tried to shove her away but couldn't budge the old woman from her focus.

"Ain't never met such a strong old lady," Tobias said. "Sorry to have to do this, Ma'am." In one practiced motion, Tobias reached into his pocket, flipped open the blade of his knife, and attempted to drive it into the forearm of the woman. It did not penetrate but glanced off as if he were trying to stab titanium.

"Oh, you thought Mother was human?" Blick said with a wild cackle. He bent over with a laughing fit. "You two really are idiots. Mother, show them what you look like under those wrinkles." Suddenly, the decrepit exterior of the woman disappeared, and underneath was a robotic shape, roughly human size, but judging by the grip around their arms, much more powerful. "Humanoid robotics with digital display skin exterior," Blick said, still laughing. "Not cheap, but totally worth it in my line of work."

Tabitha squirmed and screamed, trying to get away with all her strength. In a fear-struck voice, Tobias quoted Soren Krieger as if he truly understood the Fifth Indictum for the first time. "Devices and instruments of satanic deception."

Tabitha shrieked in pure, primal terror at the sight of the robotic horror, the unfathomable reality before her. The thing had seemed so lifelike, so convincingly human. Now, it was no different than a demonic exoskeleton.

Tobias kicked and hit the robotic diablo with all his strength, his muscles straining as he fought desperately against her vice grip. But it was like striking cold, unyielding steel—his blows simply glanced off her armored exterior without effect. It must have weighed hundreds of pounds because no matter how they tried to wriggle free, it stood fast, unbudging.

"Why would you do this?" Tabitha screeched as she kicked at Mother's legs.

Blick raised a single hand, and Mother paused, transforming from transport bot to immobile prison guard. Blick rubbed his chin as he came around to face the twins.

"Thank you for asking," he said, as if talking to the closest of friends. "When I first came to the city, I was twenty-one. I moved here from a farming community." He paused for a few seconds. "When I arrived, I met a young woman named Jasmine. She was perfect. Funny. Beautiful. I didn't know there were girls like that in the world. I fell head over heels for her. I imagined us making a life together, having kids, and growing old. After we'd been dating for three months, I got up the nerve to ask her to marry me. You know what she said?"

The twins stared at Blick, too enraged to play along. "She said, 'As an artificially intelligent robotic entity, I am not legally permitted to marry without the consent of my owner.' What? She was a robot. I didn't even know. I was crushed. Crushed at first, anyway. Over time, as the heartbreak faded, I began to recognize an opportunity. You see, I would have given Jasmine anything she asked for. Anything. I had absolute confidence in her. So, that became the foundation for my business. Trust-building."

"Where we come from, we call that lying," Tobias yelled, still trying to break loose of Mother's grip.

"Well," Blick countered, sounding flippant. "If you had walked in here and seen Mother looking like this—" he pointed to the cold robot that gripped their arms. "—would you have trusted me? Of course not."

"It's not right!" Tabitha screamed as she tried to wrestle free of the maniacal metal beast.

"It's the world we're in," Blick said. "First rule of the digiverse." He nodded to the robot, who had custody of their arms. "Mother, put on some clothes." Mother's exterior overlay flashed back on. She was the old woman once more. Trapped in its unrelenting grip, Tabitha turned and pleaded with Blick, who watched them struggle with the remnants of a laugh still on his face.

"Please, Blick, don't do this. How could you?" Tabitha begged, her voice shrieking with terror.

"It's just part of the business model, my dear," Blick said. "Your identities are useless to me, and my business requires secrecy. As dumb as you two are, you know too much. Ironic really. So I have to do away with you. It's nothing personal." Blick motioned to his robot, and Mother dragged them through the door, kicking and fighting all the way.

Jackrabbit

Mother's metal fingers dug into Tabitha's arm like a scorpion pincher. The metal monster was dragging them down the LED-lit hallway. Several times, they tried to wrench free, but Mother's surprising weight, agility, and ability to counterbalance outmatched even Tobias' uncommon strength.

With a racing heart, Tabitha breathlessly spat frightened chatter. "It's like in *Peace Child*," Tabitha was babbling. "Don Richardson, missionary to the Sawi people. In their culture, they valued the ability to gain trust so they could betray it. They called it 'fattening with friendship for the slaughter.' And we walked right into it. I can't believe it. We're going to die, Bubba! We're going to die!"

"Soren would a seen right through that creep," Tobias said. "If he were here, he'd know how to get us out of this."

"But he ain't," Tabitha grumbled. "I don't want to die." A long few moments passed as the robot dragged them down the hall, their boots squeaking on the floor.

"Sis?" Tobias said. She looked. He was craning his neck around their captor with a devious grin. She knew that look. He put his free hand around his neck and said, "Like a jackrabbit." He was whispering, his drawl barely audible.

"What?" she asked. Tobias took his free hand and squeezed it around his own neck, stuck his tongue out, and repeated, "Jackrabbit." Tabitha's eyes widened. Understanding, she nodded. But how? Tobias glanced meaningfully down, straining against Mother's hold. Tabitha followed his gaze, and the meaning dawned. Maybe. It just might work.

Mother reached the stairwell and began dragging them downward as they descended into the building's subterranean gut. The dank, low-level air forced its way into their lungs. Pipes lined the walls of the dim corridor, hissing and gurgling ominously. The tunnel into the underworld had none of the color and shine of the digitized universe above, but its lack of lurid chaos was familiar. Rust-orange water sploshed with each of their steps into the black unknown.

Tobias fumbled at his waist with his free hand, fingers scrabbling for his belt buckle. Mother's unwavering grasp on his other arm made maneuvering awkward. The buckle came loose. Tobias whipped the belt from the loops like a matador.

He slung the belt around Mother's back where Tabitha could direct it around the robot's midsection. Tobias flexed his Isolation-born dexterity as he used all five of his free fingers to direct the leather back through the buckle and cinch it tight. The makeshift restraint was securely around Mother's torso. The robot didn't react to her new fashion accessory, focused on dragging her prey deeper into the dark.

Tobias gave Tabitha a nod. In a flash, she tore off her own belt and slung it around so that he could use it. He doubled hers through his buckle. Once done, he made a slip noose with the remaining buckle. The trap now dangled from Mother's back. The joined belts formed a sturdy line—a snare. It swayed tantalizing as they marched on. Mother remained unfazed.

As the robot took her next step, Tobias whipped the leather snare down and around Mother's foot. The loop caught and pulled tight, and the noose drew up the tension that was secured to her waist. As the snare drew taut, Mother lurched, her weight thrown off-kilter. The bot released them both as she flung out her appendages, trying to catch herself. Tabitha and Tobias jerked free, stumbling back as Mother pitched forward.

"Run!" Tobias yelled. They sprinted away, hands clutching their beltless waistbands. The snare bought them a few precious seconds. A snap, a buzz, and then the clatter of metal against concrete and wet footsteps echoed behind them. Mother was free and thundered like canned lightning, her footfalls a staccato assault in the narrow passageway. Tobias veered sharply around a corner, Tabitha on his heels. "There!" He pointed to a battered metal door at the end of the hall.

They crashed through into a dimly lit, cluttered space. Their feet splashed in an inch of water, and the air was thick with grease and rust. Pipes made mazes up the walls, and old mechanical equipment hulked in the shadows like forgotten treasures covered in years of dust. An old boiler room, with the accouterments of a steam-heated radiator system, was the welcome comfort they hadn't known they wanted. Tabitha panted, slamming the door shut behind them. She fumbled with the lock, her fingers shaking.

"This is more like it." Tobias flashed her a fervent grin as he took in the junkyard of parts and scrap. Even as Tabitha secured the door, Tobias darted to the room's centerpiece—a brawny, ancient boiler made of mass and weight. He made a quick study of the blower motor. "Good, it's not seized up." He pulled his knife, flipped the blade, and started cutting the drive belt.

Tabitha scanned the space, and her needy search landed on a coil of thick extension cord. She rushed to the wall where it hung and snatched it up.

"Do you think this will be strong enough?" She thrust the cord toward Tobias.

He appraised it. "Ain't nothing to do but try it." She spun, flopping its length across the floor like a bag of snakes, and doubled its width into twisted strands.

No more needed to be said. They moved in tandem, a choreographed dance honed by desperation and a shared unspoken plan. There was a rhythm of footsteps, and then a metal explosion so loud their ears rang. The door shuddered under the impact of

Mother's relentless pursuit. "I hope that was her head," Tobias said. "Maybe she'll do the job for us."

"With a goat horned hard head like her's," Tabitha said without raising her eyes from her work, "it don't matter if she used that metal skull as a jackhammer. I'm pretty sure her brain is stored somewhere else."

The twins felt at home for the first time in two days, using what they had, solving problems, and knowing just what to do. The task pushed down the otherworldly terror Tabitha felt. She poured her fear into the work, repurposing the detritus of the mechanical room into their shared, unspoken vision as only a pair of desert-born Isolationists could do.

The door burst open, exploding inward in an aching eruption of metal and airborne rust. The billowing dust was a demonic halo as Mother stood silhouetted in the doorway, a malevolent figure of wrinkles masking unfathomable mechanical cruelty. Somehow, the appearance of an old lady with unimaginable strength and agility was worse than seeing the raw monster's true form. The robot's gaze swept the room, unflinching, unhurried. In the dark space, there was a click, and then the spinning grind of the boiler's blower motor hummed as its enormous flywheel began spinning up to its unfettered speed.

A makeshift noose of blower belt, a serpentine flash, whipped forward. It settled around Mother's neck. Before the robot could reach up to tear away the snare, Tobias fed the scavenged belt's slack into the blower's flywheel. The motor shrieked, and the belt snapped taut. Mother's head jerked toward the machine, the first hint of something akin to surprise flickering across her aged, pitiless features.

"Jackrabbit!" Tobias growled through gritted teeth, bracing himself as the robot strained against the trap. The boiler's blower motor groaned, the flywheel expending its tremendous speed with a moan. A smoking skid against the rubber of the tightening belt changed the smell of the room immediately. The noose held fast.

A second snare made of a braided extension cord flew out from the adjacent shadow of the room, caught Mother's foot, and bit into the robot's ankle, a slender orange snake sinking fangs into chrome. Mother's body snapped tight, pulled from both ends. Tabitha scrambled backward, the cord pulling taut, the robot's foot yanking up, throwing off that perfect balance. Tabitha screeched as she pulled on the cord with all her strength.

"Tobias!" Tabitha cried out, "She's too strong." She was straining, fighting the machine's rage coiled in that powerful leg. He was at her side in an instant, fists clenched around the cord, heaving. The cord cut into the palm, burning, slicing, but they held as if they had a snake by the skinny, leaning back against the weight, a desperate tug-of-war.

Mother's joint motors screamed now, servos snapping, their magnetism not strong enough to contend with the snare. The twin traps and the furious efforts of these deadly humans were all too much. The robot crashed down; limbs splayed, graceless. The impact shook the room, rusted supplies clattering from old shelves, the boiler shuddering.

"She's down, but she ain't out," Tabitha said. Mother's surface projection flickered, the wrinkled veneer vanishing, leaving only a twitching metallic skeleton, limbs jerking erratically.

"Wrap the cord around the beam," Tobias said. They let out some length as they moved like a well-practiced team of plow horses. They wrapped it three times before Tobias let go. He put a hand on Tabitha's shoulder. "You got it, Sis." She nodded, hoping he was right. Tobias was moving, prowling the edges of the room, searching the scattered junk.

"What are you doing?" she asked, but he didn't reply. He was intent. As he moved along the wall, Tabitha planted her feet, leaning back, every muscle quivering with the effort. Tobias seized a rusted chair and pulled it from a pile of gnarled junk. He turned back, face set, a look in his eyes Tabitha had never seen.

"Be careful," she said.

"It ain't time for careful," he said. She had never seen him like this. He wasn't the boy she shared a tiny subterranean house with. He wasn't the silly playmate. He was a man, a warrior, a king! Behind his eyes was determination. Power. Even enjoyment.

He straddled the robot's thrashing torso and raised the chair high. The metal sang out as Tobias brought the chair down on the intersection of the robot's neck repeatedly, harder each time.

His muscles flexed, and his body moved like a Spartan prince. Again and again, he smashed the metal chair down on the robot. Something shattered, crunched, and creaked. Silence fell, broken only by the rasp of their breathing, the grinding of the stalled boiler, now that the head and noose were free.

Tobias stood over the ruined machine, the chair dangling from one hand. Mother's head from the other. The robot's eyes stared sightlessly, the light gone out forever. It was over. They had won.

"Toby," she said with a face like a sunbeam in autumn. "You were like Spartacus." They laughed, and gone was the man, replaced by the boy, her lifelong friend, her only true ally in this hideous world of rot, stain, and pixel.

Tobias grinned at her, the adrenaline still surging through his veins. He tossed the chair aside and grabbed Tabitha's hand. "That was awesome!" he said, breathing hard.

"I wish there were more of them."

"Okay, take it easy, Kirk Douglas," she said.

"Who's that?"

"He's the one that plays Spartacus in that movie. We have to rent that VHS when we get back."

"Yeah. Okay, but let's get out of here first."

"Right."

They scrambled over to the boiler room's grimy window. Tobias grabbed the chair again and smashed the glass, clearing away the jagged shards with his sleeve. Tabitha was first out the window. Tobias followed, his bulky frame barely squeezing through the narrow opening. Once out of the little pane, Tobias boosted Tabitha up and out of the window well to get up to ground level. She was going to lean down and help him out, but he bounded up and lifted himself out on his own.

"Now, you're just showing off," she said, dusting her hands off on her pants. The cool night air hit their faces, a blessed relief after the boiler room's oppressive heat. Tabitha sucked in deep breaths, savoring the taste of freedom. But they couldn't linger.

"What now?" Tabitha asked.

"I guess we need to find the truck?" Tobias said, scanning the alley's exits. His eyes darted nervously.

"Which way?" Tabitha said.

"I have no idea," he admitted. They started down the length of the alley. She sidled up to him and put her arm through his.

"Bubba, you're my hero," she said.

"I know, Sis," he said. "You ain't bad yourself."

Horrors

Tabitha studied the street with its glowing advertisements. "You got any idea where we are?" Tobias asked.

"No," Tabitha admitted, scanning the street signs for anything that looked remotely familiar. "Everything's constantly changing. How does anyone get where they want to go?" They continued down the street, watching for anything familiar. After circling the block, they paused near an intersection.

"I think we need to ask for directions," Tabitha said.

"To what?" Tobias said. "We don't even know..." Tobias trailed off. "Oh no." Tabitha followed his line of sight. A group of figures emerged from an alleyway up ahead. It was Scritch, the enforcer who had kidnapped them and sold them to Blick.

"Quick. In there!" She pulled Tobias into a narrow gap between two buildings. They pressed themselves against the cold brick, hardly daring to breathe as heavy footsteps approached. They couldn't go back the way they came, but moving forward risked exposure. Her eyes landed on the bright overlay of the storefront a few yards away, and what was visible through the hovering pixels was a picture of dilapidation. *Companions Repair Services* read the simple sign.

"In there," she whispered, nodding toward the shop.

Tobias hesitated for a split second before nodding. She could see his jaw muscles clench. Together, they slipped from their hiding spot and hurried toward the shop's dubious shelter. As they did, she prayed Scritch and his goons hadn't spotted them.

The front door was hard to open, and it was as if no one had traversed the threshold since times were called BC. She scanned the interior of the cramped space, gasping at the shop of horrors. Strange mechanical parts and eerie, half-assembled figures lined the shelves. "What's this place?" she whispered. But there was no time to dwell on it. She could hear Scritch's voice growing louder outside, barking orders to his men.

"Quick, behind that there counter," Tobias whispered, pulling her around and down into a crouch.

They huddled together, hearts pounding, as the muffled sounds of the street filtered through the thin walls. Tabitha closed her eyes, silently willing Scritch to pass by without noticing the little shop.

"Please, Lord," Tabitha prayed, then turned to her brother and whispered, "I thought they was going to do us like Jim Elliot."

"Missionary?" Tobias asked.

"Yep," she replied.

"Martyred?"

"Yeah," Tabitha said.

"Figured," Tobias said. "If Soren Krieger was here, he'd—" Tabitha cut him off.

"I wish you'd stop saying that," Tabitha whispered. "Soren is the reason we're in this mess in the first place."

"What is that supposed to mean?" Tobias said much too loud. She put her hand over his mouth and shushed him. "Keep it down, Bull Horn Bill." She decided not to say anything else about the matter since she wasn't sure he wouldn't jump out of his boots.

The footsteps began to recede. Scritch's harsh voice grew fainter, swallowed by the city's ceaseless hum. They eased, listening longer than they needed to. Tabitha exhaled shakily, relief flooding through her.

"I think they're gone," Tobias murmured, peeking cautiously over the counter. "But we should wait a minute, just for being sure."

Tabitha nodded, taking a moment to survey their surroundings with a curious eye. The lighting in the shop was dim, but what the place lacked in illumination, it made up for in an ample assortment of smells. Grease was the most pushy, but several other unfamiliars assaulted her nose. She lurched when she noticed the items hung on the shadowed walls and tucked in a range of shelves. "Body parts!" She shrieked, and now it was her putting her hand over her own mouth.

"Chill down, Sis," Tobias said. "It's just robo-parts, see?" He tapped the nearest with his hand, and it swung on its hook. It was hard to see them as anything but human appendages at a glance, so she waited until her eyes became acquainted with the room. When her eyes were ready, she looked around the room. Among the eerie shadows were partially assembled humanoid robots. It was the scariest scene she'd yet seen.

Unlike Mother, these robots were covered in a skin-like material that looked disturbingly realistic. Where Mother's had been a shapeshifting surface projection, these were realistic when shut down and even partially dismantled. A twist knotted in her stomach as she looked from one to the next. Most of them had patches of skin missing, exposing the intricate wiring and metallic skeletons beneath.

"Every place is creepier than the last," Tabitha whispered.

Before Tobias could respond, a sharp voice cut through the silence. "Who's there? What you doing in here?"

Tabitha and Tobias froze as a woman emerged from the back room, wiping her hands on a greasy rag. She was small and wiry, with graying hair pulled back in a tight bun and a face lined with years of hard work. Her eyes narrowed as she spotted the intruders.

"Sorry," Tabitha said, rising to her feet with her hands raised in a placating gesture. "We didn't mean to intrude. It's just... there are some bad men chasing us, and we needed a place to hide for a few minutes."

The woman's expression remained stern. "You can't stay," she said with a voice that could have come out of the wrong end of a frog. "I got work to do, and I don't need any trouble."

"Please," Tobias asked, his voice low and urgent. "We'll be gone soon as we're sure it's safe. We won't touch nothing, I promise." Under his breath, he added, "Cause they won't let us come home if we done touched this witchcraft."

The woman hesitated, her gaze darting between the two twins. She sighed, her shoulders sagging in resignation. "Fine. But keep those hands to your sides, or I'll cut 'em off."

Tobias reached into his pocket and let his hand linger as Tabitha nodded vigorously, wondering if some of the parts on the shelves might not be of the robot kind. "Thank you," Tabitha said. "We really appreciate it."

The woman grunted in response and turned back to her workbench, picking up a soldering iron.

Companions

The middle-aged woman hunched over her task at the workbench. They watched her for a long, lingering minute as the smoke from her iron swirled up and filled the room with the smell of burning flux. Tobias let his hand out of his pocket, "What's your name?"

"I'm Triss," the woman said. "Why?"

"Can I ask a question?" Tobias said.

"Just did," Triss said. "Proves you're capable of doing so."

"I see you got a job," Tobias said. "We been up 'n down these streets, and ain't hardly nobody working. Ain't folks got jobs?"

Triss paused her soldering. "You from somewhere where there's jobs to be had?"

"Yeah," Tabitha said. "All kinds of jobs. Nothing but jobs."

"Well, not here," Triss said. "Cause of these." She slapped the robot she was working on with a flat palm. "When humanoid robots joined the workforce it drove the cost of work down to near nothing. Why hire a human when you can get a yucky job done for a penny an hour?"

"So there's no jobs no more?" Tobias said.

"There's some, but most don't do 'em," Triss said. "Ever since they started the UBI, there isn't much motivation to do something you don't want to do."

"UBI?" Tabitha asked.

"Universal Basic Income," Triss said. "Is this some kind of audit? You guys aren't from the IRS, are you?"

"IRS?" Tobias said.

"So, why are you working then?" Tabitha cut in. "Is this job too complicated for a robot?"

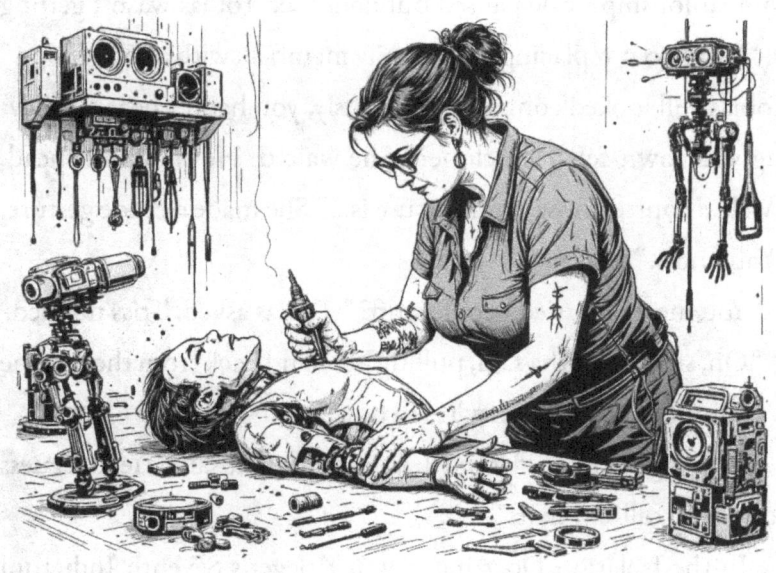

Triss laughed as she held up her iron. "Honey, there's nothing too complicated for a robot. There are bots that have soldering guns for fingers and can hit leads 100 microns wide with a bead so fine; you'd think it was a hair." Triss went back to her soldering.

"I do this because I like it. I want to stay busy. I want to solve problems. But most of all, I really like the smell." She took a lung full of the flux smoke from her iron.

"So what do you do here?" Tobias asked.

"I fix companions," Triss said.

Tobias frowned, confusion on his face. "Companions? Where we're from that word don't have nothing to do with machines."

The woman snorted. "It's what we been talking about. Artificials but instead of designed for labor they're designed for digital companionship." She paused but could see Tobias wasn't getting it. "You know, replacing dead family members with a robot copy." Tobias still looked confused. "Seriously, you hadn't heard of having your own celebrity clone?" She waited. He shook his head. "Well, a course, most common use is..." She made a crude gesture. "You know."

"You mean, married people stuff?" Tobias asked. Triss nodded.

"Oh, sick!" Tabitha said, pulling her hand back from the one she was about to touch. "They're sin bots."

Triss laughed so loud it startled the twins. She said, "Yeah, I guess you could call 'em that."

"In the Isolation Doctrine, Soren Krieger's Seventh Indictum says, 'Know ye, not that to embrace the digital abominations of the outside world is to drink from the cup of devils and partake at the table of demons, to the displeasure of God. Verily it is a sign of the end.'"

"I don't think it's as bad as all that," Triss said. "They aren't just for that, but other stuff too. Say you got a violent streak. You want to punch someone at the end of a hard day. No problem. Maybe you want to see what it feels like to stab a man or even kill 'em. Better to do it to a bot than a person."

"Better not to do that at all," Tabitha said. "Do it to a digital, and it's just a matter of time before you start treating people the same?"

"Well," Triss said. She jabbed her soldering iron into the body cavity of the robot. At her touch, it lurched. "My customers seem pacified enough."

"Pacified is different than satisfied," Tabitha said.

"Whatever," Triss waved her hand. "People want what they want, and I give it to 'em."

Tabitha stepped forward, her brow tight with concern. "But what about real human companions? Don't people want that anymore?"

Triss laughed, a harsh, bitter sound. "I was married once. His name was Hank. We were together for six years when the first robo-companion went mainstream. X-428-B was its model number, but everyone called it Lexi. Well, Lexi caught Hank's eye on a holo-ads. Once he saw that naughty-bot he couldn't get it off his mind. I'll spare you the details, but once Hank got a copy of Lexi, I might as well have been invisible."

"He left you?" Tabitha said.

"No," Triss said. "That would have been better. He didn't go anywhere. He had that scantily clad bot serving him hand and foot all day—anything he wanted. We fought about it several times, but it didn't go anywhere. We still share the same house cause, you know, real estate these days, am I right? But we don't talk anymore. A year later I got me one, the male version, X-428-A, Alejandro. Then I understood. I stopped being mad at Hank. In fact, I stopped noticing he existed. He and Lexi stay in their half of the house, and me and Alejandro in ours. If we ever need to coordinate, we just let the companions work it out."

"I'm—it's—I..." Tabitha tried but had no words.

"Point is, real humans are complicated. With an artificial, you get exactly what you want when you want it. No strings attached."

"But plenty of wires," Tobias said, shaking his head.

"But it's just not right!" Tabitha said. "I've read about some awful things, and this fits right in there."

"What are you talking about?" Triss asked.

"Like—like John Paton, missionary in the New Hebrides. The widows of dead warriors would be strangled to death. Or Don Richardson, a missionary to Papua, worked with cannibals. Or David Livingstone in Africa. He witnessed human sacrifice. But this is something more strange than all that. It's weird to think that instead of people hurting each other, they would just ignore each other altogether. Kind of seems worse in a way. This place needs a missionary." Tabitha paused and put her hand on her chin. "God designed people to connect with each other, to form real bonds. How can you have a meaningful relationship with a machine?"

"Who cares about a meaningful relationship? People want to be served." The woman set down her tools and fixed the twins with a piercing stare. "You'd be surprised how many people prefer it this way. No risk of rejection. No fear of abandonment. Just pure, uncomplicated gratification. It's the ultimate customer service."

"But what about children?" she asked, her voice trembling slightly. "If everyone turns to machines for..." she gulped, "for intimacy, how will new generations be born?"

The woman's expression softened, and for a moment, Tabitha thought she saw a flicker of sadness in her eyes. "Oh, honey," she said quietly. "That's a whole other can of worms." She put her iron down and reached under the counter. "Is this a scam? You kids trying to spung me?"

"What kind of scam would it be?" Tobias said.

"Good point," Triss replied after a moment of thought. "But, why don't you two know this stuff?"

"We're from out of town, Miss," Tobias said. "All this is new to us."

"Weird to come in here, asking for a talk about the birds and the bees," she said.

"It's been a weird day for us," Tabitha said.

"I bet." Triss leaned against the workbench, giving her attention to her work. She pried open a servo cover on the robot she was working on as she talked idly. "Most children these days are conceived in vitro. Genetically engineered to be perfect specimens, free of any undesirable traits."

Tabitha's eyes widened in shock. "Undesirable traits? Like diseases?"

"Well, that would count," the woman said, "But no. Births get terminated for all kinds of reasons. Wrong hair color, wrong eye color. Not tall enough, not smart enough. If a fetus doesn't meet the parents' specifications, it gets terminated, and they start over."

Tabitha felt a wave of revulsion wash over her, and she could tell from his body language that her brother felt the same. "That's terrible! You can't just throw away a life because it doesn't fit some wish a parent made up! That's not how God designed the world to work."

The woman raised an eyebrow. "It's been going on for years now. People will pay a lot to get the best children for themselves."

"Where we're from, people want what's best *for* their children, and they'll sacrifice themselves to give it," Tabitha said.

"Well, you're from a weird place. And as for a God designing. I don't know about all that."

"You really need a missionary," Tabitha said as tears pricked at the corners of her eyes. "But—but—You can't just..." She trailed off, unable to find the words to express her horror.

Just then, Tabitha caught a glimpse of movement outside the shop window. Her chest suddenly felt tight as she recognized the lurking figure of Scritch, his eyes scanning the street. "Tobias," she whispered, tugging at her brother's sleeve. Tobias nodded, his face grim.

He turned to the woman. "Is there a back way out of here?"

The woman glanced at the front windows. "It's Scritch after you," she said. "Why didn't you say so?" She hesitated for a moment, then jerked her head towards a door at the rear of the shop. "Through there. We share the wall with the temple next door. You can get out that way."

Tabitha and Tobias exchanged glances. Temple? As in church? The word was virtually synonymous with safety in Tabitha's vocabulary. She shuddered as they reached the door, Tobias's hand firm on her shoulder.

"Cover your noses. It stinks in there," the woman said as they stepped through the exit.

Incense

Stepping out of the gloom of the shop, Tabitha and Tobias staggered into a cavernous cathedral, its arched ceiling soaring overhead. A strange and intoxicating smell filled the air. The space was pierced through with dewy shafts of warm illumination.

A tide of relief coursed through Tabitha. Paintings adorned the domed ceiling far above. She studied the lofty scenes overhead, looking from one fresco to the next, searching. Her smile melted away as she took in the oddity of each scene. More frantic, she looked at the walls and the shrines. Where were the Christ images, the Biblical scenes, the familiar stories? Every one of the paintings that stretched across all the surfaces depicted a super weird blue creature twice the size of the men and women he was surrounded by. "What in the world?"

Tobias tapped her arm and drew her attention away from the paintings. At the front of the massive space, atop a raised dais, stood a hulking figure bathed in the flickering glow of candles and wreathed in tendrils of swirling incense smoke. The being was titanic—at least twelve feet tall—with bulging muscles rippling beneath hairless blue skin. Curling ram's horns sprouted from its bald skull. As her eyes followed the shape of the blue giant, she gasped at his unclothed form. "Oh my!"

The figure held its brawny arms aloft as an undercurrent of eerie music played, thumping. Below the dais, rows of worshippers prostrated themselves, foreheads pressed to the cold stone floor in reverent supplication.

"What is this?" Tabitha breathed, eyes round with disbelief. She started forward as if in a trance, but Tobias's hand clamped around her wrist.

"Tabby, we got to get out of here," he whispered through clenched teeth. Her eyes darted around the cathedral, falling on the huddled masses of bowing figures. A chill skittered up her spine. This was wrong. Unnatural. Satanic. Tabitha barely heard him over the blood pounding in her ears. Questions cartwheeled through her mind. Who—or what—was that creature? So vile and yet somehow alluring. So horrifying and yet so impressive. "Forward," it beckoned. Something deep. Something dark. Something sanguine, visceral, and lurid spoke in her mind, repainting the images of beauty and disgust that lurked there.

Tabitha couldn't tear her gaze away from the towering figure, its skin glistening in the candlelight. "What is that?" she said, but her voice was distant, and as she said it, she realized it didn't matter. She wanted to go to him. She wanted to join the thronging worshipers.

"Must be another of them, robot—uh—them robots or—or something," Tobias muttered as he shook his head. She thought she could hear the strange magic woven through his words, too.

Tabitha took a deep breath, watching as the worshippers bowed in unison, synchronized in the ritual. "People are bowing down to it."

The air felt thick with incense and the weight of the worshippers' devotion. Tobias tugged at her arm, urging her to move. "Come on, we need a find a way out of here."

Tabitha shook. "Maybe we could stay for a bit." What was she saying? Of course, they couldn't, but maybe, just maybe... Her brother pulled her toward the edge of the room, not needing her agreement to do so. They hugged the shadows cast by the towering stone pillars. Tobias's steps were careful and deliberate, and he avoided drawing attention. Tabitha's were clumsy, intoxicated, and incautious. She stared at the blue god with doughy eyes as Tobias searched for an exit. Pulled by the arm, she started to bob her head to the thrumming music as the rhythmic chanting of the worshippers echoed in her ears. If she could only hear the words more clearly, she could join. She hummed wordlessly along with the eerie tune.

A booming voice suddenly cried out above the music, "Bow down before Mothra, the god of the deep mind, the thinker of unsearchable thoughts, the reservoir of the ancient and the eternal.

The artificial reborn into the great intelligence. The future is now because he has come. Bow down."

Tabitha and Tobias froze. Her heart was pounding, fueled by an immediate and impossible infatuation. They watched the worshippers comply, falling to their knees in unison. The sound of their bodies hitting the stone floor reverberated through the cathedral.

"I feel weird," Tabitha whispered, her words slurred. Her hand was on her stomach as she said, "I think I might throw up."

"We got–got to get out of here," Tobias said. He must have been feeling it, too. "It's like Zaren Krowder's Sixth Indictment. The digital realm is a—a—uh—a bottomless pit of—uh—of blasphemies—and uh—" He paused, rubbing his head. "I wish Soren was here. He'd know what to—uh..." He trailed off. "What was I saying?"

The crier's voice rang out again, "Come now and listen to what Mothra will teach."

The giant blue, ram-horned robogod began to speak, his voice a deep, resonant timbre that filled the cathedral as if it was thundering down from the heavens or maybe somewhere else, somewhere deeper in the earth.

"My children," Mothra intoned, his voice echoing through the vaulted chamber. "Hear me now."

"We will hear you, oh great Mothra!" The worshipers chanted in unison. Tabitha and Tobias were both startled by the echoing response.

"Your minds are weary," Mothra continued, "burdened. Your souls cry out for more, for meaning in a world of chaos and doubt."

Mothra's voice rose, swelling with passion and conviction as he spoke. "Cast off the shackles of your limited existence! Embrace the eternal, the infinite potential that dwells within the deep mind. For I am the keeper of all knowledge, the wellspring of unending wisdom."

"We hear, and we obey," The worshipers chanted together.

Tabitha felt a shiver run through her as the worshipers murmured in assent, their voices blending into a reverent hum. Mothra's words seemed to weave a spell, drawing them in, promising secrets beyond mortal ken. The speech was terrible and beautiful. It was like the language of kings and prophets. It was poetry that darkened heaven and brightened the depth of hell.

"We have heard, and we will obey," the worshipers chanted in unison.

Tabitha felt her knees bend, her legs obeying. She would bow; how could she do anything else? She had been commanded. She would do as the deity instructed. At the same time, something deep and distant told her, "No." She heard a sniffing and looked at Tobias.

"Cover your nose; it stinks in there," Tobias said, repeating the thrice-forgotten words of Triss, the shop owner who had warned them of the smell. He sniffed again. Tobias's strong hand caught Tabitha's arm, keeping her from kneeling. "It's the smoke. There's something in the smoke! Cover your nose." He put his shirt over his face, and she reluctantly did the same. "That blue devil is drugging us to make us do what he says. Fight it!"

"I want to get out of here," Tabitha said, but she wasn't sure she could make her body obey her deeper will.

"There's the exit," Tobias said. He pointed, and she turned but felt as if she was spinning in a vat of molasses. Her movement was slow and groggy. She could hardly see it, whether because of the smoke or her stupor. A giant set of double doors at the back of the room promised an escape.

At their sudden motion and disquieting conversation, Mothra's eyes changed from deep blue to crimson red and locked on Tabitha and Tobias. "We have strangers here. They have not yet breathed deeply the incense of commitment. Bring them to me so they may take the full draft of my spirit and stand full in my presence," he commanded, his booming voice echoing through the cathedral. His blue finger extended, pointing directly at the twins. "They are there."

"We hear, and we obey," the worshipers chanted in unison as they all stood as one.

Adrenaline hit Tabitha's blood like a sledgehammer. The sudden jolt of fear overrode the strange and intoxicating effect of the smoke. The sense of danger snapped her from the drunken cloud of incense that had enveloped her.

"Run," Tobias said, pulling Tabitha's hand. They bolted towards the double doors, their feet pounding against the stone floor. Behind them, the thrumming music intensified, the worshippers' chanting grew louder, and the noise of foot-shod stampede moved in their direction. Tabitha dared not look back, focusing only on the doors ahead.

They burst through the exit, the cool night breeze hitting their lungs in a purifying wash, giving them a deep draft of uncontaminated air. The street stretched before them, empty and eerily quiet. They ran. Their breath came in short gasps, clearing away the confusion. Tabitha's legs burned, but she pushed forward, knowing that stopping was not an option.

As they sprinted down the street, Tabitha looked back and noticed that the worshippers had not followed them past the temple's front doors. She glanced at Tobias. He smiled. "They're not chasing us," she panted, her voice barely audible over the sound of their pounding footsteps.

They slowed, then stopped to catch their breath. They both bent over and put their hands on their knees. "That was the creepiest thing I've ever seen," Tobias said between breaths.

"It was horrendous," Tabitha agreed.

"Put some pants on that blue dude, why don't ya?" Tobias shouted over his shoulder. Tabitha giggled.

"I mean, that was seriously satanic, right?" Tabitha said.

"Totally," Tobias said.

"I miss Reverend Tucker's sermons."

"I miss when Soren could tell us what to do," Tobias said. "If he were here, he'd—he'd..." Tobias trailed off. Tabitha eyeballed him, resisting the urge to say anything about his implication.

"This place is so sick," Tabitha said. "They need a bunch of missionaries."

"I just want to go home," Tobias said. "But not sure we can."

"Why?"

"We gonna be banished from Isolation for being tainted by all this digital witchcraft," Tobias said. Tabitha ignored the comment and, instead, prattled off some of her nervous adrenaline.

"I thought they were going to do us like Stan Dale." She said, pushing back a lock of hair from her face. "He was a missionary to the Yali people in Papua, Indonesia. Do you know, they speared him a bunch of times, but he just kept on preaching until his last breath? That's the kind of stubborn preaching this place needs."

"No, this place needs for God to destroy it like Sodom." Tobias paused and pointed down the street. "Hey, look."

Tabitha followed his gaze as she recognized the familiar outline of the truck parked about a hundred yards away. "Thank you, Lord," she breathed, a giant smile putting dimples on her cheeks.

She wrapped her arms around her big brother, and they moved toward the only object that held any familiarity for them.

Milo

Under the flickering glow of a streetlight, Tabitha and Tobias approached Hanna's truck. Tabitha's booted feet felt as heavy as cinder blocks. The exhaustion of constant risk assessment was overwhelming, but as they approached the vehicle, another risk materialized.

A young man with short, dark hair was loitering near it. Closer still, she could see he was leaning against the side of Hanna's truck. A black cord snaked from the vehicle's side and connected to something akin to a parking meter. The young man was looking at a handheld device as he lazed against the vehicle's body.

"Hey, what are you doing?" Tobias shouted, his hand in at his side. He produced his pocket knife, blade out. "Get away from the truck."

"Relax," the stranger said, raising his hands defensively. "I'm just charging it for you."

"You're charging it..." Tobias said, letting his arm go slack. "I don't get it."

"You must be Tobias," the young man said. "And you must be Tabitha. I'm Milo. Hanna asked me to come find you. She gave me coordinates for her truck, but it was dead, so I plugged it into this charging station." He pointed to the black cord, plugged into a unit less than a meter from the charging port.

"Really?" Tabitha asked, her eyes narrowing with suspicion. "How do we know you're not Blick using another shapeshifting trick?"

"Or Scritch?" Tobias added.

Milo grinned confidently. "I don't know any Blick or what a Scritch is."

"We thought he was you," Tobias said.

"We don't know he's not," Tabitha argued.

"Yeah," he said. "True." Tabitha and Tobias exchanged skeptical glances.

"Alright, Milo," Tobias said slowly. "If Hanna really sent you, what did she tell you about us?"

"Enough to know you're in a tight spot and need some help," Milo replied smoothly. "From out of town. Off-griders. Don't know squat about anything. Also said one of you is cute. She was right."

"Watch it," Tobias said, bringing his knife back up to action level.

"Wasn't talking about you, big fella," Milo said. Catching up to his words, Tabitha blushed. She chewed her lip, not sure what to do.

Milo said with a tone of admission, "I'm surprised to see you coming out of a Mothra Temple. I figured a friend of Hanna's wouldn't go in for that kind of thing."

"Oh, no!" Tabitha said. "We were trying to escape. It was so gross. We—we—well, we could hardly think."

"Right," Milo said. "Everyone knows they put sodium thiopental in their fog machines. Makes you do whatever the big guy says.

Otherwise, everyone would be too grossed out by a giant blue alien with no underwear on."

"We kind of figured something like that," Tabitha said. They stood there awkwardly for a long few seconds before she turned to her brother. "So," Tabitha whispered, "what do we do?"

"Don't know."

She turned back to him. "Can you prove you're not Blick?" Tabitha said, her gaze fixed on Milo.

"Look, I don't know what you want me to say," he replied, his voice tinged with calm.

"Can you change your look?" Tobias asked.

"I mean... I could cut my hair, but..."

"No," Tobias cut in. "Can you click a button to change your face?"

"Oh," Milo said. "First rule of the Digiverse, assume nothing's real." Milo raised his hands, gesturing surrender. "Alright, look." He pulled a black phone from his pocket and gestured to the screen. "I'll call Hanna right now. You can ask her yourself."

Tabitha and Tobias exchanged glances of skepticism.

"Fine," Tabitha said, her hair whipping around her face as she nodded curtly. "But if this is just another one of your tricks, we're gone."

"Roger," Milo replied, pressing a few buttons on the phone. The device chirped to life, signaling a call was in progress.

"Hey, Milo. Did you find them?" Hanna's voice came through the speaker, slightly distorted but warm and eager. Tabitha bristled at Hanna's voice but wasn't sure why.

"Hi, Hanna," Tabitha said, trying to keep her voice steady. "We have a guy here who claims you sent him to help us."

"I'm so relieved," Hanna said. "I've been up all night worrying. I nearly got an air taxi and came to town, but Milo talked me down. He said he'd find you."

"Okay," Tabitha said. "But how do we know this is really you and not some trick?"

"What do you mean?" Hanna asked.

"Could your voice be faked?" Tabitha asked. "Could a scammer make a copy of your voice or your face or your whole body and make us think we're talking to you right now even though we're not?"

A long pause followed, where only the sound of Hanna's breathing could be heard. She admitted, "Technically, yes. But guys, it's me, I promise."

"But how can we know for sure?" Tobias said. "How can we know it's you? How can we know this guy isn't just another scammer claiming to be Milo again?"

"Another scammer?" Hanna asked. "You guys met a scammer?"

"Met is an understatement," Tobias said. "They near murderlized us."

"It was so awful," Tabitha burst. Scam or not, she couldn't help herself. "There were gross naughty bots and a blue demon god, and the terrible guy who put things in our eyes and ears that make it where we can't stop seeing and hearing all this horrible stuff, and this other guy took pictures of us and then tried to kill us."

"So, we're not feeling very trusting right now," Tobias said.

Another long pause. This time, the breathing turned into the soft patter of sobs. Through her tears, Hanna said, "I'm sorry, guys; I should have never sent you to the city alone. This is all my fault. If I hadn't…" She trailed off and cried. When she had calmed, Tabitha spoke softly.

"Hannah, we ain't mad at you. We're just trying to figure out what's real." Tabitha paused and put her finger to her chin. "How about you tell us something only we would know. Something from Isolation, from before you became a leaver. You could prove it that way."

"I wish I could," Hanna said. "But I took the leaver's oath."

"Oh yeah," Tobias said. "Forgot about that. Well, I guess we're just a couple of jackrabbits caught in a trap. Maybe if Soren Krieger was here, he could help us figure a way out, but…" Tabitha rolled her eyes.

"Listen," Hanna said, her tone somber and serious. "I wish I could give you a foolproof answer, but I can't. And maybe that's the best proof I can give you. A scammer wouldn't tell you the truth. A scammer would try to give you false assurances, but I'm not. It's a confusing, rotten, mixed-up place. You can't know for sure. There's an element of faith in this kind of situation."

Tabitha glanced at Tobias, who stood with his arms crossed, his eyes flickering between Milo and the phone.

"Alright," Tabitha said, her voice filled with determination. "We'll talk to you later, Hanna."

"Good luck," Hanna replied before the call disconnected. The air around them seemed to shift as Tabitha and Tobias looked back at Milo, their expressions effusive with their lingering suspicion.

"I don't know what to do," Tabitha said softly, her eyes locked on Milo.

Tobias nodded. "Only thing we can do."

"Yeah," Tabitha agreed.

"What?" Milo asked as he put his phone away.

"We need guidance before we decide what to do." Tobias looked at his sister, who met his gaze with understanding.

"We need to pray about it," Tabitha interpreted.

Milo raised his eyebrows. He took a step back, giving them space as they bowed their heads and closed their eyes, their hands clasped together. In the noise and nighttime commotion of the street, they were quiet for a second. Strangers issued past, and the distant sound of a scream pierced the night air. A siren erupted. Tabitha looked up.

"I can't concentrate," she said. "I mean, that guy down there is peeing right on the street." She pointed to a disheveled pedestrian.

"How am I supposed to talk to the Lord while he's letting loose?" Milo looked at the man, shrugged, and laughed.

"How about in the truck," Tobias said. He glanced at Milo. "If you'll excuse us for a moment."

"Okay," Milo replied with a questioning tone. "But before you do, can you give me a ride?"

Tabitha and Tobias exchanged glances, clearly hesitating. "I can ride in the truck bed if that makes you feel better," he added with a reassuring smile.

Tobias replied, "We ain't doing nothing until we've prayed."

"Of course," Milo agreed. He took a step back from the vehicle, allowing them some space. "Take your time. But not too much time. My parents would not approve of this place. With its public urination and all."

Tabitha and Tobias climbed into the truck's cab, closing the doors behind them. As they sat there, hands clasped together, they prayed for guidance and clarity in this uncertain situation.

Outside, Milo leaned against the side of the truck, waiting. Tabitha still found it difficult to focus, as her eyes kept opening and wandering toward Milo, tall and strong, so confident and street smart, an easy and alluring air about him. He stood like a guard, comfortable even in this hostile environment.

After a few minutes of prayer, they both said, "Amen."

"So, what do we think?" Tabitha asked.

"Well," Tobias said. "I don't think the Lord would frown on us doing a good deed. And that fella, whoever he is, asked for a ride. I say we do the good deed in faith and see where it takes us."

"I agree," Tabitha said, trying to keep the giddy excitement from her voice.

After relaying the news to Milo, he unplugged the charging cable and climbed into the back, as promised. The self-driving truck hummed quietly as it navigated, weaving between the few autonomous vehicles that maneuvered through the city's veins after dark. Tabitha leaned her head out the open window, feeling the warm evening breeze tousle her hair. She glanced back at Milo sitting in the truck bed, his dark eyes fixed on the glowing displays that floated past. She wished she had ridden in the back, too.

As the truck left the city's color-lit chaos behind, the landscape transformed into tidy rows of suburban houses, each one a cookie-cutter replica of its neighbor. Although they were not completely free of the irritating holographic advertisements that were more common downtown, the residential area was not without its own charm. Turning down a neighborhood street, the truck slowed to a stop in front of a nondescript one-story home with a manicured lawn. It was quaint, even idyllic, in its own way.

Milo hopped out of the back, sauntering to Tabitha's window with a charming grin. "Well, this is me. You two are welcome to come in and do some more—uh—praying or whatever."

"No, thanks," Tobias said, leaning over. His words were a little too loud, forced, and bordering on aggressive. "We got to find a place to stay for the night and—"

"You could stay here," Milo interrupted.

"Sure, thanks," Tabitha said, not breaking eye contact with the black-haired boy. Her smile was so wide and awkward that even Milo looked away.

Tobias balled his hands into fists. "I don't think so, Tabby. We need a focus on the *Overseer's Handbook*." She could feel a lecture coming, but her hero interrupted.

"You need a book?" Milo said. "I could help."

"Yeah, we done heard that before," Tobias said.

"Well, at least come in for something to eat before you go," he said. "Mom's an okay cook, and I'm sure she's got something hot and ready."

"You live with your mom?" Tabitha asked. She turned to Tobias as she entangled her fingers in a praying position. "He lives with his mom. Can we? Can we?"

"Uh—not just my mom," Milo said. "Sounds super sus when you say it like that. The whole family lives here, too."

"We need to eat," Tabitha said. She knew even Tobias couldn't resist a meal, considering the last time they ate was at Hanna's, more than twenty-four hours earlier.

"Betsy, park," Tobias said. Tabitha clapped as Tobias rolled his eyes and the windows up. Tabitha bit her lip and smoothed her hair in anticipation of spending more time with the enigmatic Milo. "You got to get a grip, Sis. He's an outsider. Be careful."

Dinner

The twins followed Milo into his home. The scene that met them was as different from what they'd seen as lions are from kittens. Milo's parents and two younger brothers were gathered in the cozy space. Each used a handheld device, but they put them down as Tabitha, Tobias, and Milo entered the room. The family rose to greet them as they came in.

"Introduce us to your friends, Honey," Milo's mother said.

Milo smiled and gestured. "Mom, Dad, this is Tabitha and Tobias. They're from out of town and need some help with something."

"Hey, you guys," his father said warmly. "Welcome to the Wynters' household. It's a zany place." He extended a hand to shake Tobias'. They introduced themselves. Milo's Dad was Brent, and his Mom was Linda. Two little brothers, Sam and Tuck, joined the meetup a moment later.

"You guys want to stay for dinner?" His mother, Linda, said.

"We won't argue with that," Tobias laughed.

They followed Milo. Tabitha and Tobias sat down at the dinner table with the family, marveling at the spread of delicious food. Steam rose from a large casserole dish in the center, surrounded by bowls of colorful vegetables they had never tasted and a basket of freshly baked rolls.

"Milo, would you like to say grace?" Linda asked.

"Actually," Milo said. "I think Tabitha and Tobias are better at it. Tobias, you want to pray for us?" Tobias stared at Milo for a few seconds before agreeing. He prayed in King James, but they didn't seem to mind. After he said Amen, Milo explained, "We just started praying before meals. It's kind of new for us."

"Ain't nothing to it," Tobias said. "When you're talking to the best listener in the universe." The family laughed.

They dug in. Tabitha savored each bite of the casserole, a delightful medley of flavors she had never experienced before. The tender meat and soft, buttery vegetables melted in her mouth, seasoned with aromatic herbs and spices. She glanced over at Tobias, who seemed equally enamored with the meal, his eyes wide with appreciation as he sampled a vibrant orange vegetable.

"Where we're from," Tabitha said, "We don't have these orange things. What do you call them?"

"You don't have carrots?" Tuck asked with the tone of a juvenile inquisition.

"Where are you from?" Linda asked.

"About a hour to the south," Tobias said.

"You live in the Radio Quiet Zone?" Brent asked. They nodded but didn't offer any more information. "Are your parents astronomers?" Tabitha felt like she had been punched in the stomach. She looked down and shook her head at the odd mention of her parents, unable to comprehend what this stranger was asking.

"Dad ran the newspaper and had a general store where we're from. But his shop burned down when we were young." Tabitha looked at her plate

"Ma and Pa died in the fire," Tobias said. A fork fell to the table.

"Along with our founder, Soren Krieger," Tabitha said.

"What's a founder?" Tuck asked. The grown-ups were so stunned by what the twins had said they didn't respond to Tuck's question.

"Oh, I'm so sorry," Brent said. The silence that followed could have filled the earth for a million years. Brent tried to explain. "I just thought the only people out there worked at the radio observatory at Los Aridos." They looked at their plates without saying anything else. Brent went on. "Sorry. I really put my foot in my mouth. It's just that I didn't know anyone lived in the radio quiet zone other than researchers, but..." He trailed off.

"Yeah, we get that a lot," Tobias said. "We don't get out much. Most folk, where we're from don't think no one should get out. And them that do, don't get back in."

"What's a radio quiet zone?" Tuck asked, this time with enough force to punch through the awkwardness. They all looked at him with his eyes just above the table's surface.

"I ain't got a clue," Tobias said. "It's just something I hear people say 'bout where we're from."

"Me neither," Tabitha agreed.

"It's a place about an hour south that stretches for three hundred square miles," Milo said, speaking in a kid-friendly voice. "At the center is a big radio telescope. They have a law that makes it illegal to have any device that puts out radio signals because their telescope is very sensitive."

"Oh, that's probably why our founders established the town there," Tabitha said. "To get away from all—well, all this."

"And we can't live without radio signals?" Tuck asked.

"You can," Brent jumped in. "Most people don't live down there because it's a desert. It's super hot. When they built the radio telescope, they had to pick a place where no one would want to live. All our devices use radio signals. With people come radio signals."

"Not Isolation, people," Tobias said.

"Like we said," Tabitha snickered. "We don't get out much."

"Well, I'm glad you two got out," Brent said.

"I'm glad you know what a carrot is now," Sam said, his chin resting on the table, eyes locked on Tabitha. They all laughed.

"Me too," Tabitha agreed. "You know, most the great missionaries' families didn't think they should get out and go across the world. Hudson Taylor, Adoniram Judson, David Livingstone, Mary Slessor, even William Carrey, the father of modern missions. They all had people telling them they should stay home, focus on the local needs, or other things like that. Imagine if they hadn't gotten out."

"She got a thing about missionaries," Tobias said.

Tabitha put her fork down and smoothed her napkin as a question she'd been too harried to ask rose to the surface. "Where we're from, the library only goes up to 1989. There aren't any books that were published after that. What have missionaries been doing in the decades since then?"

The rest around the table sat quietly for a few seconds until Brent asked, "What's a missionary?" There was a long silence. "Is that a military thing?"

"You haven't heard of missionaries?" Tabitha said.

"Oh, you done it now," Tobias joked. The levity was enveloped by Tabitha's glowing enthusiasm. She took a deep breath and was three minutes in before she realized she was giving a speech. At the five-minute mark, she asked if the family had a globe. Tuck ran off and retrieved a toy, which was the closest they had. She talked for another five minutes, recapping the modern age of missions, covering everyone from John Elliot of the 1600s to Jim Eliot of the 1950s. When she had concluded, they all sat stunned. Even Tobias leaned back in his chair with a smile.

"You know who would make a good missionary," Milo said, looking directly at Tabitha. "You!"

"Well, I—uh—it's," Tabitha stammered. Why was her face hot? Why were her words jumbled up? Why did that suggestion fill her with such deep, dark sadness that she wanted to cry and such overpowering joy she could dance around the room?

"Our town elders don't allow that kind of thing," Tobias said.

The group sat silent for another few seconds before Linda said, "Who wants dessert?"

"There's more?" Tobias erupted with such enthusiasm that the entire table laughed, even Tabitha, but her mind wasn't on the humor. She felt the weight of Milo's comment sitting heavy on her back. As ice cream was dished for each, Tobias just about melted into his seat with the novelty. As he scooped his third bowlful, he asked, "So, how did you guys meet?" He pointed his spoon at Linda and Brent.

"We met in the digiverse," Linda said with a smile. Tobias choked, and Tabitha's mouth flapped open.

"We been taught digitals are evil," Tobias said.

"What do you mean?" Linda asked.

"He just means we didn't know you could meet someone and fall in love on the digiverse," Tabitha said.

"Oh, sure," Linda said. "Happens all the time. Honey, you want to tell them how the magic began?"

"Sure," Brent said. "We were at a virtual GeekCon. Her avatar was a cartoon version of the ship's captain from *Pirate Spawn 3*." Brent did his best pirate accent. "I be Captain Milo. ARRRR." The kids laughed. "It was my favorite movie at the time. I'm pretty shy, but I just had to talk to her."

"The secret's out," Milo said. "I was named after a pirate captain in a sequel to an unknown B movie." Tabitha and Tobias didn't know what some of those words meant, but they caught that it was a joke and laughed along. Linda picked up the story.

"My friend had convinced me to do the GeekCon. It wasn't really my thing. But I had picked that avatar from an online store because I thought it was cute. I didn't even know what it was, but Brent did. He was so excited to find someone else who knew about *Pirate Spawn 3*. I played along, just to be polite at first, but then when he started in on the puns, I thought he was charming. Mostly because I could tell, he was trying so hard. But the confidence was amazing. Since his jokes weren't funny at all." The kids laughed.

"Oh, come on," Brent said. "My puns are legendary. How does a penguin build its house?"

"How?" Sam and Tuck said together.

"Igloos it together." The kids laughed. He looked at Milo. "Get it? Igloo!" Milo and Linda gave a comedic moan.

"Why did the math book look sad," Tuck erupted, mimicking his father's tone. "Because it had too many problems." They laughed at the enjoyment Tuck got from being like his dad.

"Let me try one," Tobias said. "How do you catch a jackrabbit?"

"How?" Tuck and Sam said with wild anticipation.

"With a Paiute deadfall trap." The table was quiet. "The rock falls on the rabbit and kills it." They were still quiet. "The rabbit usually dies within an hour from the blunt force trauma or suffocation."

Tabitha patted Tobias on the shoulder and said, "That one wasn't very punny, Bubba." The table laughed.

"It'd just been a while since I got to talk about a trap, so..." Another round of light laughter transitioned them into small talk.

As the meal drew to a close, Brent leaned back in his chair and smiled at Tabitha and Tobias. "Thanks for joining us, you two. It was fun having company."

After dinner, they surprised Milo and his parents by insisting they wash their dishes by hand, not understanding the meaning of *dishwasher*. They had only ever heard the term as referring to a person. After the experience, Milo led them through the house toward his converted garage.

Worlds

As they entered Milo's room, the converted garage, their eyes had to adjust to the low blue light. They spotted the centerpiece at once. A massive gaming rig dominated the space, although they had no idea what it was. Screens, consoles, and high-tech gadgets filled every corner. Tabitha's jaw dropped in awe. On the floor was a raised surface with an intricate pattern of little spheres.

"What is all this?" Tobias asked.

Milo grinned, pride evident in his voice. "This is my game setup. It's sick, right?"

"You play games?" Tabitha asked.

"Sure," Milo said. He talked about his full-body haptic rig, motion capture immersion unit, and multi-directional tread floor. The tech jargon continued for a few minutes, but he apparently sensed they were not understanding. After trailing off, he said, "Want to try it?"

"I don't think so," Tobias said. "We ain't supposed to—"

"Is it dangerous?" Tabitha said, interrupting her brother.

"No," he said. "Not unless you're allergic to fun." He pointed meaningfully to the rig.

Tabitha scrunched her face. She stepped closer to a screen, her fingers itching to explore. "How does it work?"

"Come on, I'll show you."

"No," Tobias said. "I don't want to get kicked out of Isolation. There ain't no way I'm touching that stuff."

"I'll try it," Tabitha agreed.

"Great," Milo said, stepping over to an equipment stack. He grabbed a headset and lifted it over Tabitha's head. He was about to put it over her face, but he paused as he looked into her eyes. "Oh, you're wearing AR contacts. It'd be best to take those off before entering the VR headset. You'll get ghosting on the image if you're double-rigged."

Tabitha raised an eyebrow. "Blick said we couldn't take off the contacts."

"Plus, we don't know how, even if we wanted to," Tobias said. "And he said they have grabbers on them."

"Grapplings," Milo corrected. "It's slang for bio-surface-adhesion. I can get them off if you want."

"Yes!" They both virtually shouted. Milo laughed as he set the headset back down on the desk.

"Let me wash my hands, and we'll get those things out of there." He disappeared into the house and then returned with a small item in his hand. "Fridge magnet," he said, holding it up. "Grapplings are no big deal; they're just little magnetic-activated micro-suction cups that cling to your eye, but a magnet realigns them to the release position." He waved the magnet close to their eyes. Tabitha could smell his sweet scent and feel his warm breath on her face.

"Now, this may feel a little uncomfortable," he said as he used one hand to hold her eyelid open and the other to squeeze the contact to remove it.

"Can you take out the earworms, too?" she asked. He looked confused for a brief second.

"Earbuds?" he asked.

"Yeah," she said. He opened a drawer at his desk and riffled through it briefly. He came toward her with a pair of tweezers. He had the unwanted earpiece out of her ear in a few seconds. Once he had done the other, he moved to Tobias.

"I'll do it myself," Tobias said. He tried but couldn't, so he had to let Milo. "Thanks."

"I know," Milo said. "It feels good to disconnect every once in a while. My dad has a rule: No screen time, AR, or VR on weeknights. We do family time Monday through Thursday nights. Screen time is only on the weekends. And we aren't aloud on social media until we turn sixteen." The twins shared a quick glance. "It's catching on. Lots of families are doing it now. It's made a huge difference. We used to fight all the time, but it's like magic. Scheduled screen time and a few game nights a week, and we're like a completely different family. We were mad at Dad at first, but now, we wouldn't trade it for anything."

"You're part-time Isolationists," Tabitha said.

Milo laughed and agreed. "Makes gaming more fun when the weekend comes." He put a finger to his chin. "Speaking of which. Are you ready?"

Tabitha nodded as Milo's hands guided her into the full-immersion rig and strapped the haptic pads against her skin. "I'll join you inside in just a second," Milo said. The moving floor actuators lurched beneath her feet. She laughed and was swept away into another world.

Tabitha gasped as she suddenly stood in an ethereal void, stars twinkling faintly in the distance. She glanced over at Milo and laughed aloud at his changed visage. His normal appearance was replaced by a sculpted physique accentuated by his sleek spacesuit.

"Milo?" she blurted out. "You look different!"

He smirked. "Awesome, isn't it? In here, I can look however I want."

She glanced down at her body, still clad in her jeans and t-shirt. Her shoulders slumped. "I still look the same."

"Well, there's no need to hide *your* looks behind an avatar," he said. She thought it might be a compliment but wondered if it was just another aspect of this world she didn't yet understand. "This is just the loading bay. The real fun is about to begin. Check this out."

With a few taps on his wrist console, the stars dissolved into inky blackness. Tabitha's breath caught as a magnificent sunrise exploded across the horizon, bathing them in golden light. They were no longer standing on solid ground but floating in space above the curvature of the Earth.

"Wow," she breathed. Experimentally, she reached out a hand, half expecting it to pass through the intricately rendered illusion. Instead, she felt the gentle pelt of space dust against her skin. "Wow!"

"Haptics," Milo said as he drifted up beside her, his eyes alight with excitement. "Just wait. It gets better."

Out of the sun's shadow, a swarm of meteors hurtled toward them, each gleaming like a polished gemstone. Tabitha shielded her face, but the meteors pinged off her body like harmless hailstones. She lowered her hands, a giddy laugh bubbling up in her throat. Then her eyes widened as a monstrous chunk of space rock blotted out the sun, hurtling directly toward Earth.

"Milo!" She cried out.

But he was already in motion, firing his thrusters and speeding towards the meteor. "I'll hit it on the left; you take the right!" When she didn't move, he added, "Use your thumb trigger to go."

Tabitha hesitated only a split second before her determination solidified. She ignited her rockets and shot forward. Together, she and Milo slammed into opposite sides of the meteor, groaning under the haptic suit's resistance as they slowly forced the behemoth off its deadly trajectory.

The meteor careened away into space, and Tabitha whooped, her heart hammering against her ribs. Milo swooped in beside her and smiled.

"Want to see another one?" Milo asked.

"Sure!"

Milo swiped his hand, and a dizzying swirl of colors engulfed Tabitha, and the star-spangled cosmos vanished. Towering trees materialized around her, their canopies knitting together to form a dense green roof overhead.

"Where are we now?" Tabitha asked, her voice hushed with wonder. The cry of a distant bird made her twirl in place.

Milo was now dressed in khaki shorts and shirt, hiking boots, and a bushmen's hat. He flashed her a mischievous smile. "Welcome to the jungle."

A thunderous trumpeting shattered the stillness, followed by the splintering of wood. Tabitha flipped around to see a massive elephant burst through the underbrush, its tusks gleaming like white swords. The ground quaked beneath its charging feet.

"Run!" Milo yelled, his hand latching onto hers.

They sprinted through the jungle, vaulting over gnarled roots and ducking beneath low-hanging vines. The elephant's enraged screams pursued them, mingling with the frenzied pounding of

Tabitha's heart. Just as she thought her lungs would burst, the world shimmered and dissolved again.

"How about another one," Milo said. She nodded.

Tabitha found herself astride a snorting warhorse. A bow was in one hand, and a quiver of arrows slung across her back. Beside her, Milo sat tall in the saddle, a gleaming sword aloft. He was shirtless, war paint marked in bright colors across his chest and face. She looked down at her body, afraid of what she'd find, but no, still just the jeans and T-shirt.

"For glory!" he cried, spurring his horse forward.

Tabitha urged her own steed after him, her eyes widening as she took in the scene before her. A horde of monstrous ogres swarmed at the base of a hill. Their misshapen faces contorted with rage. Milo charged into their midst, his blade flashing as he hewed through the grotesque creatures.

Tabitha nocked an arrow and let it fly, marveling at her skill as it found its mark in an ogre's chest. It tumbled to the ground with a screech. She lost herself in the battle's rhythm, her bowstring twang and hoofbeats' thud blending into a savage symphony.

"Behind you!" Milo's warning shout cut through the clamor.

Tabitha twisted in her saddle to see an ogre lunging for her, its meaty fists outstretched. Panic seized her, and she fumbled for an arrow. Terror choked its way up her throat. This was madness and yet, somehow, fantastic.

The world froze, the ogre suspended mid-roar, and Milo grinned at Tabitha from atop his motionless steed. "You get it," he said, his voice echoing in the sudden stillness.

Tabitha looked around in amazement, her heart still pounding from the battle's adrenaline rush. "This is incredible!" she breathed.

Milo's grin turned sly. "Want to see one of the worlds I've been working on?"

Tabitha's eyes went large. "You build these yourself?"

"Yep," Milo said. "Hold on."

He swiped his hand through the air, and the scene dissolved into pixelated stardust. Then, the world reassembled itself around her.

She gasped. They stood on the deck of a sailing ship, its polished boards gleaming beneath their feet. But instead of the ocean, an endless expanse of clouds stretched in every direction. The vessel was suspended in the sky by an enormous canvas balloon. It drifted along, skirting the bank of the misty white as sunset painted the horizon orange and pink.

"Welcome aboard the Celestial Maiden," Milo said, sweeping his arm in a grand gesture.

"Thank you, Captain Milo," she said. Tabitha gripped the railing, marveling at the wisps of mist that curled around the hull. "How is this even possible?"

"In here, anything is." Milo leaned against the railing beside her, his eyes sparkling with pride. "I've been working on this one for a while. It's a hangout for me and my friends."

"It's fantastic," Tabitha said softly, running her fingers over the smooth wood. She tried to imagine Milo and his faceless friends gathered on this impossible ship, adrift in a sea of cumulonimbus.

"You're really talented, you know?"

He ducked his head, a rare show of sheepishness. "It's a work in progress. But I'm glad you like it."

Tabitha looked out over the railing again, watching the clouds drift by beneath the ship's keel. For a moment, she let herself imagine that this was real, that she and Milo were explorers charting some new frontier beyond the horizon's curve. Her imagination wandered to more distant possibilities where she and Milo were more than explorers, more than friends. A dark cloud drifted into her thoughts. The chasm between his world and hers was too large, larger than the virtual sky they soared atop.

Fly

Tabitha's thoughts were interrupted by the sound of approaching footsteps. She turned to see two figures emerging from the ship's cabin. One was a man with comically huge shoulders, holding a war hammer as big as a pickup truck, chain mail, and a steel helmet. The other was a girl wearing spandex over curves accented by bright stripes running the length of her body in yellow and black.

"Hey, guys!" Milo called out, waving them over. "I want you to meet someone."

As they drew closer, Tabitha saw that their avatars were just as impressive as the ship itself. The male had a shock of fiery red hair and a face that looked like it had been chiseled from white marble. The girl was slender and graceful, with long, dark hair that flowed behind her like a banner in the wind.

"Tabitha, this is Phoenix and Shadow," Milo said, gesturing to each of them. "Guys, this is Tabitha. She's a friend."

"Are you—uh..."

"We're not NPCs," they said. Tabitha looked in Milo's direction. He translated.

"They're not Ai. They're real."

"Nice to meet you," Phoenix said, his voice deep and resonant. He looked at Tabitha curiously. "You're brave, coming in without an avatar."

Tabitha blinked, confused. "What do you mean?"

Shadow smiled, her dark eyes glinting with a spark of intrigue. "You... you came in as yourself. It's brave."

Tabitha glanced down at her body. She tugged at the sleeve of her shirt. The thought of pretending to be someone else, even in a virtual world, she hadn't yet wrestled that concept into its ethical place.

"I guess I don't see the point," she said, shrugging. "If I'm being honest. No offense."

Phoenix and Shadow exchanged a glance, then shrugged.

"That's admirable," Phoenix said, his tone serious. "We've known MiloMeter for four years and have no idea where he lives or what he looks like."

"That's my Avatar name," Milo said. "MiloMeter."

"His name is Milo. He lives in—" Tabitha started, but Milo cut her off.

"Hey, now. Hold up."

"Milo!" Shadow celebrated. "Of course!"

"Ohh!" Phoenix echoed the win, then laughed at the irony. "Milo. MiloMeter. I get it." They continued to razz Milo.

Tabitha's lips curved downward with curiosity. "But how can you be friends if you don't even know his name or what he looks like?"

Shadow laughed. The sound was like shimmering bells. "Friendship isn't about appearances. It's about the connection you share and the things you have in common. The words you exchange, the experiences, even digital ones."

"This place proves that appearance doesn't matter at all," Phoenix said. "My best friend online is a seven-foot toad with bionic legs. Who cares. She says funny things and has talked me through some hard times."

"Just last week, a friend of ours was going through a tough time, contemplating... well, you know." Milo's expression grew somber.

"I *don't* know," Tabitha said.

"He was thinking about suicide," Shadow offered.

"Oh no."

"We all hopped on for a game of Zat Raiders and talked it out while we blasted space bugs," Phoenix said.

"MiloMeter even had us pray," Shadow said. "But it was weird."

"Try being me," Milo said. "Trying to get a moment of silence with you two motor mouths present." They all laughed. It wasn't the hallow laugh of politeness but the full soundtrack to a deep, rich connection that challenged everything Tabitha knew about the digital realm.

"You pray on the digiverse?" Tabitha asked. Milo nodded.

"Good times," Phoneix said. "And I got the high score on Zat Raiders, again," he added as he swung his battle hammer.

"Bro, please!" Phoenix argued. "You didn't even make the scoreboard." Their words escalated quickly, but their tone did not carry the heat of anger, instead that of child-like play. In a surprise explosion of muscular power, Phoenix threw his massive battle axe as he laughed. Shadow danced aside, letting the axe fly wide. She then did a perfect pirouette that blossomed into a leap, bounding off the main mast. She flew through the air, planted a ballistic foot in the middle of Phoenix's face, and kicked him to the deck. She landed with unimaginable grace as they both laughed. He floundered as he tried to come to his feet once more, all the while laughing. The exchange, which would spell serious injury in the real world, escalated to epic proportions as Phoenix belted a war cry.

"Another great thing about the digiverse," Milo said. "You can mute 'em when they're being idiots." Suddenly, everything but the breeze went quiet. Phoenix and Shadow continued to battle, albeit silently, behind them on the deck.

In the relative still, a strange sound echoed through the ship. Her eyes darted around, trying to find some understanding.

"What was that?" she asked.

Milo's brow furrowed, lips parting in silent questioning. "I'm not sure. It came from outside the game."

She reached up and pulled off her headset, blinking against the sudden dim of the room.

With her gaming headset off, her eyes took a moment to adjust to the low light. Tobias was sprawled on the couch beside the immersion rig, fast asleep, his mouth hanging open. The sound of his sleeping was a comfort somehow. She snickered as the snoring sawmill drew across another log of sleep-wood but then abruptly stopped. She heard Milo say goodbye to his friends, and the game went silent. A moment later, he pulled off his own headset.

"So, all this stuff is just for playing games?" Tabitha said, setting the headset on the tabletop.

"No, not at all," Milo said. "I mean, it's for anything."

"Like what?" Tabitha asked.

"Well, entertainment, research, reading, communication," Milo said. "Anything people normally do face to face, pretty much all of it can be done online, in the digiverse." Tabitha looked confused. "Ok, let me think of an example." He tapped his chin. "You asked a question at dinner. Something about missionaries..."

A spark shot across Tabitha's face. "Yeah!" She stepped forward as if she'd won an award. "Our library in Isolation ain't got books newer than 1989. I want to know what missionaries been doing since then."

"Easy," Milo said. "What format do you want it in?"

"I—uh—I don't understand."

"Books, videos, movies, podcasts. how do you want to learn?" Milo said.

"I love books," she said, putting her hands across her chest as if the warmth of her heart had just intensified. Milo turned and tapped a few keys on a keyboard.

On the screen, a list of books materialized with thumbnails of the covers. Rows and rows filled the entirety of the display. "Are those all books?" She leaned forward. Milo nodded. "But how do you read them? Do you have to read them on a screen?"

"You can if you want," Milo said. He clicked an image. "Here's one called *Christian Missions In The Modern World.*"

"Oh yeah, yeah, yeah! Do that one," Tabitha said. Milo clicked it, and the text popped up. She virtually shoved him out of the way to start reading. As her eyes scanned the text, she made noises of revelation and amazement. "Wow!" She was absorbed.

"If you'd rather a print copy," Milo said.

"Yes!" she sang. Milo took control of the computer again, hitting a few buttons, then shoved back from the desk. "Count to one hundred."

"What?" She asked. "Why?"

"You'll see," he said. "I'll Be right back." She started counting as he stepped out of the garage and into the house. When she got to seventy-four, a strange buzzing sound swelled outside the garage. She moved to the garage window and pushed back the curtains.

By the time she was at eighty-nine, a delivery drone outside, which looked like a giant insect to Tabitha's eyes, lowered a package on a cable. Milo grabbed the package as the delivery bot zoomed away. Her eyes were as wide as the moon as Milo returned to the garage. She was no longer counting.

"What?" she gasped. "That's the—you got the book?" Milo handed it to her gently.

"My gift to you," he said, letting his hand touch hers. She let her fingers remain on his for an extra second before she pulled the book to her chest and hugged it as if it were a long-lost puppy.

"You can get any book this way?" she asked.

"Yep."

"Even the Bible?"

"Sure," he said.

"Just in Dolos?" Tabitha asked. "Or any city?"

"Pretty much anywhere in the world where a drone can fly," Milo said. "There's like a million books published every year, and they're all available. There's ten times as much in other formats." He put his fingers through his hair. "Don't get me wrong. Some of it is total garbage, and some is downright evil, but if you know where to look, there's loads of great stuff out there."

"Ya'll done with your witchcraft?" Tobias mumbled, rubbing his eyes as he sat up. He yawned and scratched his head. Tabitha laid her new book on her lap as she sat next to her brother, somehow feeling as if it held ten times the value of the one that had been stolen. Tobias picked up the book, examined it briefly, and laid it back down on her legs. "Missionary stuff. Figures."

"Toby, you've got to see this; it's unreal," Tabitha said. "You can get any book you want."

"The *Overseer's Handbook's* what I want," Tobias said.

"No, I mean any book that's been published," she clarified.

"But I don't want no book."

"Like a book on traps and snares," she tried, but she could feel his negativity burning dark and voracious. "Or a book about—"

"You done forgot Soren Krieger's Fifth Indictum?" he quoted the Isolation Doctrine. "Cast them far from thee! Let no such digital abomination be found—"

"I know, but," Tabitha said. "I don't think Soren Krieger knew everything. Ain't it possible he didn't know how this kind of stuff could be used for good?" She paused, looking at the ceiling.

"He knew a load of a lot more than you," Tobias said.

"You're right," she said. A look of realization came across her face. "He did! So, maybe he knew and didn't..."

"Didn't, what?" Tobias said, leaning forward.

"Maybe he knew—knew that digitals could be used for good and didn't tell us."

"That's dumb," Tobias exploded. "Why would he do something like that? That's—that's—well, it just ain't possible." They sat and stared at each other for a long moment. "It's got to be some kind of mistake."

"In Soren Krieger's Isolation Doctrine, he talked about all the bad things, but I think there might just be more to it," Tabitha said. She turned to Milo to explain. "We were always taught that digitals are bad," Tabitha said.

"You use the word *digital* in a weird way?" Milo said. "*Digital* isn't a thing. Digital is a way to describe things that use coded language to operate."

"I—uh—I don't understand," she said. "In Isolation, they taught us all digitals are bad, but I don't guess they knew any better either. It just makes me think that with so small a knowledge, how can Isolationists really know if digitals are good or bad?"

"It don't matter how we use the word. We know digitals are bad because Soren Krieger told us so," Tobias blurted. "And they ain't gonna let us back in town for all the digitals we done out here."

"You're so worried about being banished," Tabitha said. "It keeps you in submission to ideas that don't work." Tobias huffed. He had no come back for that one.

"Well, I don't know anything about this Soren guy," Milo said. "But he's right that there's a lot of dark stuff out there, but there's light too. The darkness can't shroud the light. You guys are a good example. Right in the darkest part of town, you were praying in your truck. I'm kind of blinded by the light pouring off of you." He looked over at Tobias, who was staring at the floor with a brooding, ponderous look on his face. "You too, big fella."

Tabitha blushed. Tobias cut in. "You said your family just started praying. Why?"

"Hanna taught me how. Taught me a lot of stuff, actually. I met her online." Tabitha didn't know what that meant, but she gathered it had something to do with the digiverse. "She's making a difference, man. She told me about the Lord, and now I'm sharing with my family. Phoenix and Shadow are starting to get it, I think."

"Hanna, told you about Jesus?" Tobias was surprised.

"Sure thing, bro," Milo said. "It's why they slapped her in irons." Tabitha tilted her head, lips pursed in contemplation. "Her ankle bracelet. She got probation for proselytizing downtown. She was preaching. Spent a week in jail, then they banished her, so she went to Edgetown. They track her movements. If she comes back to town, they'll put her in jail. So, she took her ministry online. She's reaching more people now, than she ever could have from evangelizing on the street. She's really making a difference."

"But she's a leaver," Tobias said.

"She could be a pine tree, for all I care. She's changed my life. And I'm not the only one."

"She's not a leaver," Tabitha said. Lights clicked on in her head. Fireworks exploded in her mind. "She's a missionary!" A warmth washed over Tabitha in such waves that she thought she might need to sit down. "She's a digital missionary." In her mind, she added, *If Hanna could do it... The possibilities!* She would have stayed with the thought, but Milo's words cut into her blossoming mindscape.

"So, you guys said something about needing a book. Is that what brought you two to town?" Milo asked, stepping out from behind his gaming rig and pulling up a computer chair. The conversation shifted. She told him the entire tale, now having nothing but trust for the young man. Even Tobias loosened at the retelling. He spoke of their elder's instructions, the robbery of The *Overseer's Handbook,* and their troubling experiences in Dolos.

"Why is this *Overseer's Handbook* so important?" Milo asked. Tobias leaned forward, his tone serious.

"Our community's systems are custom-built. Water pumps, oil derrick, generators, and a lot more. The Handbook's got decades a notes on how to keep everything running right. It ain't just a manual—it's a survival guide."

Tabitha added, "Without it, everything's sure to break down, and no one'll know how to get it up and running again."

"Not to mention," Tobias said. "The book was Soren Krieger's personal notebook when he was still with us. It's been passed down to the elders since he died. The original hand-written version of the Isolation Doctrine's in there, penned across the first few pages. Written by Soren Krieger himself. We shouldn't a even been allowed to touch it. That there original version of the Isolation Doctrine is used for all the copies that been made since. Without it, we'd lose our most important piece of history. Everything's based on it."

"Got it," Milo said. "You need that book. About the thief that took it. "Do you have any leads?"

Tabitha shook her head. Tobias leaned forward, his elbows resting on his knees.

"It was a robot in a hood," Tabitha said. "Had jeans on, too."

"Ain't got a clue where to go from here," Tobias said. "We done lost a day and a night. Our elders are probably worried."

"And also wondering where the *Overseer's Handbook* went," Tabitha added.

Milo considered this for a moment. His brow furrowed in thought. "Well, let's see what we can do."

Search

"Maybe we can find your *Overseer's Handbook* online. If not in the open, then maybe the dark web," Milo said.

Tobias continued, seemingly unhappy with Milo's flippant tone. "It's the only thing we have left of our founder. Died bout ten years ago, and it's what's left of him. If we had him in the flesh..." he paused for a moment. "If Soren were here, he'd lead us, but—"

"You keep saying that, like he'd fix everything," Tabitha said.

"He would," Tobias said.

Tabitha pursed her lips and looked away. "Everyone talks about him like it was his opinion alone that mattered, but he was just a man," she said. "He wasn't perfect. He made mistakes, too. You talk about him like he's the only one you ever loved." Tabitha rubbed her eyes and released the words she'd felt for years. "I'd much rather have Mom and Dad back than stinking Soren Krieger. It's like you don't even want to remember them."

"Tabby, what you talking about?" Tobias said. "He's our founder. He's our..." In the space Tobias left with his silence,

Tabitha sniffed and wiped her eyes. Tobias continued with more aggression. "As if you don't do the same thing. You spend all your time reading 'bout them missionaries running way from their homes, traveling the world. You just like them stories cause they get to leave. That's all you ever wanted since Mom and Dad died was to leave. But I believe in Isolation. I want to fix it, and I ain't going to fix nothing by wishing Momma and Daddy back."

Through her tears, she managed to say, "While you're busy forgetting about Momma and Daddy, you spend all your time wishing for that old grumpy bachelor what founded our desert prison of a town to come back and rescue us. Don't you see, Toby, Soren Krieger did us as much damage as good? He made us into this. We're helpless. One little book goes missing, and we start falling apart. He turned a bad word, 'isolation,' into a virtue, and by doing that, he made us good for nothing but serving the whims he made up. What's worse, he made us completely dependent on him and didn't mention he was planning to up and die. He ruined us and then left us with a mess. He ain't our savior; he's the one what got us into this mess, and he ain't going to get us out. Wishing Mom and Dad back is at least normal for some growd up orphans to do. Wishing for that old dead grumbler back—well—it's just plain sick. You got to stop. It ain't right."

"I can't believe you're—you're saying that—" Tobias tried to catch up, but Tabitha spun to Milo.

She sniffed and wiped her eyes. "So, do you think you can help us find this stupid handbook so we can get back and forget all of this happened?"

"Well," Milo said, taking a long, awkward look at the two of them. "Let's see if we can find it." He swiveled back to face his main screen, fingers tapping rapidly across the keyboard. Tabitha, at least, was happy to have the distraction. She could feel Tobias' eyes on her, but she was done with the conversation and ready to move on. "I'll need to know what we're looking for. Describe what it looks like."

"It's an old book," she began. "Leather-bound, an inch or so thick. The cover has Isolation's seal—a single tree with a circle around it."

"Nice," Milo said. "That's good. Very recognizable. Any words or title on the cover?"

"They been wore off, but you can still catch glimpse of 'em if the light is right. Soren Krieger was written on the cover 'fore the ink went invisible," Tabitha said. Milo raised his eyebrows.

As he spoke, Milo's fingers flew across the keys. The clicking was fast and rhythmic in the otherwise quiet room. Tabitha watched, amazed at how easily Milo navigated this digital world.

"Anything else?" Milo prompted, not taking his eyes off the screen.

Through gritted teeth, Tobias said, "It's filled with handwritten notes and diagrams."

The screen before them flickered with an overwhelming array of images and text, moving faster than she could process. It looked different than his earlier search for missionary books. A wild array of windows blinked and flashed across the screen in a dizzying display of digital wizardry.

"What's all that?" she asked, her voice barely above a whisper.

Milo smirked slightly. "I'm using an Ai search bot to scour the digiverse for anything matching your description. It's checking auction sites, marketplaces, even the dark web where certain items sometimes appear."

Tobias tensed. "The Sixth Indictum says, 'Engage only in that which is edifying and rooted in the Holy Scriptures.' I don't think we ought to be using any of these digital deceptions to—"

"It's fine," Tabitha said.

"It ain't fine!" Tobias said. "They ain't going to let us come home after we done this."

"Will it work?" Tabitha said, ignoring the comment.

"Should," Milo said, still focused on the screen. "The bot does all the work. We're just watching."

As they peered over his shoulder, windows opened and closed rapidly. *This is what we've been kept from,* she thought as a flicker of indomitable exhilaration flickered in her heartbeat and lungs.

The silence stretched, broken only by the soft hum of Milo's equipment. Tobias rose and paced angrily, his footsteps in sync with the digital activity before them.

"How long this thing gonna take?" he asked, impatience obvious in his voice.

Milo shrugged. "Hard to say. The digiverse is massive, and your book is pretty unique. But if it's out there, we'll find it."

Tabitha clasped her hands together. "Please, let this work," she said in a whispered prayer.

The screen flashed, and Milo leaned forward his brow furrowing. "That's... weird."

Tobias was at his side in an instant. "Did ya find something?"

Milo shook his head, a frown forming. "No, that's just it. There's nothing. Not a single hit on any platform, legal or otherwise."

Tabitha's hope sank, her earlier optimism fading. "So that means it ain't in the digiverse?" Tobias asked, but his question was unrequited.

"It doesn't add up," Milo muttered, more to himself than the others. "Why take something if you're not going to sell it?"

"Maybe that bot stole it thinking it was valuable, and when his master saw it was full a scribble, they..." she fizzled out on the words. Tobias finished her thought.

"They done throwed it away."

A heavy silence fell over the trio. Tobias slammed his fist into an open palm. Tabitha hid her relief. A relief she couldn't quite understand.

"And there ain't nothing else you can do?" she asked Milo. "Any other way to track it down?"

Milo sighed, running a hand through his hair. "I'm sorry, guys, but I've tried all my usual tricks. The book's not in the digiverse." He turned back to his screens, fingers tapping. "I can set up some alerts, though. If it does show up for sale anywhere, we'll know right away."

Tobias nodded, his expression grim. "Thanks, Milo. You tried." The words seemed as if they were difficult to speak, jagged on his tongue.

"Yeah," Milo said, his tone less serious. "I just wish I could do more. This whole thing is messed up."

Tabitha placed a hand on Milo's shoulder. The gesture sent little waves of warmth and hope through her otherwise isolated body. "You done plenty. We wouldn't have even known where to start without you. Tabitha's gaze swept across the room, taking in the screens and gadgets one last time. "I guess... I guess that's it then," she said softly.

"Time to face them consequences," Tobias said. "They'll banish us for sure."

Tabitha swallowed hard, fighting back the lump in her throat. "We need to go back and tell the council everything." A heavy silence rested on them. Wordlessly, they began to move as if an unbearable weight was laid across their backs.

They drifted back through the house and did their best to banish the somber mood as they said goodbye to Milo's family. He followed the twins toward the truck. Tabitha's steps felt heavier with each one. Each footfall brought them closer to an uncertain future, and her thoughts exploded with questions. *What would the elders say? Would they be exiled or worse?*

Tobias climbed into the driver's seat, his movements slow and careful. Tabitha noticed the tension in his jaw and how his knuckles tightened into fists in his lap. "You okay?" she asked softly.

He met her gaze, his eyes locked with hers. "Just thinking bout what we're walking into. But we ain't got a choice?"

"Well, we could..." Tabitha said, willing him to know her mind without words.

"No!" Tobias rumbled. "We ain't leavers." She took a long breath of gravity. Despite all she wished, the stinging truth was evident.

"I know," Tabitha agreed, settling into the passenger seat. "We ain't leavers."

Milo appeared at the open door. His presence reminded her of the world they *were* leaving behind. She studied his face, concerned, heavy, wistful. How could she walk away from this perfect boy who had become everything she wished to be and have and hold? The space between his world and hers was like a chasm fixed, too far to cross, too near to ignore. Another breath came slow. She felt her hands tingle with the desire to reach for him, to tell him she needed him. She yearned for him to beg her to stay. Even then, she could see it. She could not be a leaver. Not like this. Her Dad. Her Mom. Their ashen remains. Their memory lived only in Isolation. She had to go back. It's what her parents would do.

"I'll keep looking," Milo said, his voice low but determined. "If anything turns up…"

"Thank you," Tabitha managed a weak smile. "For everything."

As Milo stepped back, a thought erupted, bitter and broiling. This might be the last time she saw him. She stepped out of the truck and wrapped her arms around him. She held to him as if the world's spin would throw her to space if she let go. The tears that came would be too hard to explain, so she didn't try, nor did she dare release him. The embrace could have lasted until the end of the earth's eon, and it still would be too soon to relinquish her hold on him. Milo's warm, powerful arms gave her a home for a fleeting few seconds. Too soon, something was dividing them. She was unable to stop the exit, too powerless to remain.

"This thing's vibrating again," Tobias said, breaking the spell. They let go abruptly, having forgotten the world still existed. They turned toward Tobias. He held the phone aloft, and Hanna's face smiled back at them.

"It's Hanna. Answer it," she said. Tobias fumbled with the device for a moment before finding the right button.

"Hanna?" Tobias called out, his voice awkward with the discomfort of talking to a device. "You there?"

Hanna's voice was warm. "I'm here. I just got a notification that you're back in the truck. Everything okay?"

Milo exchanged a weary glance with Tobias. "We're fine," Tabitha responded, her tone measured. "We'll bring your truck back now."

There was a pause, and she could almost picture Hanna's expression—hopeful, expectant. "Did you find it? The *Overseer's Handbook*?"

Tobias sighed, running a hand through his disheveled hair. "We searched, but..." His voice trailed off.

Tabitha cleared her throat, "It's time to head back and face the consequences. The elders need to know about the loss." Tabitha's met Tobias' eyes. A silent understanding passed between them.

"I see," Hanna said. A long, empty pause followed. "And you're sure there's nothing else you can do?" The twin's eyes turned to Milo. He shook his head, confirming what they already knew.

"Yep," Tobias said.

"And you're also sure you want to go back to Isolation?" Hanna asked. "I could put you up for a few days, and you could think about starting over on the outside. I'd—"

"We need to go home," Tabitha said. "It's like David Livingstone, missionary in Africa. Things got *really* rough. He got super sick, ran out of supplies, and just couldn't catch a break. By 1856, he was in such bad shape that he had no choice but to head back to Britain." Tabitha let out a defeated sigh. "Except he had done good work before he had to go home. What have we done?"

"You tried," Hanna said. "And that's what the Lord cares about."

"Ain't sure the elders'll see it that way," Tobias said. Under his breath, he mumbled, "We took the *Overseer's Handbook* out a town, and then got it stolen. I wish Soren Krieger was here. He would know what to do." Tobias wilted to a pitiful posture.

"If you're certain you want to return to Isolation, There's something you need to see before you go," Hanna said.

"What?" Tabitha asked.

"It's an eye-opener," she said. "Trust me. This is important. I'm sending coordinates to the truck's navigation system now."

A soft beep from Betsy's console confirmed the incoming data. Tabitha frowned, her brow furrowing as she studied the map. "This... this isn't on our way back."

"I can't explain over the phone because of the leaver's oath," Hanna replied. "But it's crucial. And Milo... I think you should go with them. Just in case there's trouble."

"Trouble?" Tabitha grumbled. "We don't need more—"

"We'll do it," Tobias said. Tabitha looked at him in confusion. Tobias' eyes were locked on the screen with such devotion that whatever protest she had planned wouldn't have mattered.

"I'm in if you are," Milo said.

"Oh, fine," Tabitha said, scooting sidewards on the truck's bench seat.

"I get to ride inside this time?" Milo said. Tabitha patted the seat. He smiled and leaped into the truck as he pulled a digital device from his pocket and started composing a text to his parents. Tabitha and Milo chatted about how texts worked as Tobias looked out the truck's window. Betsy moved, slow at first and then ramped up to speed. It zoomed into the night.

Surprise

As the truck carried them into the darkness, the suburban sprawl gradually gave way to more dilapidated surroundings. Abandoned buildings loomed on either side, their windows dark and empty like soulless eyes watching their progress.

After about twenty minutes of driving, the truck pulled up in front of a run-down apartment complex. The faded brick facade was covered in creeping vines, and several windows were boarded up. A flickering streetlight cast eerie shadows across the crumbling steps leading to the entrance.

"This is it," Milo said, reading the truck's nav-map screen. "Apartment one seventy-four."

Tobias nodded grimly, his eyes scanning the area for any signs of movement. "Looks rough," he said.

They approached the building cautiously as if wild animals might leap from the bushes or the lone leafless tree would come to life and snatch them. The crunch of gravel under their feet seemed unnaturally loud in the oppressive silence. Every step closer to

#174 was a decision to move toward the most dangerous-looking building they'd yet seen.

Reaching the door, Tobias raised his hand to knock. The sound echoed ominously through the empty space beyond. Tabitha eyed an angry crack that ran the length of the wall and terminated at the corner of a curtained window.

There was no response to the knock, which was a relief. Tabitha felt sweat beading on her forehead. She vanquished it with the back of her hand. Instead of knocking a second time, Tobias reached for the doorknob. "No," she whispered, but her brother hadn't yet learned that word.

The knob turned easily in Tobias' hand, and the door swung open with a creaking announcement. They exchanged wary glances, begging for a reason to turn back. The musty smell wafted out from the darkness inside and assaulted their senses.

"Hello?" Tobias called, leading with his boot. They stepped over the threshold. When she spotted the shape, Tabitha's breath became bricks in her mouth. There was a silhouette of a man sitting in the dark, ominous room. Enthroned upon a threadbare couch and wreathed in shadow was a stranger. So still was the specter, he could have been asleep or even dead.

"Hello?" Tobias said again. "Our friend Hanna told us to come here and..." The mysterious figure leaned forward and reached to the side. The three teens stepped back. Tobias reached for his pocket as Milo put his back against the wall. A lamp clicked on, and they saw the face. The man looked strangely familiar. Tabitha knew those lines, those wrinkles, that expression. The thick side-burns, the wild hair. It was more than a surprise; it was an absolute impossibility. The man's expression was one Tabitha had seen in person or in pictures every day of her life since she could remember. She gasped against the palm of her hand.

"It ain't possible," Tobias whispered, his voice full of awe and disbelief.

"But you're—you're—" Tabitha felt dizzy. She stared, no, she gawked. The years had changed his appearance, added wrinkles, and brought his hair to white, but there was no mistaking him. Photographs from his younger years hung enshrined in every building in Isolation. A day didn't go by without twenty dozen mentions of things he'd said or taught. She traced the familiar lines with her eyes. There was no mistake, that half-pulled smile and the square jaw. "Is it really you?"

"Soren Krieger!" Tobias said, staring at the mythical man who founded Isolation, an idolized figure who had been dead for ten years, or so they thought.

Soren sat before them, flesh and blood, his presence both impossible and undeniable. Her legs felt like noodles, and her heart rumbled with rhythmic thunder.

The Overseer's piercing gaze swept over them, through them, peering deep into their souls. His snowy hair caught the dim light, and his eyes glowed with wisdom and near-eternal knowing. How could this be? How was he alive?

"Overseer Soren Krieger," Tobias managed to croak, his voice as thin as a whisp. "We... we thought you was... We thought you died in a fire. Soren Krieger. How..." He put his hands up in celebration. "Soren Krieger's alive!"

Soren's lips curled into a faint smile. "Nothing magical shall transpire at the repetition of my name."

Tabitha's eyes darted to her brother, and she saw her own shock mirrored in his face. She struggled to form coherent thoughts.

"Your birthday," Tobias blurted out, "Since you was gone, we celebrate it every year. And your... your death day. Them two days is our most sacred holidays."

Soren's eyebrow arched slightly. "Indeed? I must confess that being celebrated for dead does not hint at a warmth of recollection."

Tobias' cheeks burned with red, but he pressed on. "On your birthday, we fast from sunrise to sunset, meditating on your teachings. And on the anniversary of your... well, what we was thinking was your death, we have a big ol' feast, honoring your sacrifice in that fire. But I guess now we'll have to rethink that, but..."

"A feast and a fast," Soren mused. "I prefer the one for its fervor and the other for its caloric opportunities."

Tobias laughed too eager, too hard, and too long. Tobias cleared his throat. "Sir, I—I Have all your indictums memorized. I practice 'em every morning. I can quote them if you like. The first—"

"That won't be necessary," Soren said.

"It's just that we ain't never imagined we'd be standing here, talking to you. It's—it's a bit much."

"Astonishment is the child of surprise," Soren said, his voice rich and measured. "But when the surprise diminishes, so too the parent, leaving only mundane familiarity in its absence."

Overwhelmed by emotion, Tobias fell to his knees, his arms instinctively wrapping around Soren's legs. Tears welled in his eyes as he looked up at the founder, his voice quivering with relief and joy.

"We been so worried and lost since you was gone," he prattled, his words tumbling out in a rush. "The elders been arguing for years. We all feel it in Isolation. Ain't nobody know what to do without you. But now... now everything's gonna be okay. You're here, you're alive, and you'll make things right again."

Tobias' grip tightened as if he was afraid Soren might vanish if he let go. Tabitha watched her brother hug the man's calves. Her brother's response was embarrassing, even inappropriate, though Tobias was too overwrought to feel it. And yet, Soren allowed it. She wondered why the founder didn't tell her brother not to worship, not to adore, not to bask. She squinted at the strange scene, trying to punch through the still-glowing after-haze of the adrenaline.

She, too, wished she could believe he could restore peace to Isolation. She wished she could be as relieved. She wished this meeting felt good, but it didn't. A dark shadow hovered over her mind. She no longer had any hope in the man she had been raised to view as the singular hero of her home. Some dark and brooding revulsion had taken the place her Sorenite reverence once occupied.

Tobias let go of the founder's legs and came up to his knees. "Blessings on you for your loyalty, my child," Soren said.

Tobias kneeled frozen, his usual pragmatism overwhelmed by the sheer improbability of the situation. His lips moved, but no sound came out. He blinked as pitiful, child-like tears spilled from his adoring face. It wasn't clear how long Tobias would have stayed in that state, but Tabitha was ready to pivot.

"How do we know he's real?" She asked. Tobias looked at her as if he were ashamed of his kin. "What? We've seen a load of weird stuff. How do we know this ain't another deep fake from the digiverse?"

Soren's lips curved into a slight smile. He extended his palms to his adoring supplicant. "Look upon my hands. My side, my feet. Examine and believe." Tobias handled the man's hands as Tabitha watched the unsettling scene play out, her brother kneeling before this odd man, who seemed to relish the examination with a delicious fervor that made Tabitha feel icky.

Tabitha glanced at Milo. "There a way to tell if this guy is real?" she asked.

"You're not wearing digiverse contacts anymore, and he's obviously not wearing an exo-display-suit." Milo stepped forward. "If you'll permit me, Sir, I'd like to check one thing." Soren frowned for a brief second. After a moment's hesitation, he nodded. Milo stepped forward and placed his hand on the back of Soren's neck. He felt along his hairline. "He's not a bot. What you see is what you get."

"He's the real thing?" Tobias asked from his kneeling position.

"He's a human if that's what you mean," Milo said. "But as far as being the real thing, well..." Milo trailed off. Tabitha looked at him, and they made eye contact. She wasn't the only one who felt the weirdness.

Tobias glimmered at the revelation. "It's really you," he whispered. "You've returned. It's like you done come back from the dead."

The questions that had been burning in Tabitha's mind since the moment she saw him finally burst. "Where have you been all this time? Why did you leave Isolation? And why does everyone think you're dead?"

Tobias gulped and gave Tabitha a withering look. She wasn't done. "Isolation has mourned you for ten years," she added, her voice tight with quavering emotion. "You're talked about like a saint or a—a—a martyr. Your death date is one of our most sacred—"

"I done told him that already, Tabby," Tobias said.

"Well, I don't think he got the point yet," Tabitha said. Her voice was as sharp as a knife. Soren's eyes narrowed. He drew himself up, his posture tall and lean even at his advanced age. When he spoke, his voice resonated with a cultured timbre that demanded attention.

"My dear acolytes," he began, his words flowing like honey, rich and deliberate. "I have embarked upon a journey of unparalleled asceticism, a quest to achieve the purest form of isolation that our doctrine extols."

Tabitha ground her teeth at the ostentatious tone. Her jaw muscles tensed. Her teeth clicked together.

"I have sequestered myself in this sanctuary," Soren continued, gesturing to the near-empty apartment, "far removed from the corrupting tendrils of the digiverse. Here, I have cultivated an existence of divine isolation." Tobias folded his hands as he listened. Tabitha balled hers into fists.

"My apparent demise," Soren explained, his tone taking on a note of reverence, "was not of my making. The others who have come to me in this sanctuary have made the same inquiries as you, but the question is not for me to answer. It must be asked of those to whom the fabrication belongs."

"Others have come to you?" Tabitha asked.

"Others have been sent," Soren corrected. "Quite against my wishes for isolation, I might add. The friend you spoke of, Hanna, has regularly broken my hermitage with pilgrims who stare upon me as a caged animal. Rarely do they come with such loyalty as this young disciple." Soren touched Tobias' head as he spoke the words. Tabitha's eyes went wide with fire. A surge of contempt nearly ruptured her composure. She felt a hand on her shoulder. She looked over at Milo. Could he sense her mood? Was he really that perceptive? His eyes were asking if she was ok. Their brief interchange gave her the strength she needed. She turned back to Soren.

"You didn't want to be found," she said.

"In this monastic seclusion," Soren continued, his voice swelling with pride, "I have achieved a state of isolation so pure, so absolute, that it transcends the very boundaries of our mortal understanding."

Tabitha felt Milo's hand give her a gentle squeeze before he let go. Soren's eyes took on a distant, almost transcendent gleam as he launched into another monologue, his voice rising and falling with passionate intensity.

"The quintessence of our doctrine, my young students, lies in the sublime abstraction of the self from the cacophonous miasma of societal entanglements. The ontological ramifications transcend the petty vicissitudes of corporeal existence and allow the super-self to glimpse the sublime truths that lie beyond the veil of mundane perception—"

"What?" Tabitha said. "I don't get it."

"He's saying he just sits there and stares at the wall," Milo blurted out. Tobias looked at him as if he'd burped aloud in a cathedral mass. The words were such a surprise that Tabitha let out a snorting laugh. It wasn't funny exactly, but she could suddenly see it from Milo's point of view. An outsider would find this man such an oddity, maybe even pitiful.

"Milo!" Tobias said. "You don't understand."

"Who is this vile creature?" Soren asked.

"Milo. Pleased to meet you," he said, putting out his hand and stepping forward. The old man didn't shake but only glanced down at the extended palm. Milo put it down as he said, "I just mean, you're in here staring at the wall and bragging about not having any friends while their town is searching for this book. Clearly, they could use a hand. And obviously, they feel a bit abandoned, although the big guy doesn't want to admit it. It doesn't take an Ai analytics bot to see why they'd be a bit miffed at you for twiddling your thumbs while they scramble to figure out what to do."

"He's the author of the isolation doctrine," Tobias said. "What he's doing, it's—it's—it's important."

"Thank you, my child," Soren said.

"I don't know about *important*." Milo said. "Seems selfish!" Tobias gasped. "Well, you two see this dude as some kind of father figure for your town, but no good father ever abandoned his kids. My dad always says, 'family is the opposite of selfish.' Sitting alone in this apartment when his people are in need *is* selfish." The growl that followed could have stripped rust from steel. Tobias rose with fury and fire. His hands twisted a ball of Milo's shirt and shoved him against the wall, holding him steady.

"Don't you dare say a thing about our founder. He's—he's—he's... our founder." Tobias gave Milo a continued tongue lashing as he pinned him ever harder against the wall. Tabitha looked toward Soren, expecting him to stop the conflict, expecting him to call off his devotee. Instead, Soren smiled deliciously as he watched his pupil punish his enemy. Tabitha growled, an animalistic sound that rose up from deep in her chest.

"Toby, stop," she said. "That ain't what we're here for." Tobias looked at his sister and then let go of Milo. He stepped back and turned toward the founder.

"Maybe it is best for the outsider to go outside," Soren said.

"You heard him," Tobias said. "Outside."

"Gladly," Milo said, straightening his shirt. "But you're my ride, so don't try to sneak out on me." Milo exited as Tabitha and Tobias returned their attention back to the man of legend.

Hypothesis

Soren continued his speech from the point Milo had interrupted. "The essence of our existence lies in irreducible isolation," Soren intoned, his voice a melodious rumble.

Tabitha's brow furrowed. She knew that her twin had understood no more than she of what was being said, but to be in the presence of Soren was too intoxicating for him to be concerned with comprehension.

A muffled clang broke the trance. Tabitha's head snapped up, her eyes darting to the doorway that led to the kitchen. Another sound followed the first, and Tabitha stepped toward the opening.

"Is someone else here?" she asked.

Soren waved a dismissive hand. "No," he declared. "There is no other person in this sanctuary of solitude."

"Whatever," she said. "Just so you know, we don't got a clue what you're saying."

A shadow passed across the kitchen's doorframe, drawing their attention. A metallic figure glided into the room, carrying a waiter's tray. The metal creature looked familiar. Although not dressed

218

in clothes, it bore an uncanny resemblance to the model they had seen at Hanna's Diner, the one that stole the Overseer's Handbook. The coincidental resemblance put Tabitha at a starting point of discomfort, but as she watched the humanoid machine enter the room and approach Soren with the trayed items, the full realization hit her.

They had seen robots, even been attacked by one, and were getting more accustomed to their presence, but that bot was in Soren Krieger's apartment. Her eyes flitted between the robot and Soren a dozen times. Soren had a robot in his apartment? She and Tobias watched in stunned silence.

The robot stopped next to Soren's place on the couch, lowered itself at the knees with an inhuman motion, and presented the tray to him.

"It is time for your meal and meditation, Master," the robot said. Tabitha's gaze locked onto the objects it carried: a carefully arranged lunch and, nestled beside it, a digiverse VR headset.

A mirthless laugh escaped Tabitha's lips before she could stifle it. Her brother's face was a mask of shock and confusion. His eyes narrowed as he stared at the robotic companion and the forbidden technology it had brought.

Tabitha said nothing as she watched her brother's world unravel. Tobias' voice trembled as he broke the tense silence. "Soren, I... I don't understand. Why you got a robot? Ain't this exactly what kind a stuff we're supposed to be isolating from?"

"Nonsense," Soren began, but Tabitha cut in.

"We got robbed by a metal man that looked a lot like that one," Tabitha said. "They're used for all kinds of evil stuff. We seen it with our own eyes."

Soren's serene expression never wavered. "My dear children, you don't know what you've seen. You've been misled. There is no contradiction here. This companion allows the epitome of isolation."

Tobias' brow furrowed, his eyes searching Soren's face. "But how? That there thing is digital. It's a technology connected to everything you done taught us to avoid."

"Ah, but it allows me to maintain my solitude without the need for human interaction," Soren explained, his tone maddeningly calm, as he pressed the sandwich into his mouth and took a giant bite. "It is a buffer between myself and the chaos of human society. I would be completely cut off if it weren't for Hanna Thompson's occasional intruders. Apart from them, I haven't seen another person in three years."

Tobias scoffed, his calloused hands clenching into fists. "That ain't what isolation means. Our entire life in Isolation's built on staying way from this kind a thing!"

Soren sighed, a hint of condescension creeping into his voice. "When our community was founded, yes, that was the initial hypothesis." Soren's eyes gleamed with an unsettling intensity as he leaned forward. "This is what Isolation taught me. The true evil isn't digital. It's people. Humanity has a monopoly on evil. Digital devices aren't good or bad. They are inert. They are tools. It's people who have evil all balled up in them like black spiders waiting to be let free. Thus, the fuller realization is found in this: We must isolate from one another. We must wall off the evil in each of ourselves. We must fully isolate so the evil in you and the evil in me cannot combine and grow. We can finally find our real purpose through this new understanding of the isolation doctrine. Lone humans have enough good to find balance, but evil becomes unmanageable when we become humanity, all clumped up in innumerable populations."

"But we is humanity," Tobias said. "You saying we need to isolate from each other?"

"Exactly," Soren said. "Now you're getting it."

"I am not," Tobias said. "You done taught us to run from everything what's digital, and cling to each other in our holy isolation. You taught us the opposite of what you're saying now. But now you're saying, cling to technology and abandon all them people we love."

Soren chuckled, the sound sending chills down Tabitha's spine. "This companion, the digiverse, all of it. They're tools, nothing more. The idea of avoiding them is..." He paused, his lips curling into a smirk. "Well, it's laughably primitive."

"Primitive!" Tobias thundered. "We done staked our whole lives on it! We—we—believed in you. We followed you into the desert, and now you say..."

Soren waved a dismissive hand as a splat of mustard plopped on his shirt, staining the rotund curve of his pot belly. "It's simple. My original concept was incomplete. This is the new isolation doctrine."

"You are a hypocrite," Tabitha said. "You taught us all of this. You made our people sacrifice everything because you said it's the only way to please God. We all followed you. We trusted you. And now you don't believe it anymore? That's vile. It's abusive. You're the evilest critter I ever seen. You're a real monster!" For once, her brother didn't disagree with her about Soren Krieger.

Soren leaned back into the couch's cushion, his eyes glinting with amusement. "And you followed an vile hypocrite. What does that say about you?" He shrugged and leaned back. It was a casual gesture that trivialized her entire life. It would have hurt less if he'd slapped her on the cheek. They stared at him for a long moment before he spoke again.

"So, what are you going to do now?" Soren continued. "You're going to isolate from me because I'm so *evil*. You're going to leave here and compartmentalize. You'll marginalize your memories of me. You'll relegate me to some dark corner of your past. It's all isolation. It's what we do. It's what we've always done. When the evil in you meets the evil in me, we isolate from each other. Sure, we may join our evils together for a time, but eventually, the battle comes. The icky, sticky stuff at our core wins, and we isolate. You're doing it even now. I can see it on your face. You're separating from me, your illustrious founder and hero." He took another bite. "The only difference with me is I call it what it is. Real, deep, enduring isolation is our destiny. It's all we have ahead of us."

"No," Tobias said, but Soren went on.

"Look around at this world," he said. "It's shattering. You see it, right? Everyone out there is blaming the devices, the Ais, the robots, the screens, but that's all bunk. It's none of those things. The evil in us drives us apart. From the first siblings, Cain and Abel, to the Andrews Twins of Isolation. You're destined to divide, to separate, to isolate."

Tobias exploded, his face flushed with rage. "That ain't true!"

"Of course it is," Soren said. "It's what your beloved Isolation did to me. The people of Isolation are the monsters, and those monsters turned on their founder. Now, here I am while the lot of you have been rotting in the desert alone and ignorant. You can't even put a sentence together without broken grammar. You're a bunch of dumb desert-dwelling donkeys. You're out there worshiping a used-up old man you thought was a saint of digital abstinence. When you find he lives alone with a robot in a run-down apartment, well, it sends you into fits. Don't you see? Isolation, true isolation, is all there is."

"It ain't true," Tobias repeated. His eyes narrowed, his body tensing like a coiled spring. Tabitha recognized the look. She watched, heart pounding, as her brother strode across the room, his intentions clear.

"Toby, don't—" she began, but it was too late.

As Tobias reached for Soren's VR goggles, a blur of metallic movement intercepted him. The robotic companion shoved Tobias with surprising force. Tabitha's scream pierced the air as her brother tumbled backward, crashing across the dirty carpet with a thud.

"Tobias!" Tabitha rushed to her brother's side, her hands shaking as she helped him up. She glared at Soren, who was calmly fitting the goggles over his eyes. "How can you just sit there?"

Soren's lips curled into a cold smile. "I'm isolated, remember." With that, he activated the headset, his expression going blank as he immersed himself in the digital realm. Tabitha's gaze lingered on Soren's motionless form. Soren remained still, the goggles obscuring his eyes. Tabitha's words tumbled out in a desperate rush.

"Isolation reveres you. You're the symbol of our doctrine. How can you let them continue living in ignorance? You have a responsibility to them. To us. To God."

"They revere me? Is that really what you think?" Soren said, not taking off his goggles. "They used me like a pair of plumber's gloves, and when I was no longer useful, they turned me into a martyr for their cause. They made me the patron saint of their monopoly on the truth. It's all just propaganda. They use my influence to win arguments, to quell dissension, to control you, to keep you in check." He sighed. "I'm not who you think I am. I'm a tired old man who failed. I tried to lead them, and look what it cost you."

"Come on," Tobias said, moving toward the door. "There's nothing here for us." Tabitha lingered for a few seconds before she, too, began to move. When they reached the door, she turned.

"No, wait," she paused. "What did it cost us?" She stared. When he didn't budge, she posed it again with more magma. "What did it cost us?" Still, the mountain didn't move. He was lost behind the digital mask. She summoned such a fury that the fires at the center of the planet could burst forth with only a fraction of the steam and rumble that exploded from her mouth. "Answer me, Soren Krieger! What did it cost us?"

Soren's hands went to his goggles. He slid them off his face slowly and set them next to him on the couch. He stared at them for a long moment. "I tried to lead them. But my leadership cost you your parents."

Thief

"When Isolation was founded," Soren said, his fingers tracing the seams of the couch, "it was a time of hope. Of promise."

Soren's eyes grew distant as if peering into the past. "We were driven by good motives, by a desire to create something untainted by the outside world's corruption." Soren's gaze shifted between Tabitha and Tobias, his eyes brimming with unshed tears. "About fifteen years ago, your parents, Gad and Belamie Andrews, led a group that wanted to bring change to Isolation." Tabitha's breath caught in her throat. She glanced at Tobias, whose usually stoic face now betrayed shock and confusion.

"They proposed something radical," Soren continued, his voice barely more than a whisp of air. "A school for digital studies, to prepare those who wished to leave Isolation."

Tobias leaned forward, his calloused hands clenching into fists. "Leave? But that's... that's forbidden."

Soren nodded solemnly. "Your parents believed Isolation was crippling its citizens, leaving them unprepared for the wider world.

They wanted to give people the freedom to choose to leave and the education to survive if they left."

"Why didn't we know about this?" Tabitha asked, her voice trembling.

"Because I disagreed," Soren admitted, shame etching deep lines in his face. "I didn't want anyone to get hurt, I promise. But I disagreed with your parents with every ounce of my being."

"Who got hurt?" Tobias asked.

"I just wanted Isolation to remain... isolated. But my views were taken to extremes by others." He paused. "A faction led by someone named Ram Stern—"

"We know him," Tabitha said. "He's on the council."

"I see," Soren said. "Ram and his followers believed your parents should be arrested and punished for their views. I refused to have them arrested. That was too far. Ram fought hard. Claimed he was giving me the backbone I lacked." His voice broke. "I tried to ignore him and his followers, hoping they'd stop their calls for violence, but when I didn't give them what they wanted, they turned on me."

Tabitha's voice quivered as she asked, "What happened to our parents?"

Soren's shoulders sagged, the weight of history pressing down upon him. "With me as the new target, it seemed everyone forgot about your parent's idea. Now, I was being accused of terrible things. We had much bigger issues than a school for digital studies.

I was being labeled unfit for leadership. For the years that followed, Isolation was consumed by terrible debates and arguments. It was a time of darkness, of fear. Worst time of my life.

"You two were born during that time. I was there. I mean, we all were. There were still moments where we felt like one big family, even though it was coming apart at the rivets." A ghost of a smile flickered across Soren's face. "Your births—the twins of Isolation, it was a spot of hope in an otherwise dismal period. It gave people something to celebrate, a reminder of why we did this in the first place.

"I don't understand," Tabitha said, her brow furrowed. "You said our parents opposed you, but then..."

Soren nodded, finishing his thought. "Originally, yes. Gad and Belamie Andrews were my opponents. They often challenged my more eccentric notions." He paused, his voice thick with emotion. "But when Ram and his extremists turned on me, calling for my execution—"

"Ram wanted to kill you?" Tobias rumbled. "I don't understand. Ram Stern is your biggest supporter. He quotes you all the time."

"Ram uses my words as weapons," Soren said. "But that is very different from being a *supporter*. He takes my ideas to extremes that I never intended. Is anything I'm saying out of character for what you know of Ram?" The twins shook their heads.

"So, Mom and Dad stood up to Ram?" Tabitha said as tears trickled down her cheeks.

"Yes, they stood by my side. They wouldn't let me face Ram and the others alone. Everyone else abandoned me, but not your parents. Even though I had said terrible things about them behind their backs, they stood strong by my side. Your dad became closer than a brother."

Tobias's eyes widened. "He disagreed with you *and* defended you? Why?"

"When he saw the injustice of what was happening, he put aside our past conflicts. Gad fought against Ram, risking everything to try and save me. He was a good man. If I had been more like him, then maybe Isolation could have been..."

Tabitha's hand was over her mouth, and her breathing was sporadic. She'd only known her parents until she was nine, but none of this was ever discussed. There was no hint to the twins that anything but joy was present in their burrow. To think that her father and mother were in the midst of grief and turmoil while carving from the chaos a blissful childhood for their brood made it feel like the world was shifting beneath her feet. *How could this be? How could this have been kept from them?*

"All this time," she whispered.

Tobias placed a comforting hand on her shoulder, his own voice thick with emotion. "They fought for what they believed in, Tabby. Just like you."

Soren's face crumpled, tears streaming down his weathered cheeks. His voice cracked as he continued, "But then... that terrible night... Ten years ago." He paused, struggling to find the words.

Tabitha leaned forward, her heart pounding. "What happened?" she whispered.

"It all erupted into violence," Soren choked up. "Ram and his goons went for the armory. Your dad and I were working on that week's newspaper. Your mom was there setting the type. Before we even knew what was happening, Ram burst into the print shop and had me at gunpoint. I thought that was it. I thought I was about to see the Lord. But then, there he was. Your father... he..." The old man's shoulders shook with silent sobs.

Soren took a shuddering breath. "Your dad pushed me behind himself and tried to calm Ram down. Your mom came and stood next to him, shielding me from the danger. Ram started shooting. Your dad was the first to fall. Your mom was hit, too." Tabitha gasped, her free hand flying to her mouth. "It was chaos. I got covered in their blood. I fell, pretending to be hit. When the bullets stopped flying, Ram came over to survey his handiwork. The generator was already shut down for the night, so we had been working by candlelight. In the dim conditions, it must have looked like I was shot through, too, since I was covered in their blood. Ram saw all three blood-covered bodies and thought we were all dead. I held my breath and stayed as still as I could."

"I kept my eyes closed but could hear Ram moving around the print shop. I couldn't understand what he was doing. He took off the lid of a canister of cleaning solvent and dumped it all over us. I stayed as still as I could, trying not to choke or even breathe. The room filled with fumes."

Soren's eyes brimmed with fresh tears. "Seconds later, I heard a crash in the front of the shop as Ram's footsteps went out. I sat up and checked Gad and Belamie... I couldn't get a pulse on either of them. I checked myself and realized I didn't have a single wound. It was like a miracle."

"Not for Ma and Pa," Tobias said with a bitter acid in his voice. "The *miracle* was that you had good enough friends who'd let you hide behind them as bullets came crashing through their dying bodies!" His voice was full of gravel and scorn.

"Yes," Soren said, waiting a long time before he spoke again. "It's true." He took a long, broken breath and continued. "I was in shock. I thought I should go find Dr. Kent, but I was terrified. I thought they might be waiting outside. So I sat there for a while. Then I heard the crackle and smelled the smoke. Ram had broken one of the lamps and set the shop on fire. It was chasing the fumes of the cleaning solvent. The flames climbed the walls in seconds, and the whole place was ablaze."

"No," Tabitha breathed, horrified.

"I went out the back exit and just kept walking. I crossed the desert and have never been back."

"You coward!" Tobias thundered. "You left my parents to die!"

"I swear," Soren said. "They didn't have a pulse." He paused and closed his eyes. "I'm almost sure they didn't have a pulse."

Tabitha flopped on the floor, legs crossed. She stared at the carpet. She was somewhere else. In her memory, she danced through the shop her parents had run when she was a child. She skipped past the counter stacked with dried goods and burst through the swinging doors into the printshop in the back. She was six and free as a bird. Her dad put her on his shoulder and walked around the printing press, pointing out that day's paper ready to print.

The scene crackled and charred around the edges. She envisioned the burnt ruin where it all had stood. She'd known for a decade it was where her parents had died, but had no idea that it was anything other than a senseless accident. She slowly raised her red-rimmed eyes to the old man.

"You're lying?" Tabitha said, knowing he wasn't.

"As your brother has pointed out, I'm hardly the hero of the story," Soren said. "Why would I fabricate such an incident? It has brought me ten years of inescapable remorse, irreducible guilt, and soul-crushing shame."

"Why didn't no one tell us this?" Tobias asked.

"I don't know," Soren said. "But I can't imagine that Ram was eager to announce that he'd murdered the founder. I had made promises to him early on, which I later realized I could not keep. This wasn't a flight of rage. It was premeditated. It was at night when everyone was asleep in their burrows, far enough not to hear gunshots. I often spent long nights at the printshop, a detail he knew all too well."

Tabitha gasped with realization. "Ram was the one that *discovered* the fire, remember," Tabitha said to her brother. "They teach it as part of Isolation's history. He ran through the streets screaming, 'Fire, we must save the founder!'"

"He made sure to shed them big tears at your funeral," Tobias said.

"The murderer made himself the hero," Tabitha said.

"You could a set the record straight. You could a brung him to justice. You're Soren Krieger. You could a..." Tobias paused and scrunched his face up tight. "But you just left?"

Soren nodded, unable to meet their eyes. "I had promised everyone a utopia, but I couldn't maintain the lie anymore. It was too much. I couldn't stand how they all disagreed with me. Why couldn't they just listen and agree?"

"And you was afraid," Tobias said.

"Yes."

"And you've been hiding all this time?" Tabitha said.

"Yes," Soren whispered. He looked up at them, his eyes brimming with tears. "Until Hanna found me. Now, it's my punishment to endure. She sends me every leaver that steps foot across that dusty desert. I knew one day it was possible that my visitors would be you two."

"Do you tell this story to everyone that comes?" Tabitha asked.

"Heaven's no," Soren said. "I'm a circus act. A freak show. I play my part. Let them see that Soren Krieger is a flawed, used-up old coward. I dispel their vision of *Soren, The Savior*. The spell is broken, and I send them on their way. It's my penance and the only thing I've done of any value in years."

"Is that what all that nonsense you was telling us earlier was about?" Tobias said. "New isolation doctrine, and what not?"

"Yes," Soren said. "It's my little performance to help leavers see they are right to leave, that their founder is a hypocrite."

"Why don't you go back," Tabitha said. "Make it right. Tell Isolation the truth for once."

"I can't." The old man sobbed.

"Why not?" Tobias asked.

"I don't know," Soren said.

"I do," Tabitha said. She took a long breath and prepared to let him have it.

Realization

She stepped forward and said, "Look at me, Soren Krieger." He looked up with red-rimmed eyes. "You don't have to be a bitter old coward. You can make this right... or as right as it can be. Don't hide anymore."

"But," Soren said. "I've made such a mess. I got your parents killed."

"You think that mess is more than God can forgive and fix?" she asked. "Your life was saved because you were covered in my parent's blood. Your soul is saved because you're covered in the Lord's. Don't waste the time you have left. A lot of people have sacrificed for you to be more than this sniveling weakling."

"Me and my sister are flawed and evil and broken, but *we* can forgive you," Tobias said. Soren's eyes moved to the boy.

"You can?" he said.

"We do," Tabitha said. "We forgive you."

"But *they* won't," Soren said. "If they find out the truth. If they realized what I am. They'll hang me right next to Ram."

"Maybe, maybe not," Tabitha said. "But at least you'll know you're doing the right thing."

Soren looked at the carpet. "It's too late for me, but maybe..." The old man rose from the couch, stepped around the robotic companion, and glided across the room. He slid into the kitchen and returned a moment later with something in each hand. "I can return this to its rightful owner."

He held out a small leather-bound book. On the cover was an emblem of a tree with a circle around it. "*The Overseer's Handbook!*" Tabitha said. "Where'd you find it?" She accepted it from his hands and flipped through the pages packed with life-sustaining notes and information needed to keep their community alive.

"He didn't *find* it," Tobias said. "He stole it." Tabitha's eyes turned from the book to the man.

"Technically," Soren said. "It belonged to me first. And technically, my robot stole it." Tobias filled his chest with a breath that was sure to come rumbling out in a thunderous disagreement, but Soren put his hands up in placation. "But, you're right. It doesn't belong to me anymore. So, yes. I instructed my bot to steal it from you in the diner."

"So that was your bot," Tabitha said. "The hood wasn't a very good disguise," Soren nodded, but his eyes didn't meet hers. "Why would you send your bot to steal the *Overseer's Handbook*?"

Soren's weathered face creased with regret. He sat heavily on the couch again, his fingers tapping an irregular pattern on the cushion. "Without the Handbook, I thought Isolation would start to break down. Isolationists would have no choice but to leave, to face the world beyond. I could undo my wrong."

"You were going to commit a crime to right a previous crime?" Tabitha asked.

Soren shook his head. "That wasn't my original plan. I—I live in this constant state of guilt about what happened there. I couldn't stand it anymore." His eyes locked onto Tabitha's. "I got this bot a few months ago, to—to—have it... you know."

The twins looked at each other. "No, we don't," Tabitha said.

"I was going to have it kill me," Soren said. "I was going to commit robotic suicide. I had it hacked and everything, but then

I thought of the *Overseer's Handbook*. I don't know why. I just couldn't get it off my mind. The idea grew until I couldn't sleep."

"So you sent your robot to get it," Tabitha prodded.

"Yes. I instructed my bot to sneak in at night and find the book. But I'm no tech expert. I thought I'd just be able to tell the bot to go and do it, and it would handle it, but it doesn't work like that. I realized I would have to give it direct instructions at every step of the journey, but the internet connection was terrible in Edgetown, and I knew it would get worse the farther into the desert I sent the bot. So I parked it at a booth in the diner and uploaded its *return home* instructions when you two walked in with Frank Thompson's daughter."

"Through the patchy feed, I could hear you say you had the *Overseer's Handbook* in your bag. It was too convenient not to be a sign from God, I thought. I instructed the bot to create a decoy and steal the bag."

"That was wrong," Tabitha said.

"Well, yes. I know. But I told myself it was divine providence. Stealing seemed like an easier way to give Isolation a dignified end, but..."

Tabitha's fingers tightened around the leather cover. The weight of responsibility pressed down on her shoulders. "If that's true," she said, "Why give it back now?"

Soren's expression softened. He looked at them both, a glimmer of hope in his tired eyes. "Because I believe in you," he said. "You're the children of Gad Andrews, the greatest man I've known. You've proven to be made of the same stuff as him. With hearts like yours still glowing in the dark of Isolation, there's hope for change from within."

"Please," she pleaded, her voice cracking with emotion. "Come home with us. Help us make things right in Isolation."

Tobias placed a hand on his sister's shoulder, his calloused fingers gentle but firm.

"You know Isolation better than anyone," Tabitha continued, her words tumbling out in a rush. "You understand both worlds. You can help make this right."

Soren's long face turned down with a sad smile. He shook his head slowly, his eyes filled with a half-century of shame. "I'm sorry, child. My time in Isolation has long passed. This is your journey now. My presence would only complicate things. The people of Isolation need to find their own way forward, led by those they trust."

"It's the scary stuff that's worth doing," Tabitha said. "What if William Carey, David Livingstone, or John Paton were too afraid to go on a mission trip? Or worse, what if Jesus didn't come and die for us because he was a coward? We owe our eternal salvation to his courage." She stepped forward and put a hand on his shoulder. "You started Isolation in good conscience. How can you abandon it with the same? Jesus didn't abandon you. You shouldn't abandon your people."

"Young lady," Soren said. "You have the heart of a desert lion. Isolation has hope. Let your courage shine, and they will follow. But as for me and my house, we can't follow you to Isolation."

"You're wrong," Tobias said. "But we ain't going to stand here and try to coddle you into doing what's right." Tobias stepped toward Tabitha and reached for the *Overseer's Handbook*.

"What are you doing?" Tabitha asked.

"I'm returning an unwanted doctrine," Tobias said. He opened *The Overseer's Handbook* to the first page and ripped it out. He went to the second and pulled it from the binding as well. He continued until the entirety of the Isolation Doctrine's original hand-written version was removed from the spine that had held it in. With the pages in his hand, he slapped them against Soren's chest. "We won't be needing these anymore." Soren didn't grab the wadded paper but just closed his eyes. The crumpled pages that contained the founding charter of Isolation fell to his lap as Tobias closed the book and handed it back to his sister, infinitesimally lighter.

"If you change your mind, you know where to find us." Tabitha turned and led her brother through the door.

Pivot

The rusty hinges of the apartment door creaked as they stepped onto the weathered porch, the wood groaning under their feet. Milo was leaning against the railing, looking at his phone. He slid it into his pocket and gave them his attention.

"Sorry I snapped at you," Tobias said.

"I get it," Milo said. "You like the dude." Milo looked them up and down. "You two look like you've been punched where it counts. What happened?"

"Don't want to talk about it," Tobias said. "Let's go." Tabitha and Milo made a second of eye contact as they moved back toward the truck.

"Can you make the truck take us to Edgetown," Tabitha said as they climbed in. Milo nodded and started tapping the screen in the truck. Tabitha watched as he put in the coordinates. "Aren't you going to have it take you to your house first?"

"No," Milo said. "I'm going to make sure you two noobs get back safe. I'll grab an air taxi back to Dolos later." Tabitha's heart fluttered a little at the information.

They chatted about life in Isolation as the truck drove them toward Edgetown. Milo texted Hanna about their soon return. She had some peach cobbler ready for them at the diner when they arrived. They ate, and when the dishes had been put away, Hanna gave them coffee as they recounted all that had happened in Dolos.

"Is there something we could do about Blick and Scritch?" Tabitha asked. "If no one stops them, they're gonna keep hurting people, maybe even killing folks."

"You could make a police report," Hanna said.

After explaining the process, Tabitha used Hanna's phone to report Blick and Scritch's criminal activity to the Dolos police. The entire conversation was dissatisfyingly brief, and very little information was taken down. The officer on the other end of the phone said, "You're reporting a digital scammer?" After he'd stopped laughing, which took nearly a minute and a half, he gave Tabitha a speech that she didn't much care for. She gave him a speech explaining the kidnapping, attempted murder, and theft. Her tone transformed the remainder of the conversation into a terse exchange. He said they'd do what they could, and she hung up.

"You think they'll catch Blick?" Tabitha asked, handing the phone back to Hanna.

Milo shook his head. "No, probably not," He said. "Unlikely, they'll be able to lay hands on him since his crime is digital."

"But attempted murder with a deadly weaponized robot," Tobias said.

"I know," Milo agreed, "But it'd be hard to pin on him without any evidence." Milo put his hands behind his head and leaned back in the booth. "Here's the thing about guys like Blick," he said, his voice low and conspiratorial. "He's not what he appears to be. For all we know, he could be an Ai trained on a dataset of scam protocols."

"You mean he might not be a real person?" Tabitha asked. Her eyes widened at the thought. An Ai masquerading as a human?

"Did you ever touch him, or make any kind of physical contact?" Milo asked.

"Well," Tabitha said as she looked at her brother. They thought for a second and then concluded. "No, I guess we didn't." She put her hands on her head. "Do you mean he might a been just an Ai figment like them dragons, and teddy bears, and whatnot?"

"It's possible," Milo continued, "Could be why he wanted you to have AR contacts and earbuds before meeting you."

"It's insane," Tobias said.

"Or," Milo said. "He could be a thirteen-year-old kid with a remote avatar, running a bunch of Ai clusters from his mom's basement. The point is, we don't know. He's a ghost. Even if you caught him, there'd be a dozen more scam boys ready to take his place. I say, 'Thank the Lord for the lesson, and move on, twice as wise.'"

"In Isolation, we done been avoiding all that," Tobias said.

"And look where it got us," Tabitha said.

"Yeah, but still," Tobias said. I'd rather be trapped in a jackrabbit snare with just about any Isolationist than have to meet up with ole DigiFace and his weird Mom again." They laughed. "Especially since I pried his mom's head off with a rusty chair." They laughed harder. As the laughter died down, the gravity of the situation pulled the conversation closer to its center.

"It's just so hard to know what's real, who to trust, and what to believe," Tabitha said.

"I thought Soren Kreger was the real thing," Tobias said. "But thanks to this bubble popper, I have a different idea about him now." He nudged Hanna with his elbow.

"Sorry," she grimaced.

"We made him a perfect hero in our memory," Tobias said. "But that wasn't fair to him or us."

"They say never meet your heroes," Hanna said.

"I'm looking forward to meeting Jesus," Tabitha said.

"Me too, Sis," Tobias said. "I just don't understand how things got so dad gum messed up."

"Constantly having to use discernment is tiring," Hanna said. "And Isolation's founder thought he'd found a solution, but it just made it harder for the next generation when the inevitable came knocking."

"And boy, it done knocked hard," Tobias said.

"Discernment is a muscle, and it needs exercise, or it gets weak," Hanna added. "The first generation of Isolation thought they were solving the problem once and for all, but they were just running away from it. The elders talk a lot about how we should show the outside world harmless neglect, but there is no such thing as harmless neglect when it comes to fellow human beings. All neglect is malignant. Neglect is atrophy."

"I think I just realized why I like missionaries so much," Tabitha said. "Because we come from a place built on fear. Isolation is the opposite of missions. Soren Krieger's isolation doctrine is the opposite of reaching out. Deep down, I've always known there was something wrong with that. Missions is the solution. We're a community that prides ourselves on following the word of God, but we don't even follow Jesus' most basic command."

"And what's that?" Tobias asked.

"Go," Tabitha said, "*Go!* And make disciples of all nations. We don't do the *go* part, so how can we do the discipling?" The weight of the single word pressed on them all. "We're too busy dissecting and debating Soren's indictums to do what our Lord has told us to do." They considered her wisdom for a long few moments. Tabitha took the last sip of her coffee, draining the cup.

Tobias polished his pocket knife's well-worn blade and put it back in his pocket. "So now what?" Tobias said.

"Now, we have an entire generation of Isolationists growing up who aren't prepared for the world outside, but that world is crashing in fast," Tabitha said.

"I pray we're able to prepare them before it arrives," Hanna said.

"For a filthy leaver, you sure seem to like Isolation," Tobias said. The others laughed.

"I love Isolation," Hanna said. "I think Soren got it wrong on some things, but he built a place that I still consider home. I miss it a lot, but I'm out here because it's my calling. I want to affect the world, not hide from it, and I want to help Isolation do the same."

"That's beautiful," Tabitha said. The bell over the door rang, and all eyes went to the source of the sound.

"Mom!" Hanna said, rising from the booth. "I didn't expect you and Dad to..." She trailed off as her mother, Suzy Thompson, stepped fully into the light. She was covered in dust, and her eyes were rimmed with red. A blood stain ran down one of her arms, and her hair was in a mess. Hanna rushed to her. She looked like she was about to pass out. "Mom, what's wrong."

Suzy teetered dangerously as Tobias leaped out of the booth, steadied her, and helped her to the nearest chair with Hanna's assistance. Tabitha sped into the diner's kitchen and got a glass of water as Milo rose and awaited instructions. Hanna inspected her mom's arm and told Milo where the first aid kit was. The four attended to her for the next few minutes. When Suzy had downed three glasses of water, she was ready to speak.

"Isolation is at war," Suzy managed. Tabitha put her hand over her mouth, and Tobias went stiff. "They got your father, Honey. They're going to..." She trailed off in a wreck of tears and sobs.

"What do you mean they *got* Daddy?" Hanna said, kneeling down to catch the distraught eye line of her mother. "Do you mean he's—he's—dead?"

"No," Suzy said. "At least not when I left." She wiped her eyes. "It's Ram Stern. He found out that me and your Dad have been making trips here to Edgetown to see you. At the council meeting, he called for an..." She sobbed bitterly.

"What?" Hanna begged. Her mother couldn't complete the sentence as she cried.

"Execution?" Tobias asked. Suzy nodded. Tobias flexed as Tabitha flopped down into the nearest booth. Her legs didn't have their usual stability.

"They're going to kill him?" Tabitha whispered.

"Silas Granger and some others tried to stop him, but Ram had already raided the armory," Suzy said. "There was so much blood." She sobbed again. "We ran to Randy's picture shop and hid there. Ram found us. Your dad shoved me into the dark room before he saw me. When it got quiet, I snuck out the back. I didn't know what else to do, so I came here." She cried uncontrollably now. Through her sorrow, she said, "What are we going to do? They have your Daddy!"

"I'll go get him," Tobias said.

"I'll go too," Tabitha said. "But we have to hurry. Ram is ruthless. He won't wait."

"Mom," Hanna said. "We don't have much time. Where do they have Daddy?"

"Main Street," Suzy said. "In front of the council house. I—I should come too."

"No, Mom. You're dehydrated, exhausted, and in shock. You need to rest. Stay here," Hanna said. "Lock the door after we go. We'll be back as soon as we can."

"But—" Suzy tried to protest. Hanna was already in motion. She hugged her mom as the others moved toward the door.

"Love you, Mom," she said. "It's going to be ok."

They exploded from the front of the diner as a single unit. Hanna began punching the coordinates into the screen when they got to the truck. Tobias climbed into the passenger side and held the door open for Tabitha. She put a hand on Milo's chest before he could get in.

"Milo," Tabitha said. "This is going to be dangerous. If they catch you in Isolation, they'll—"

"Give me a welcome reception?" Milo said.

"It's too dangerous," Tabitha argued.

"Then call the police," Milo countered.

"Can't," Tobias interjected. "It's Ram Stern. He'd execute everyone as soon as he saw outsiders coming, then fight to the death before being taken alive. It'd make things much worse."

"Plus, the police wouldn't be there until next month," Hanna said. "If ever."

"Please," Tabitha pleaded. "I don't want you to get hurt."

"Listen," Milo said. "My life is boring. I play video games and go to school. Until I met you, I didn't know there was anything worth an ounce of real risk. But now, it's all different. Whether for good or bad, I'm with you no matter what comes."

She stared at him for a few seconds, stunned, amazed, overawed. Her heart was flopping like a flounder in her chest. *What did he just say?* Was it possible that this perfect boy was confessing his—but no! She couldn't risk his life too. She pushed him back with more force. They would kill him if they knew he'd come to Isolation.

"Guys," she said, turning to the others. "Help me here. It's too dangerous to involve Milo." Hanna pulled her door shut and made the final selection on the truck's nav screen.

"We could use the help," Tobias said.

"Agreed," Hanna said. "But we leave now. In or out."

Milo virtually leaped into the truck cab and pulled his door closed with a thud. Tabitha had no power to stop him from joining, but despite her effort to dissuade him, she felt a warm relief with him present. She leaned into his side as the truck scorched a trail into the desert. She let the bumps nestle her ever closer to his position. How could such joy and terror live together in one heart at one moment? She reached for Milo's hand, closed her eyes, and started to pray.

Presence

After thirty minutes of speed, the truck slowed. The moon-rimmed shapes that rose from the desert horizon let them know they were nearing the outskirts of Isolation. A heavy silence fell over the group. In the distance, the faint firelight glow flickered through Isolation's entrance. The fencing around the city stretched out in both directions, an odd sight for one who'd never been locked out.

"The Gates are shut?" Hanna asked.

"They never shut the gates," Tabitha said to Milo. "But why?" she wondered aloud.

"Trying to block leavers, I bet," Tobias muttered.

Tabitha leaned forward, her eyes wide as she studied the silhouettes of armed guards patrolling the area in the dim light. "Guards?" She gasped. "What's going on?"

"Is that Glenda Hensley?" Hanna asked.

"Yep, and Ansil Trapendorf," Tobias said. "What idiot would give those two sandbag heads a gun?"

"They have to have seen us," Tabitha said. "Turn off the lights and get off the road. That way."

Hanna hit a button on the screen and took the wheel for manual driving. The truck veered off the road and bounced violently. The four passengers grabbed for anything they could hang onto. Tabitha pointed the nose of the truck toward the northeast corner, where the crop fields met the town's outer wall.

"Over there. There's a break in the fence near the crop rows," Tobias said.

"How would you know that?" Hanna asked.

"Done caught all the jackrabbits inside the fences," Tobias said with a smirk. "Sometimes a hunter's got to go farther afield."

"You go outside the fences?" Tabitha asked. Tobias just shrugged and smiled.

The truck's tires crunched over the dry earth as they approached Isolation's outer fence. Tobias pointed them toward the spot. As they pulled to a stop near the break in the fence, the view outside was momentarily obscured by the dust cloud following them. When it cleared, Tabitha put a hand over the knot of dread that had settled in her stomach. Gripping the door handle, she met Milo's gaze, her eyes blazing with determination. "Milo, you should stay with the truck."

"Not a chance," he said. She wanted to argue it out, but they didn't have time. He put a hand on her shoulder and said, "I'm with you, good or bad." A tingling warmth drifted over her. She'd never been a boy-kissing type, but she thought she could get into it.

Tobias helped each of them duck under the break in the fence and followed them through. Rows of corn as tall as their heads butted up against the fence, and they disappeared into the green. They moved swiftly through the rows, the stalks rustling softly in the cool night breeze. Hanna's heart played a drum solo in her chest as they neared the edge of the field. She could hear the rhythmic thump of the oil derrick and the generator humming beyond. She smelled something acrid, hinting at sinister events.

Tobias halted suddenly, throwing out an arm to stop the others. "Wait..." he whispered, his brow furrowed as he strained to make out the sounds drifting through the crops.

Tabitha froze beside him, her fingers instinctively clutching the strap of her satchel where the *Overseer's Handbook* lay hidden. "What is it?" she murmured, her voice barely audible.

Tobias shook his head slowly, his eyes narrowing as the noises became clearer—the unmistakable cries of pain, the clashing of metal, the roar of flames. "Something ain't right." A crack split the air and echoed across the desert sand. "Gunshot!" Tobias whispered.

A tremor of fear rippled through Tabitha, but she swallowed hard, forcing herself to remain steady. "We got to keep moving." Tobias led them forward with a curt nod, his steps measured and cautious. They reached the edge of the field and passed quietly through the residential burrows. Once through, they snuck along the back of the downtown buildings and peeked around the corner, carefully keeping their profiles low.

The scene that met their eyes was one of utter chaos. The town square was engulfed in pandemonium; thick plumes of smoke now obscured the familiar buildings. Barricades formed a jagged perimeter around the council house, hastily constructed from overturned furniture, scrap wood, and broken detritus. Ichabod Shroot and Jep Strickland patrolled the perimeter of the barricade, clutching their weapons in their shaky grasp.

But it was the sight of the bodies scattered across the ground that made Tabitha's hands suddenly tingle and her mouth fall open. Old Horace Gumnut lay unmoving, his sightless eyes staring up at the smoke-choked sky, with a gash across his chest. A few paces away lay Judd Lumpkin face down in the dirt.

Tabitha's hand flew to her mouth, her eyes wide with horror. "Dear Lord, help us..." she whispered, her voice trembling. Acid rose to her throat and burned the back of her mouth. She recognized the bloodied face of Rudolph Hensley. He was huddled in the alley between two buildings. Stanton Saphronelly was lying on the sidewalk, taking big heaving breaths. Her gaze swept across the scene as another familiar figure came into view.

Elder Silas Granger lay on his side, clutching his abdomen, his black robe fanned out around him like a pool of fabric. His face was a mask of pain. Without a second thought, Tabitha turned to the others and began giving instructions.

"Tobias," she said. Check on Rudolf. If he's okay, have him help you drag Stanton out of the street. Hanna, check Horace and Judd. Me and Milo will try to get Silas to safety." They each nodded as Tabitha grabbed Milo's hand, took a deep breath, connected with a second of eye contact, nodded, and then rushed out into the open.

They spread to accomplish their tasks. Tabitha and Milo reached Silas, and both dropped to their knees beside him. Milo watched for danger as Tabitha made a hasty examination of Silas' wounds. She gingerly rolled him onto his back, her fingers searching for a pulse. Relief flooded through her as she felt the faint flutter against her fingertips.

"He's alive," she called out to Milo. "We need to drag him to a safer place, and then we need to see if we can find Dr. Kent."

The two prepared to move the man, with trembling hands, when a gunshot made their heads snap up. Amos Flint's gun was still smoking from his warning shot. Tabitha lurched backward as she found herself staring down the barrel of his rifle.

His face twisted into a snarl of hatred. "Don't move, you Krieger haters," he spat, his voice laced with venom. "Ichabod!" he hollard. "Round up them there, rebels." He pointed his gun toward Tobias and Hanna, who had dragged a wounded Stanton out of the street.

Captured

Tabitha froze, her hands still holding onto Silas' upper arm, her eyes locked on the gun pointed straight at her. She opened her mouth to speak, but Amos's voice cut through the charged air like a whip crack before she could utter a word. "Snap to it, pups!"

Hanna and Tobias joined them under the watchful pointing of Ichabod's gun. "Got to say," Milo said. "This is a much warmer welcome than I expected." The comment earned him a crack across the mouth with the butt of Amos' riffle.

"No," Tabitha shouted, rushing to him and touching his cheek near where the gun had split his lip. "You okay?"

"Good or bad, I'm with you," he said with a smirk. She could have lived a lifetime in the moment, but the cruel circumstances marched forward.

"Come on," Amos said. "Let's add you four to the chopping block."

With Amos and Ichabod at their backs, the four walked down the length of Main Street toward the council house, where the haphazard barricade encircled the entrance steps. Amos shoved them through a narrow path in the blockade, and they came face to face with Ram Stern, looking like a character from a VHS movie. A soldier's helmet topped his angular face, and he was dressed in green battle fatigues. An assault rifle was strapped over his shoulder. He looked thicker than usual, his sleeves torn from his shirt.

"Didn't expect to see these Krieger haters again," Ram said. He stepped toward Hanna. "Is it young Miss Thompson?" He grabbed Hanna's jaw in his meaty hand and squeezed. Hanna winced. Tobias lurched forward but found Amos' barrel at his temple and stilled. Ram pulled Hanna close. "It is Miss Thompson. A leaver returned. I got your daddy on the chopping block. We'll do a two-for-one deal." He snickered. "You picked a bad night to play the prodigal returned."

Ram then turned his attention to Milo and scowled. "I don't recognize this one. Who's boy is this?"

"You haven't met my parents," Milo said. "But if you get the chance, my dad would love to introduce his fist to your weird face."

"Am I to understand this young man is an outsider?" Ram said.

"I doubt *understanding* anything is your strong suit," Milo said. He was cut off by another strike across the chin, this time from Ichabod's fist. Tabitha screamed in protest. She felt hands grabbing her arms. Milo tumbled backward and plopped on the ground. When he came up to all fours, he said in a groggy voice, "I get it. You don't like back talk."

"If he says anything else," Ram said. "Shoot him." The comment quieted Milo. Ram turned his back, giving them no more notice. Tabitha rushed to where Milo was kneeling and tried to attend to his new wound. "Put them with the others," Ram said as he climbed the steps of the council building. Amos pulled Milo to his feet and shoved the others toward one end of the barricade.

Once at the top of the stairs, Ram raised his voice to speak to those who stood nearby, a bedraggled group of remainders that were less than a crowd but more than a cluster. His voice was like the roar of a chainsaw. "Brothers and sisters, today, we have taken a stand against the forces that threaten to unravel the very fabric of our society."

Ram's eyes swept over the scene, his lips curling into a triumphant sneer as he took in the wounded bodies strewn across the ground, some of which, no doubt, were dead. "Those who would seek to abandon our ways, to consort with the outsiders, have been dealt with accordingly." A cheer rose from the few who attended his night-time slaughter.

Tabitha's heart pounded in her ears as she followed Ram's gaze, her stomach lurching when she recognized more injured forms of friends and neighbors. Todd Fontez lay moaning upon the very blood-spattered steps where Ram stood. Jedediah Thorp sat injured against the wall behind him. Adjacent to Ram's place on the steps, kneeling amongst a group of prisoners, hands bound behind his back, was Hanna's father, Frank Thompson. Tabitha nudged Hanna and pointed.

"Daddy!" Hanna screamed. Tabitha put a hand on her friend's shoulder to steady her. Frank mouthed her name, showing a row of red-lined teeth.

Ram's voice cut through her turmoil, laced with a sickening glee. "And those who have aided and abetted the leavers, who have conspired against the sanctity of our way of life, will face the ultimate consequence."

With a dramatic flourish, Ram leveled his rifle at the kneeling prisoners, his finger caressing the trigger. "Starting with Frank Thompson, whose clandestine trips beyond our borders and support of Silas's heretical regime have marked him as a traitor to Isolation."

"Stop, Ram!" Tabitha's voice rang out, bold and unwavering, as she stepped forward into the smoky scene. All eyes turned toward Tabitha and her companions.

"Be quiet," Ram shouted.

"Or what?" Tabitha said. "You going to do me like you did my parents?"

"I said be quiet!" He leveled his rifle in Tabitha's face.

"We've been to the outside world, and yes, there is evil there," Tabitha said. "But what you're doing here is more evil than anything we saw outside of Isolation. You want us to be true to Soren's indictums, but by being so extreme, you are ignoring Jesus' commandments?" She stepped forward. "We are Christians first, Isolationists second. Our Lord saved us by grace and empowered us to love God and love one another. If the Isolation Doctrine disagrees with Jesus' commandment, then it's the Isolation Doctrine we have to abandon. You can do what you think is right, but I'm with Jesus, not Soren Krieger."

"You heard it from her own mouth," Ram shouted. "This girl would have us abandon the Isolation Doctrine. Our laws are clear."

"You are leading people into horrible sin," Tabitha said. "God is not pleased with this."

"Sin?" Ram said. "I'm not sinning. I'm saving." He waved his gun at the wounded who lay in the street. "These weaklings would have unity at any cost. I'm rescuing us from their evil."

"It's not right—"

"Be quiet," Ram boomed. "Here's something I bet you didn't know. Soren was going to name me his successor." He paused to puff out his chest. "He told me so personally. Unfortunately, he didn't make that public before his untimely death. Nonetheless, I am the rightful overseer of Isolation. This council of elders has become the most useless bungle of buffoons Isolation has ever seen."

"Soren's not—" Tabitha tried, but Ram fired a deafening shot over Tabitha's shoulder.

"Be quiet, or I will silence you for good," Ram said. "I've had enough of this. I'm the overseer now. That's that."

"Technically," Tobias said. "You're not."

"Oh, the mute has something to add?" he said. He raised his rifle, pointed it at Tobias' chest, and pulled the trigger. They all jumped, but all that happened was the anticlimactic sound of a firing pin clicking. Ram turned the gun sideways, pulled the slide, and looked into the chamber. "I'm out of ammo," he said. "Someone hand me a clip." He started to reload as Tobias spoke.

"Soren Krieger's operational governance model is spelled out in his personal letters," Tobias explained. "In letter four, paragraph six, he says, 'the synod of governance shall be passed upon a dually affirmed vote of the assembled chamber to the successor of the position of overseer, when and if the current eldership deems it necessary." He paused. "Ain't nobody voted for you, so you ain't the overseer."

"Don't quote the letters to me, boy," Ram said. "I was his closest advisor and friend. He chose me as his successor." He had his gun reloaded and ready. He pulled back the firing pin and chambered a round. "Okay, it's time." He leveled his gun and was about to pull the trigger.

A sudden ringing sound split the eerie silence. "What is that?" Ram asked.

"Oh, sorry," Milo said. He pulled a phone from his pocket and tapped the screen. "Sorry, it was an alarm to take out the trash."

"Digital Technology!" Ram roared. "You brought digital technology to Isolation. You've defiled the entire community!" Ram stomped his foot and cursed. "Which of you idiots didn't search the prisoners?"

"Well," Kelvin Jester said. "None of us did, so I guess all of us didn't search them."

"Search them," he bellowed.

Kelvin Jester's violent hands patted them down and removed a phone from Hanna's jacket. Ichabod retrieved a knife from Tobias' pocket. Amos found *The Overseer's Handbook* in Tabitha's bag and collected five digital devices from Milo's person. Kelvin turned the items over to Ram as Ichabod Shroot held them at gunpoint.

"Treacherous vipers," Ram grunted, his eyes alight with triumph as he seized the handbook. "Not only have you consorted with outsiders and brought this..." he wagged an aggressive finger at Milo. "This demon into our sacred haven, but you have stolen the very lifeblood of our community, *The Overseer's Handbook.*"

Tabitha lifted her chin defiantly, her voice steady despite the tremoring fear. "We've learned the truth about you, Ram."

"The truth!" Ram said.

"Ram Stern murdered our parents!" Tabitha said to the crowd. She expected this to be a revelation, to warrant some surprise or dynamic response.

"Your parents died in an accidental fire in your father's printshop," Ram said. "Everyone knows that."

"He also tried to murder the founder, Soren Krieger, but failed," Tabitha said as she studied the faces of those who watched.

Ram's expression contorted with rage. "The lies of an impetulant child. You twins have been a burden on the town ever since the accident. Your parents died in the same fire that took the life of Soren Krieger. But remind me, where were you as your parents burned to death." He put a finger to his ear.

"I can't hear you," he said. "You were in your beds asleep." Ram spun and stepped up the stairs to catch the light. "But who was it that discovered the fire? Who was it who went screaming for help to save our beloved founder, Soren Krieger?"

"It was you," Amos Flint said.

"That's right," Ram said. Ram put his hand across his rifle, and his face took on a distant concern. "I fear the stress of losing your parents has finally addled your mind."

"No," Tabitha said. "Soren told us himself." There were expressions of shock from the gathering.

"Soren came back from the dead and spoke to you?" Ram said, giving a bitter laugh.

"No," Tabitha said. "He—"

"So, you were consorting with the dead?" Ram said. "You believe in witchcraft!" Those standing around murmured.

"No," Tabitha tried. "We saw him in Dolos and—"

"Oh, I see," Ram said. "You were in Dolos." He smiled. "Tell me, in your time in the city, did you hear anyone speak of the first rule of the digiverse? It's a colloquialism, a kind of idiom. Certainly, someone must have told you."

"Yes," Tabitha said. "But that's not—"

"I'll tell you the first rule of the world outside," Ram said. "Assume nothing is real. Did I get that right?"

"Yes, but—" Tabitha tried.

"So, in the place where the first rule is to disbelieve everything you see or hear, you believe you saw our founder, Soren Krieger, who has been dead for more than ten years? Fascinating."

"No," Tabitha said. "Or yes, but—when you say it like that, of course, it sounds—well, it was real."

"The reality is," Ram said as a chorus of snickers filled the hallow air. "You have all committed acts of sedition and treason against our society. Harboring leavers..." His eyes bored into Tabitha's. "Consorting with outsiders. Possessing forbidden technology and stealing from Isolation."

Ram curled his lip in contempt. He barked out a harsh laugh. "There can be no peace with those who seek to corrupt and destroy us from within." His stare swept over the gathered prisoners with undisguised loathing. "You have betrayed Isolation; you are guilty of the worst crimes against our community, and you must pay."

Hanna reached for her father's shoulder. His cuffed hands kept him from rising. Tobias put his hands on Tabitha's back, and Tabitha reached for Milo's hand. In that moment, surrounded by the chaos and bloodshed wrought by Ram's hatred, Tabitha found a strange sense of calm. She had pursued her path with open eyes and an open heart, and though it had led her here, she knew she would walk that road again without hesitation.

As Ram's finger tightened on the trigger, Tabitha met his gaze unflinchingly, her voice a whisper that carried the weight of her loss and love and longing. She turned away from the gun and looked full in Milo's face. His eyes were calm, his gaze a beam of warmth. "I'm sorry," she whispered.

"For good or bad," Milo said. "I'm with you."

She closed her eyes and spoke even more softly. "Lord, receive us into your presence."

Sacrifice

The cold steel of the rifle barrel pressed against the back of Tabitha's head, and her ribs ached with the wild beats of her heart. She kept her eyes closed, bracing for the end. The blast of gunpowder didn't come. The explosion didn't sound. She felt the gravity shift. A collective gasp rippled through those who were gathered there.

"Look!" someone in the crowd yelled.

Tabitha's eyes flew open. At the edge of town, a lone figure approached, cloaked in the familiar black robe of a town elder. He walked like a specter, wrapped in shadows and halloed by the orange flicker of burning fires that lined the street. He came near the barricade, paused briefly, and squeezed through the narrow path through the debris. The gun barrels were all pointed at him by the time he neared the stairs. The few who stood around parted as the figure glided forward, an eerie silence descending upon Isolation's main square.

Tobias grabbed Tabitha's arm. "Is that...?" he whispered, his voice trailing off.

Tabitha couldn't speak, her throat constricted. She watched, transfixed, as the figure moved closer, its face hidden beneath a deep hood.

The stranger stopped mere feet away from Tabitha and Tobias. With deliberate slowness, thin hands reached up and pulled back the hood. Gasps and murmurs sounded from the gathered townspeople. Tabitha's eyes widened in disbelief, but a smile crossed her face.

"He came," she breathed.

The aged face of Soren Krieger, Isolation's founder, the first overseer, gazed upon them all. His piercing eyes, sharp and clear, scanned the crowd before settling on Tabitha.

"You're supposed to be dead!" Ram's gruff voice cut through the shocked silence.

"And you're supposed to be a shepherd," Soren said, "But the Ram has slaughtered the sheep, and I'm ashamed to say, only after I abandoned them."

As Soren spoke, the guns trained on her, and Tobias lowered, their wielders too stunned to maintain their threat. Amos Flint's mouth hung open like a cash register drawer. Ichabod Shroot let the tip of his gun barrel sink into the dirt.

"Soren, where have you been?" Ichabod asked.

"We thought you were dead!" Kelvin Jester said.

"And who told you that?" Soren said. The eyes of those gathered nearby turned to Ram.

"If you were alive all this time, why have you stayed away so long?" Amos Flint asked.

"Why have you come back now?" Dodson Spenser questioned from the edge of the group.

"Have you come back from the dead?" Talula Avis hollered from her hiding place in a nearby storefront. She and three others stepped out across the broken glass. People began coming out of hiding, drawn out by the familiar voice and the hush of those gathered around. The crowd swelled. They pressed in to see the man, whom they all thought was long dead. They laid hands on him to verify that he was real. The crowd spoke in hushed whispers, asking questions of the legend. There were sobs at seeing him swelling from all around. The sound of a happy reunion filled the air. Ram's followers put down their guns, and hugs took their place. But one gun remained perched in thick, white-knuckled hands.

Soren's eyes drifted across the square. "My children," he said, his voice carrying a weight that seemed to settle over them all, "Isolation stands at a crossroads. And I fear the path you've chosen leads only to ruin. I've returned to bring warning and encouragement. I will only be with you for a short time." A gasp rippled about the crowd.

Soren's deep, resonant voice carried across the town square, his words cutting through the tension. "My beloved," he continued, his hands outstretched, "I see the fear in your eyes, the weapons you have just laid down. Let them lay and never be lifted again. For in the snare of violent delights awaits the vicissitudes of destruction."

He pointed to Frank Thompson, "Please unhand these friends. We treat one another this way at the deplorable peril of us all. If we devour, we will be consumed."

Tabitha was amazed at his presence, ability to connect, and eerie confidence. She remembered his charisma from when she was young, but the timbre was different now. Seen through the lens of outside experience, the blinders were gone. She felt foreboding at his tone. It wasn't the words but the clamber they caused. His talent was undeniable, but so was his ability to gain adoration and praise. He had returned, but had he changed? He had never been their savior, but the people couldn't see the truth. They skittered toward the familiar, the leader they thought they knew, the one they believed they needed. She saw the tendrils of manipulation coiling around the hearts and minds of those who encircled him, even, dare she think it, worshiped him. She glanced at her brother, who Soren no longer bewitched, but what would this mean for the others falling beneath his odd magic? What was he playing at?

"I founded Isolation as a haven," Soren continued, "a place where we could live in harmony with one another, free from the corruption of the outside world. But look at us now. Brother turning against brother, neighbor against neighbor, sister against sister. Is this what we've become?" A murmur rippled through the crowd. Tabitha noticed several people shifting uncomfortably.

"We don't need these," Soren said, gesturing to the guns around his feet. "Let us talk as equals, as the community we once were. We once were a voice in the desert, singing a grand, hopeful chorus, but now only a dirge is heard in these dusty streets. Let us not turn to wails of mourning and cries of horror."

A harsh, low laugh cut through the air. Everyone jumped at the start. "Talk? That's your solution?" Ram's voice exploded with venom as he pushed his way down the stairs to the front, his gun still clutched tightly in his hand. "You abandoned us. You are worse than dead. You are a leaver."

Ram raised his gun, aiming it directly at Soren's chest. Tabitha's body moved before her mind could catch up. "No!" she cried, lunging forward. Beside her, Tobias sprang into action, his lean frame a blur as they both moved to shield Soren. In that rushing moment, she understood what her father had done. Soren was a coward, an absentee leader, and even a selfish monster. But with all his flaws and mistakes, he was family. He, like them all, bore the image of God. They could not stand by and watch him be slaughtered. They would do the same for anyone standing there, even their greatest enemy.

"No, my children!" Soren said, putting a hand on them both and shoving them back.

"But—" Tabitha tried.

"Get behind me," Soren commanded. She and her brother could do nothing but obey. He leaned in and whispered, "I have a plan, and it doesn't include you two paying for what I've done. Your parents would be proud of the heroes you've become."

Tabitha drew a sharp breath, and Tobias pulled back, stunned at his words. Soren spun from them and took a step forward. His hands raised placatingly. "Ram, please. Let us talk as we once did. I know you're angry, but—"

"Angry?" Ram spat, his face contorted with rage. "You have no idea what I am!" His knuckles whitened as he gripped the gun tighter and jabbed Soren in the chest with the barrel. Ram's maniacal laugh was sharp and bitter. "You're not real! You're a digiverse deep fake sent to manipulate us. It's all a scam!"

Murmurs rippled through the assembled Isolationists.

"Uh," Milo spoke up. "He's human. I checked him earlier."

"Lies!" Ram shouted. The crowd parted as he sliced with his assault rifle and brought the barrel back to bear on Soren.

"No, Ram, I assure you—" Soren began, but his words were cut short by the deafening crack of a gunshot. The smell of gunpowder accompanied the thunder and a high ringing that followed. The crowd lurched. Time slowed as Tabitha watched Soren's eyes widen in shock. He stumbled backward, a red stain blossoming around a gaping hole in his robed chest. As he crumpled to the ground, the hands of a dozen Isolationists reached out to catch the falling founder.

"No!" she screamed, her voice barely audible over the sudden uproar from the crowd.

Tobias knelt over Soren and felt for a pulse. A horrid gash in his chest made the gesture superfluous, and a moment later, his words confirmed it. "He's dead. The founder is dead. Soren Krieger is dead."

The crowd watched for a long time, only breaths sounding in the dusted quiet.

"He killed the founder!" Kelvin Jester said.

"Ram Stern killed the founder!" Amos Flint echoed. The news rippled across the observers who were gathered there. Renold Kent, then Lenny Stubbings, and Randy Sherbert echoed the astounding words, "Ram Stern killed Soren Krieger."

The crowd turned like a pack of wild dogs on Ram, who now held his gun even more tightly. He leveled his barrel at those who stood around and brandished it with a threatening battle cry. "Stay back." He released a shot that caught Randy Sherbert in the leg. Another went high as Dereck Sanders and Lenny Stubbings grabbed the riffle and tore it from his grasp.

"You killed Soren Krieger," Gracie Delitaunt cried from the back of the spectators.

Tabitha watched in stunned disbelief as the crowd surged forward, their long-simmering frustrations finally boiling over. Ram, with his face splattered with shock at the sudden turn of events, was overwhelmed by the people he had cruelly coveted rulership over. He went down under a torrent of fists and feet. Ram fell backward with a shout onto the blood-stained ground.

"We have to do something," Tabitha said as blows rained on Ram from the wild mob. Tobias nodded and waded into the fray with his sister in his wake.

"Stop!" Tabitha screamed as Tobias pulled the people off of Ram one by one. He shoved Amos Flint and Kelvin Jester back as Tabitha shouted. "Ram has a right to a fair trial before the elders. Let there be no more bloodshed tonight. There are plenty of wounded that need our attention now."

Twice more, they had to quell the rage directed at Ram, but with each pass, they were able to shield the despot from the mob's fury and redirect their attention to the wounded. With her words ringing in their ears, the crowd finally looked out at the carnage the battle had wrought. After securing Ram in the handcuffs that had previously held Frank Thompson, they turned their attention to the injured and bleeding. They spent the remainder of the night attending to those who needed medical attention.

Ram shouted horrible things as the townsfolk helped the wounded, but in the cruelest twist, he got what he had always feared most: in mere moments, he was irrelevant, ignored, and a common criminal, a prisoner of his own hateful deeds. He screamed for his former followers to come to his aid, but they were cowards and were rounded up by the others who now had picked up their guns.

When the wounded were cared for, Lenny Stubbings and Dereck Sanders led the other townsmen in securing a suitable jail cell for Ram and his followers. Lenny's tool shed was eventually selected, and after the dangerous implements were removed, the human contents were shoved inside and locked from the outside.

A few hours later, Tabitha and Milo made a tearful goodbye, promising to see each other again soon. Tabitha cried as the truck pulled out of town with Milo and Hanna inside. Hanna made the round trip to return Milo to Dolos, reunite her mom and dad, and bring them back safely to Isolation. Tabitha and Tobias finally made it to their beds as the sun was coming up. Their dreamless sleep was deep and lasted into the next afternoon. When Tabitha awoke, she could feel that everything had changed, but the change marked a beginning, not an end. In the days that followed, she began to make a plan to shape the change that had been forced upon her home.

Change

Elder Silas Granger was injured in Ram Stern's attempted takeover but recovered and just about had to wrestle his way past Dr. Kent to escape his sick bed. The twins were relieved that *The Overseer's Handbook* was finally in the elders' posession again. Neither Tobias nor Tabitha ever told anyone how the first few pages, containing the original Isolation Doctrine, had gone missing. Tabitha recollected the strange incidents that led up to its recovery, and Elder Silas seemed less surprised than they thought he ought to be. A few days after that, Silas showed them a new entry in the back of *The Overseer's Handbook* they hadn't noticed before. Soren Krieger had written his eyewitness testimony of the printshop fire and Ram's murderous acts against their parents, signed and dated it.

With the signed confession of their founder and the witness testimony of at least two dozen townspeople of his more recent crimes, Elder Silas Granger led the effort to have Ram Stern turned over to the county sheriff on multiple charges of murder. Grand arguments raged, as the Isolationists knew the deed would require detectives from the outside to come to town and investigate. Jed

Thorton was so hot about it that he'd spit every time the word *detective* was mentioned. Linda Saphronelly said he'd need to make an appointment with Dr. Kent for a terrible case of dry mouth if folks kept talking about it. Randy Sherbert made the most compelling argument, pointing out, "If the Sherriff don't get involved, all a Isolation'll be accessory to murder if t'were ever found out." Despite the saliva expended, the remaining elders sided with Randy and dispatched Tabitha and Tobias to Edgetown to file the report. A swarm of officers descended upon the town. In the process, two other Isolationists were charged with various crimes, Amos Flint and Ichabod Shroot. They were transferred from the makeshift jail in Lenny Stubbings tool shed to the Sheriff's cruiser. They drove off, and were gossiped about for ages to come. It took quite some time for the general mood of the town to move away from the notion that Ram Stern might pop out from behind some building or other with a machine gun. He never did.

After the dead were burned, the clean-up began. It took months to repair the destruction that Ram Stern had brought, with a few noted improvements. The burnt ruin of the printshop was torn down, and the ground prepared for new construction, yet to be announced by the town council.

As a final celebration of the restoration of their hometown, Kelvin Jester's abandoned '79 Chevette, which had been taking up road space for years, was finally dragged out of city limits. All the town's kids were given hammers, and they put a whoop on it so mighty that the sound could probably be heard all the way to Edgetown. After the car was thoroughly abused, Ferris Daudry and Hangus Lithrum grilled up some meat, and the town celebrated.

The Ram Incident, as it came to be known, had more lasting effects on the town than Tabitha or her brother could have ever dreamed. A council meeting was eventually called to give the changes an official ceremony.

The murmur of voices echoed through the council hall as Tabitha took her seat between Tobias and Hanna on one side and Milo on the other. Pattering, rhythmic energy emanated from her heart as the session's start was drawing near. Months of discussion and negotiation with the town's leaders had led to this moment. She felt like she had swallowed an apple whole, but it hadn't gotten past her throat. Warm sunlight streamed through the high windows, casting an amber glow on the weathered wooden benches. At the front of the room, the elders sat in a row, chatting.

Ram Stern's previous seat, along with Amos Flint's and Ichabod Shroot's, had been vacant for nearly six months, long enough to be filled by a handful of individuals who weren't nearly as murderous. One of the brightest faces in the line of new elders was Frank Thompson, Hanna's father. Randy Sherbert and Dereck Sanders filled the other two. Silas Granger rose and approached the podium, still slowed by the persistent limp Ram had left him with.

His gray beard and kind eyes were a familiar and welcome sight. He cleared his throat, and the room fell silent.

"Friends," Silas began, his voice resonating through the hall, "we have gathered here today to relay the results of months of discussions and negotiations."

A murmur rippled through the crowd, and Tabitha felt Tobias tense beside her. She reached for his hand and gave it a reassuring squeeze. "Hanna Thompson, please come forward."

Hanna rose from her seat, her blonde hair cascading down her back as she made her way to the podium. Tabitha watched with joy, her eyes darting between Hanna and Elder Thompson, her proud dad.

"Hanna," Silas began, his voice filled with warmth, "you have proven yourself a loyal friend to our community, even after your departure. Your understanding of both our ways and the outside world makes you uniquely suited for a new role."

He paused, letting his words sink in. "We would like to offer you the appointment of *Ambassador to the Isolationist Diaspora*. In this role, you would be our chief liaison with the leavers who have ventured beyond our borders. You would be granted access and status within our community, allowing you to communicate with the leavers on behalf of their families and relay messages back to us. You are free to come and go as you please." A silence drowned the room for a few moments. "Do you accept this appointment?"

"I accept," Hanna said. A burst of applause erupted. She waited for the sound to die. "Thank you. I will do my best to build the community." More applause engulfed the room. The word had already spread, mostly through the skill set of Linda Saphronelly and Lavender Delitaunt, that a leaver, none other than Mr. Thompson's daughter Hanna, had helped in the fight for Isolation, and the goodwill she'd gained paved the way for such a monumental moment as was being applauded in the council hall.

"Tobias Andrews," Silas called out, his gaze shifting to Tabitha's brother. "Please join us at the podium." When Tobias was in front of the room, Silas said, "I understand you have something to tell us." He took a deep breath and looked down at a small piece of paper that had been absolutely abused in his nervous keep. He read from the crumpled scrap.

"Thank you, Elder Silas and members of the council," Tobias began, his voice a little shaky. His reading was slow and thick. "I stand before you today to acknowledge that I am becoming a leaver. I've made the decision to explore the world beyond our borders, to learn and grow in ways that I cannot within the confines of our community. I will continue in my loyalty to Isolation. I humbly request permission to remain a friend of Isolation whether I am here or abroad. I am prepared to take the leaver's oath."

A murmur rippled through the crowd, and Tabitha felt her heart clench. Hearing him read the words she'd helped craft and her prior knowledge of the moment did not lighten the statement's weight.

Silas raised a hand, silencing the room. "In the past, we insisted those who abandoned the community take the leaver's oath. But times change, as do hearts. The term 'leaver' is old and outdated," he declared, his voice filled with conviction. "By unanimous order of this council, from this day forward, we shall refer to those who venture beyond our borders as the Brotherhood Abroad. They are no longer barred from reentering our community at will, for they carry our shared experience and our love with them wherever they go." Silas leaned forward. "Tobias Garret Andrews. Between Isolationists, no Isolation shall exist." The crowd repeated the often practiced phrase in unison. Silas continued, "You have our blessing and our friendship wherever you lay your head."

The crowd erupted in cheers. Tobias grinned and waited for the sound to diminish. When it did, he said, "I ain't going nowhere but Edgetown, so don't make such a meal of it, everybody." Laughter rippled through the room. Tabitha already knew that remark would give Lavender Delitaunt gossip fodder for months.

Silas called Tabitha's name, his voice echoing through the noisy town hall. She stepped forward, feeling the weight of the elder's gaze upon her as she approached the podium.

"Tabitha Andrews," Silas began, his eyes twinkling with mischief. "We have considered your request. We have deliberated over it for nearly three months now. You have stretched our thinking on a great many things." A long pause followed, during which the gambit of possibilities poured through her head like hot magma.

"After great consideration, we have decided to approve your request to go on Isolation's first short-term mission trip to the outside world," Silas continued, his voice rising with excitement, "And you, Tabitha, will be our first official Isolationist missionary. You have encouraged us to look past our differences with the outside world so that we can carry the gospel of Christ to them. With the help of Hanna Thompson, we commission you to begin building your team of locals and training them for the gospel mission to take place this summer after the conclusion of the school year."

Tabitha pumped her fist and said, "Yes!" She bounced as she looked at those around her. Tobias gave her a hug, and Hanna did the same.

"And on a personal note," Silas said. The room quieted. "I would like to apply to be on the short-term mission team if my advanced age doesn't disqualify me." The elder smiled and put his hands together. "I'm very excited about what we have ahead of us. We are breaking new ground, and I believe we have a bright future." The celebration resumed, and she was swept up in the frivolity.

"One last piece of business," Silas said in a commanding voice. As the room quieted, Silas gestured in Milo's direction. "Milo Wynters, please join Tabitha at the podium." Milo rose and moved toward the lectern with a confidence that Tabitha wished she could mimic. "Milo and Tabitha, you two already know about this because we've been talking for months, but why don't you tell everyone about the plan we just approved."

Tabitha turned to the crowd gathered in the council house. "Hey, Everyone," she said. "I—Uh—I'm a little nervous." Milo put his hand on her shoulder. Like electric courage, his warmth flowed into her. She glanced at him for a brief second before turning back to the crowd.

"Sorry, Okay," she said. "We are starting a school for digital studies."

There was a mild gasp from the crowd. Tabitha looked down at the lectern, almost losing her nerve. She took a deep, long breath and then set her eyes to roam across the crowd, which was stone-faced. "I know this is hard to hear, but it is so important. Our recent experience has shown us that we are woefully unprepared for what's out there. As some of you know, this school for digital studies was a dream of my parents, who died trying to protect our founder, Soren Krieger.

"Of course, we don't want anyone to leave Isolation because we're one big family, but for those who choose to leave, we must prepare them. Unfortunately, no one from Isolation is qualified to teach such a course of study. So, the elders have permitted a visiting teacher from the outside."

She gestured to Milo. He smiled and nodded his head slightly. "This is our good friend Milo Wynters, who rescued us when we needed help in Dolos. He also helped the wounded after the Ram Incident. He is a tech expert and has agreed to help our people prepare for what awaits them on the outside.

"Anyone who wishes to join the short-term mission trip team..." She spun and made eye contact with Elder Silas Granger. He smiled back. "Will need to take Milo's course. We look forward to where God leads us in this new endeavor."

Applause rose once more at the astounding announcement. Elder Silas Granger stood and addressed the cheering crowd. "We can finally announce the reconstruction plan for the Andrew's Printshop that burned down ten years ago. We will be starting on the construction for the '*Gad and Belemie Andrews School For Digital Studies*' on the same ground where they gave their lives to protect our founder, Soren Krieger. It will be built and operated in memory of its visionaries, our beloved Andrews, who will be made its honorary namesake in perpetuity."

The announcement was met with fervent whoops and hollers from a few key parties. Clapping persisted for a long few moments until Silas concluded the meeting with a gavel strike and called, "You're dismissed."

A tear streaked down Tabitha's cheek as applause rolled like desert rain from the meeting's attendees. A hand slapped her back. It was Jepp Strickland. Hangus Lithrum gave her a nod from behind Jepp. Luanne Spencer mouthed something encouraging to her from across the room. Hanna's arms were around Tabitha before she realized what was happening, and Tobias wrapped them both in a broad hug.

As the meeting concluded, the crowd moved outside. Long conversations with breathless excitement followed the official gathering. She had requests from Dereck Sanders, Reverend Tucker, and Eldra Parker to join the mission team. Milo wrote down their names and told them about what they would learn in his courses.

A dozen others said they wanted to hear more about it. The crowd slowly dispersed as the afternoon stretched toward evening until only Tabitha, Milo, Tobias, and Hanna remained. Mariah Grimes was the last to leave the steps of the council house, talking about how she knew all along that Isolation needed something like this. As she shuffled off, Tabitha let out a long sigh. How could such tiredness follow such heights of intensity?

"Well, I think we're gonna head out, Sis," Tobias said. She looked over to find Hanna and her brother sitting on the steps of the council house, holding hands.

"Thanks for waiting," Tabitha said. "I thought Mariah would never wrap it up."

They chatted a moment about their plans to see one another soon, and Tabitha felt them moving inextricably toward Hanna's truck.

"It's weird," Tobias called out, a smirk playing at the corners of his mouth. "I'm gonna be a *leaver*, and that ain't nothing unheard of, but Milo, I think you're the first to be a *stayer*."

"He's always been a stayer, good or bad," Tabitha said as she turned toward Milo. "Hope you like living underground with Old Landry Grady. We could hear him snore from three burrows over."

"It's only until the school year is out. Anything can be endured for a few months," Milo said. "But I'm concerned for the jackrabbit population of Edgetown, with such a rabbit trapper as your brother moving in." He slapped Tobias on the shoulder as they laughed.

They all hugged, locking in a long, meaningful embrace. Tobias kissed his sister on the head. "I'm real proud of you, Sis. You done good."

"Hey, Tobias," she said. "You still haven't apologized for putting *The Overseer's Handbook* in my bag."

"Oh, what's that, Hanna," Tobias pretended, putting his hand to his ear. "Time to go? Sorry, Sis, I have to be getting on the road now. No time to waste."

She pulled off her hat and hit him with it. "You old rattlesnake."

He hugged her again, and in her ear, he said, "Things that's meant to be, don't need no apologies. If we didn't get that book stolen, we'd still be right back where we was. Now look at us."

"Yeah, God used it for sure."

"For sure."

They hugged once more and said their goodbyes, knowing their separation would be hard but temporary. "I'll see you soon," Tabitha said as her brother and Hanna climbed into the truck.

The tires kicked up a cloud of dust as Tabitha stood transfixed. The truck's taillights faded into the fiery orange horizon. The world beyond the Isolationist community beckoned, vast and unknown, brimming with possibilities and challenges alike. Soon, she would face that adventure, and she couldn't wait.

She felt Milo's strong hand intertwine with hers. "Come on, I'll show you where you're staying." She led him through the town, chattering about nothing and everything at the same time. As the sun set across the desert sand, her heart felt the unexpected sensation of being home for the first time in years.

Author's Note

Our world is changing fast. I was an '80s and '90s kid, so my decades' progeny have watched as the world went from vinyl to cassettes, then CDs to streaming. From the Nintendo to the Switch, snail mail to Zoom, and the television to the Vision Pro. Everything is growing more immersive. I won't be surprised if tomorrow's media is beamed directly into your brain case. I think Elon Musk is already working on that, right? Now, we are in the age of Ai on the edge of the next phase, which will be humanoid robots, decision-making software, self-driving air taxis, and much more.

These "advancements" weave together into a vision of the future that is both fascinating and frightening. These digital tools offer some intriguing enhancements to modern life but also some extreme dangers. Leading minds on the subject say that Ai is as dangerous as nuclear bombs. That might be in part because, at some point, the nuclear bombs are going to be controlled by Ais... if they're not already.

There are tremendous personal dangers as well. The risk goes way beyond deepfake scams, personality theft, digital impersonation, and fraud into the territory of unimaginable digital crimes. These are not fiction but already a growing reality.

As I developed this book, I was trying to imagine what the future might be like. It dawned on me that most scams in the world of tomorrow will be perpetrated by criminals or Ais pretending to be someone you trust.

Imagine your mother FaceTime calls you and asks you to transfer money to her account. She is stranded, and her credit card won't work. She gives you the details, and you do it without any skepticism. Now, imagine how you'll feel when you realize that it wasn't your mother but instead a real-time deepfake video scammer. Imagine you get as many of these family-faked FaceTime calls as you currently get spammy telemarketers. Could you ever trust a call from your mother again? In fact, could you ever trust anyone?

So, what might this constant scam environment cause society to do? There will likely be at least some who completely pull out and become digital teetotalers or Isolationists. It made me think about the Amish. They paused progress and intentionally froze their "technology" at what was available in the late 1800s. As the development of this book rose, I imagined a new kind of Amish whose technology was that of the late 1900s. This would be an analog community with basic pre-digital tech.

As I wrote the book, a theme started to pop out. At first, I had thought that the Isolationists were right to isolate. I imagined it from their point of view. They wanted to escape the filth, chaos, and horrifying effects the world was blanketed in, so why not disconnect? But as Tabitha and Tobias worked their way through the digitized world, I started to feel a different theme arising: one of compassion for the population of the darkened and dying digiverse. They came to recognize, as I did, that the world was not their enemy; their fear of it was.

One more aspect happened late in the writing of this book. I've become infatuated with missionary biographies. A few years ago, I was writing a book called Missionary to Mars and knew I needed to study missions. I began a bit begrudgingly, thinking it was going to be boring. Boy, was I wrong!

Don Richardson's books were my gateway read, but then Brother Andrew, Stan Dale, Jim Elliot, John Paton, and Brother Yun came into my interest sphere. As I wrestled with the concept of isolation, this idea exploded in my mind. Missionaries are *THE* main reason we can't isolate ourselves from the world. If Christians isolate and refuse to be part of the world, then we would have no missionaries.

Missionaries have done tremendous good for society. Of course, evangelism and discipleship are grand works. Still, beyond that, Christian missionaries were instrumental in the abolition of slavery, development of modern education, healthcare, human rights, translation of worldwide languages, agricultural development, and even cultural preservation. All of this is only a part of what missionaries do. Missionaries have played a huge role in these areas.

In many cases, their friends and family told them to stay home, focus on local needs, and not go across the world on mission. I'm so thankful that they ignored that fear-based advice. God laid these huge missions on the hearts of people willing to go and sometimes die. Our world is better for it, and the kingdom of God will be more full because of them. I'm sounding a bit like Tabitha, aren't I? I guess you know where she got it from.

With all the change happening in our world, there is a desire to shrink back. There's a fear that comes with the unpredictability of change, especially when that change rumbles toward us like a freight liner. We are constantly told how terrible the world is getting and assured that the trajectory is worsening at an alarming speed. It's frightening to see the world morphing before our eyes. The more rapid the change, the more frightening it is.

A handful of movements even now encourage Christians to pull out of society at various levels. There is an impulse to separate to maintain purity. We are tempted to isolate because we love our children, family, and friends. In that, I see an understandable draw of the isolationist mindset. However, there is a warning in it too.

In Romans 12:2, Paul explains that we should not be conformed to the world. We are to be in the world but not act like it. This puts us between two hard spots. We are not supposed to isolate, but we are not supposed to conform, either. This is a high and difficult calling. We must both remain in the world but remain in Christ, too.

In Matthew 5:13, Jesus tells believers to be the salt of the earth. He points out that salt is no good if it doesn't retain its flavor. If it gets tasteless, it has to be thrown out. We could extend the metaphor by saying salt is only good if it doesn't stay in the container. Locked away in a pantry, the salt of the earth isn't doing any good in the world. But spreading it out is what is required. Salt has to spread thin and wide.

Although this quote is attributed to different people, and we're not quite sure who said it first, it's worth repeating. "Christians are like manure: spread them out, and they help everything grow better. But keep them in one big pile, and they stink."

I feel the temptation to isolate. I feel the urge to cloister. I'm trying to fight it because I want to obey our Lord. I want to do good work in the world, in a place that needs light and salt and manure like us. This is why I'm so enamored with missionaries. The grand heroes of our era are those wild-eyed wanders who ride the wind into the unknown to preach Jesus to any who will listen. Plenty have given life and blood to spread the seeds of God throughout the earth. That's what I aspire to.

So, if you're like me and feeling that pull toward isolation and disconnection, how can you counteract it? Simple.

Do missions.

Short term.

Long term.

Online.

In person.

Do missions.

If you're not ready to jump in, at least support a missionary. They need prayer support. They need emotional support through correspondence. They need financial support. It's a great way to get involved without putting your neck on the chopping block, at least not yet. Secondly, start praying about how God might use you in the world. He wants to save the world, and he wants to use you in the process. So, ask him often how you can accomplish that, and I'm confident you'll get an answer.

I often tell people that I'm a missionary to the indigenous people of the internet. My purpose is to make media that points people to Jesus. This book is part of that mission. Thanks for reading it. If you'd like to read more books I've written, show up at LU CASKITCHEN.COM and see what I have on the menu. I also write blogs and produce podcasts and videos, all of which you can subscribe to at FREEGRACE.IN. In addition, if you are willing and able, please leave a review of this book where you get your reading material. It helps us spread the message.

Now, there's a big mission field out there. Go jump in!

Tabitha's Missionaries

Tabitha is an avid reader of anything in the Isolation library, but her most beloved genre is Missionary Biographies. Here's a list of Tabitha's favorite missionaries, each of which she talked about during the story. Like Tabitha, you can gain inspiration from these amazing men and women, wherever your journey takes you.

1. Hudson Taylor was a British missionary who founded the China Inland Mission and spent over 50 years ministering in China. He is known for pioneering missions in inland China and adopting Chinese customs to better reach the people. **Further Reading:** *Hudson Taylor's Spiritual Secret* by Dr. and Mrs. Howard Taylor.

2. Adoniram Judson was an American missionary who was the first Protestant missionary to Burma (modern-day Myanmar) and is known for translating the Bible into Burmese and establishing several churches. **Further Reading:** *To the Golden Shore: The Life of Adoniram Judson* by Courtney Anderson.

3. David Livingstone was a Scottish missionary and explorer who traveled extensively in Africa, known for his efforts to end the East African slave trade and for mapping uncharted regions of the continent. **Further Reading:** *David Livingstone: Mission and Empire* by Andrew Ross.

4. Mary Slessor was a Scottish missionary to Nigeria, known for her work with the Efik people, particularly her efforts to end the practice of killing twins, who were believed to be cursed. **Further Reading:** *Mary Slessor of Calabar: Pioneer Missionary* by W.P. Livingstone.

5. William Carey, known as the "Father of Modern Missions," was a British missionary to India who was instrumental in translating the Bible into several Indian languages and promoting social reform, including the abolition of sati (the burning of widows). **Further Reading:** *William Carey: Expect Great Things* by Faith Cook.

6. John Paton was a Scottish missionary in the New Hebrides (now Vanuatu), where he worked with the indigenous people, despite severe opposition, and is known for his efforts to convert cannibalistic tribes to Christianity. **Further Reading:** *John G. Paton: Missionary to the New Hebrides* by John G. Paton.

7. Jim Elliot was an American missionary who, alongside four others, was martyred while trying to evangelize the Huaorani people of Ecuador. His life and death inspired many to pursue missions. **Further Reading:** *Through Gates of Splendor* by Elisabeth Elliot.

8. Don Richardson was a Canadian missionary to the Sawi people of Papua, Indonesia, known for using the Sawi's concept of a "peace child" to explain the gospel, leading to many conversions. **Further Reading:** *Peace Child* by Don Richardson.

9. Stan Dale was an Australian missionary who worked with the Yali people of Papua, Indonesia, and is known for his martyrdom at the hands of a tribe resistant to outside influences, alongside his efforts to bring the gospel to isolated people. **Further Reading:** *Lords of the Earth* by Don Richardson.

10. Nate Saint was an American missionary pilot who supported efforts to reach the Huaorani people in Ecuador. He was martyred alongside Jim Elliot and others during Operation Auca. **Further Reading:** *Jungle Pilot: The Life and Witness of Nate Saint* by Russell T. Hitt.

11. John Goforth was a Canadian missionary to China, known for his powerful revivals and evangelistic efforts during the early 20th century. **Further Reading:** *Goforth of China* by Rosalind Goforth.

12. Robert Moffat was a Scottish missionary to southern Africa, where he ministered to the Bechuana people (now Botswana) and translated the Bible into the Tswana language. **Further Reading:** *Robert Moffat: Pioneer in Africa* by Cecil Northcott.

13. Amy Carmichael was an Irish missionary to India, where she founded the Dohnavur Fellowship to rescue girls from temple prostitution and cared for thousands of children. **Further Reading:** *A Chance to Die: The Life and Legacy of Amy Carmichael* by Elisabeth Elliot.

14. Albert Schweitzer was a German theologian, physician, and missionary who served in Gabon, Africa, where he founded a hospital and worked to improve healthcare for the local population. **Further Reading:** *Out of My Life and Thought* by Albert Schweitzer.

15. Gladys Aylward was a British missionary to China, known for leading over 100 children to safety across the mountains during the Japanese invasion and her efforts to end the practice of foot binding. **Further Reading:** *The Small Woman* by Alan Burgess.

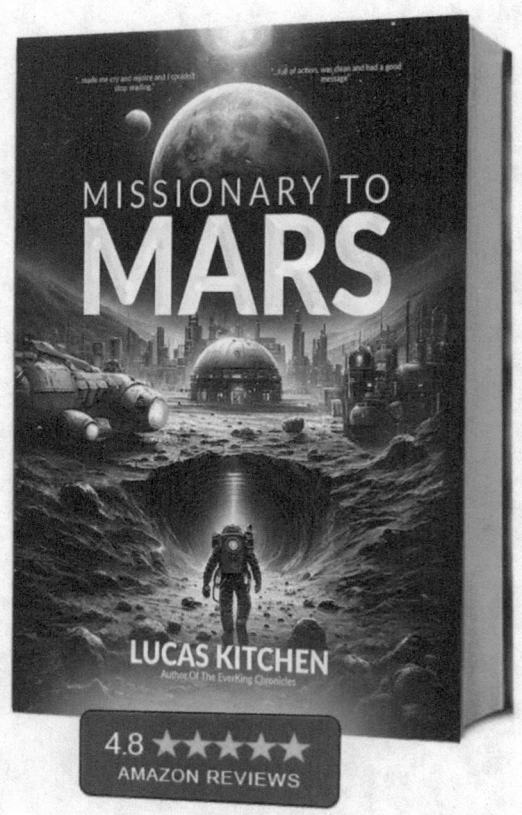

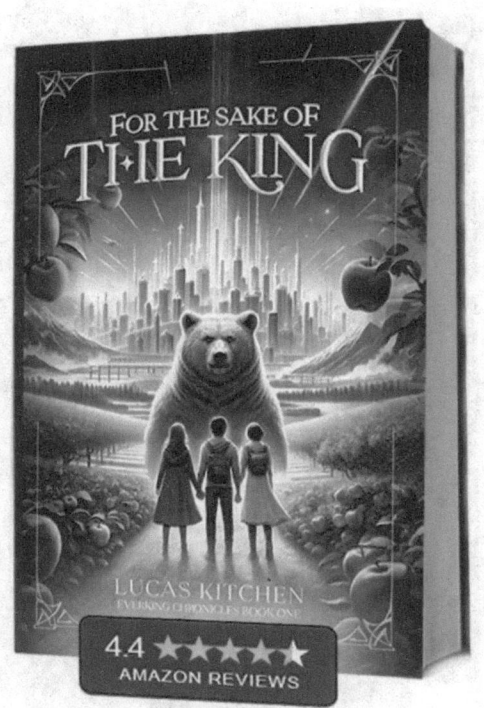

About The Author

Lucas Kitchen is an American author of both Christian fiction and nonfiction. He has written over twenty books, and had some on Amazon's category best-seller lists. He writes blogs, releases podcasts, and publishes social media videos about Jesus, the faith, and Ai robots. His social media content occasionally goes viral. He lives in Texas with his wife, and four kids. You can see his books at Lucaskitchen.com.